VENGEANCE

VENGEANCE

BRIAN FALKNER

Falkner Books

2018

This edition published in 2018 by
Falkner Books
www.brianfalkner.com
Copyright © 2013 by Brian Falkner

First Publication: Walker Books 2013

ISBN 978-0-6482879-4-0

For Sarah Foster
Your vision, guidance, and support
have meant the world to me

RECON TEAM ANGEL

The lifting of the official veil of secrecy, and the subsequent publication of the diary of Lieutenant Trianne Price, has revealed astonishing revelations about the events at the end of the Bzadian War.

The role that the brave young men and women of Recon Team Angel played in those extraordinary times has never before been fully revealed.

This, finally, is their story.

Many fought, and many fell, in pursuit of liberty for Earth. May their names live on in history.

DESERT PRAYER

[Nazca Valley, Peru, 43 BC]

The snake scraped across the dry desert floor in front of Ching'wua, in search of water. It stopped, sensing Ching'wua's presence and raised its head in his direction. It was small, just a narrow necklace with bands of red, yellow and black. A coral snake: deadly but not aggressive. But if it was desperate enough, that could change.

Ching'wua watched the snake for a moment until it lowered its head and rasped away across the dry stones of the desert.

"Run snake," he called after it. "Run well, or I will catch you and drink your blood."

He rubbed the knuckles of his right hand, still bruised and scabbed from the fight the day before. One of the scabs had broken off, and was bleeding, but lightly.

"You, Ching'wua," a voice came from behind him. "You stop to gossip with the desert?"

Ching'wua said nothing, and took a tight grip on his digging tool. He rammed the sharp end of it into the loosely packed red stones of the desert, loosening them, then reversed the tool, using the scoop end to lift the stones and reveal the whitish-grey substrate.

The High Born behind him walked up alongside as he spread the red stones across the desert to the side of the digging. Ching'wua glanced up, but only for a second. Any longer would bring the sapling whip down across his shoulders, which were already red and raw from the days of unrelenting sun.

The High Born – his name was Gochua – was a longhead, one of the last. His skull was long and narrow and his eyes were large. He was not born that way. Only the gods were born that way. At birth Gochua had had boards strapped to his skull, forcing the bones of his head to grow into the unnatural elongated shape. The High Born did it because it made them look like gods. But they were not gods.

Real gods could fly through the sky like birds. They could heal the sick and change the weather.

The High Born could do none of that.

Looking like a god did not make you a god, Ching'wua thought bitterly, feeling Gochua's eyes on his back as he hacked again at the red stones.

The true gods had gone, many years before, and soon after they had left, so had the rains. Without the rains, the crops had failed, and that had brought starvation and death to his people. Even now the taste of the land snail was sour on his tongue. That had been their only food for days. He would rather have joined the gatherers, on their eight hour walk to the coast, to collect seafood and shellfish, than to be here, scratching out a message in the desert to gods who would never come.

The gods will return, the High Born insisted. They will answer our call. They will bring back the rains.

But they had not.

The High Born had drawn the first message high on a mountain, where it would be easy for the gods to see. Ching'wua had helped dig it: a circle inside a square, a design that the gods had shown them. But the gods had not seen it.

So the High Born had surrounded it with smaller circles, a message in a language that only the gods could understand. But still nothing. They had dug pits and heaped piles of precious food in them as offerings to the gods. Many people had starved to death to send this message, but still the gods had not listened.

The gods are too far away, the High Born said. Our message must be louder. So they had drawn huge designs on the desert floor, animals, birds, spiders. The lines of the pictures were ten shoulders wide, and stretching out of sight into the distance.

But even with these giant silent pleas, still the gods did not see.

Ching'wua had heard of other lands, not far away, high in the mountains, where fresh water still flowed, and plants and wildlife were abundant. He, and many others, wanted to leave, to seek a new place where his people could live. But the High Born said no, the gods will bring back the rain.

The previous day Ching'wua had had to fight to defend his family's water gourd from a villager, crazed with thirst, who had tried to steal it. The man had fought like a cornered jaguar for the water, and much of it had spilt as Ching'wua had wrestled it off the man, and beat him into unconsciousness.

He did not blame the man. Thirst could do terrible things to a person.

"We must leave here," Arua said. He was working next to Ching'wua. He seemed tired, his digging tool barely ruffling the surface of the stones. Ching'wua glanced quickly at him.

Arua looked unsteady on his feet. Just yesterday Aura had lost a child, a young girl, to the endless thirst.

"Speak quietly, or not at all," Ching'wua said. "Gochua is near."

"I will no longer listen to Gochua," Arua said, "Or any of the other High Born. We will all die if we stay in this place." His tongue sounded heavy and his words were blurred.

"The High Born say the gods will return," Ching'wua said.

"The High Born lie," Arua said.

Ching'wua was silent. He hoped Gochua had not heard that. Accusing the High Born of lying was punishable by death, and it would be a long, slow death.

"The High Born lie," Arua said again, loudly.

"You, Arua," Gochua said. "What do you say?"

"He said nothing," Ching'wua said. "It is just the sun. He babbles."

"I said you lie," Arua said. "The gods will not return. We waste our energy and our lives."

"Take him," Gochua said, and two soldiers stepped down into the grey-white path, Ching'wua did not see where they came from.

"Ching'wua agrees with me!" Arua cried as they grasped his arms.

"I said nothing!" Ching'wua cried out, horrified, as Gochua's gaze turned towards him.

Gochua said nothing but nodded towards Ching'wua and two more soldiers were suddenly upon him, wrenching at his arms, forcing him up onto the stony ground in front of Gochua, pressing him to his knees.

There was a burst of movement next to him and one of the

guards holding Arua staggered backwards. Now somehow Arua was free, running for his life, slipping and skidding on the harsh stones.

The first spear missed, whistling through the air over Arua's head as he slipped and fell, but now he was back on his feet and the second spear did not miss, impaling his leg and driving him down into the desert. The third spear entered his stomach and it was then that the writhing and the screaming began.

Gochua's ceremonial dagger was at Ching'wua's throat. Ching'wua had been wrong. This would be a quick death, Gochua was only waiting for the attention of the other diggers before slicing the life from Ching'wua's body. A quick gush of red, on the red stones, and Ching'wua would join his ancestors, no more than a skull on rope carried by a priest.

"I said nothing," Ching'wua cried again, cursing his bad luck to be digging next to Arua.

"See the non-believer," Gochua called out to the waiting masses around them. Still Arua flailed and screamed in the distance.

Ching'wua's heart beat like that of a hummingbird, and his ears now were filled with the drumming of his own blood through his body.

"You said nothing, but you thought it," Gochua said, the blade of the knife slipping a little and cutting the skin at Ching'wua's throat.

"I said nothing!"

"Did you think it?" Gochua asked, his voice rose to a shout.

Ching'wua no longer saw the High Born. Instead his vision was filled with his wife, and their two young sons. If he died, they would die, without his protection. To save himself was to save them, but to save himself he would have to lie, because Gochua was right. He had been thinking those things. And a man could not lie before the gods, even if those gods were far, far away.

"I..." he stumbled over his words. "I..."

The drumming in his ears was louder now, a roaring sound, and it was not the sound of his own body. The knife eased from Ching'wua's throat as a strange shadow briefly blocked the sunlight . A cloud, in a cloudless sky? A bird, large enough to create a shade? No bird was that large.

There was a gasp from the crowd and the soldiers holding Ching'wua's arms loosened their grip. Ching'wua twisted free, and to his surprise the soldiers did not resist.

He turned his head to the sky, with the others, and as he did the shadow again covered the sun.

The square and the circle, was his first thought. For in the sky was a large dark square, larger than anything he could imagine. Within the square was a circle of blue fire.

This rock, in the sky, impossibly large, grew even larger as it neared, and now winds began to stir the usually windless desert, brushing at Ching'wua's clothing, whispering into his hair, kicking at the stones around his feet.

Closer, now, lower, still the great thing from the sky descended on its glowing blue tail. It was low enough now that Ching'wua could see that the square was the base of a much larger shape, triangular on the sides, a great city in the shape of a pyramid floating above them, and slowly descending towards them.

The High Born chewed the ingakuwo weed and it gave

them visions, but Ching'wua had been chewing no weeds and this was no vision. This was real.

"The gods have returned," Gochua said, dropping to his knees. His voice, so strong and full of confidence before, was now an anxious whisper, the sound of dust shuffling across the desert floor. Even Arua's screaming had stopped.

Ching'wua prostrated himself on the ground, staring at the dirt, no longer even daring to peek at the floating city that sank slowly to the ground before him.

"The gods have returned," Ching'wua agreed.

BOOK ONE:
NEW BZADIA

War changes technology. Technology changes war.
General Harry Whitehead

TURNING TIDE

[Mission Day 1, July 1st, 2033. 0355 hours local time]
[Tasman Sea, off the coast of Australia]

The sixth Angel sat below, in the cabin, out of sight.

How quickly things changed, Price thought. Less than five months ago it would have been unthinkable to have Angel Six on this mission. On any mission.

But five months ago this whole mission was unthinkable.

The world had taken a strange, surreal turn.

"Tacking now," Angel Two, Specialist Janos (Monster) Panyoczki, called from the rear of the yacht.

Angel One, Lieutenant Trianne Price, ducked her head down, ready for the swing of the boom. It happened suddenly with a hiss of ropes through pulleys and the shush of the sail, the flapping of the sailcloth as it slackened, then the crack as the ropes snapped tight.

It was so loud that Price felt sure the enemy would hear it, although in reality she knew the sound would not travel far. And in the deserted bay they were heading for there was nobody to hear it anyway.

They had been launched from a frigate, a stealth boat that had sneaked almost within sight of the Australian coast before using its crane to lift the yacht off the cradle at its stern.

Once they hit land they would have to find whatever transport they could. Only one thing mattered. The rendezvous time. By nine o'clock they had to be in Canberra. The beating heart of the Bzadian Empire.

The yacht straightened for a second or two as the boat tacked, then settled back onto a steep, uncomfortable angle. Price had been sitting on the low side of the boat, her back against the railings, but now she was on the high side and had to put an arm over the top rail to stop herself from slipping off the seat.

Angel Four, Specialist Retha Barnard and Angel Five, Specialist Hayden Wall were looking after the ropes (called 'sheets' on a sailboat according to Monster). Angel Three, Specialist Dimitri (The Tsar) Nikolaev, was watching the scope. There was nothing for Price to do. She closed her eyes, enjoying the feel of the boat as it rose and surged against the waves, feeling useless, but not really minding.

This brought back memories, no, not exactly memories, more vague feelings of those early days of her life. Before it had all changed. Perhaps because of that this didn't feel like a mission. It felt like a holiday. That wouldn't last for long, she knew that, but for now there was a moment to be enjoyed.

The sails rustled for a moment in an indecisive breeze, then filled again with air. The bow of the yacht lifted and chill sea spray stung her hand. She didn't mind. After the hell of the Bering Strait mid-winter, she would never complain about the cold again.

The spray brought with it the smell of the night ocean: a deep, cleansing smell. Millions of years ago, scientists said, the distant ancestors of the human race had crawled out of the ocean. Maybe that was why humans always felt drawn to it, she thought. Maybe there was some connection, deep within their souls, with the vast expanses of water that covered the planet.

The next puff of breeze brought with it a different smell, the smell of land. Price wasn't sure how she knew that, but she did. There was a subtle difference between the clean fresh smell of the night sea air and the musk of nearby land.

The ocean spray was in her nostrils, and in her mouth, a slight saltiness. The unadulterated taste of nature. But more than that: it was the taste of freedom.

That thought made her look at the door to the cabin. Angel Six was in there. Freedom meant different things to different people, Price thought, and Angel Six would never be free.

* * *

[Mission Day -1, July 1st, 2033. 04:00 hours local time]
[Pacific Ocean, 100 km South of New Caledonia.]

The boat showed up on Zane's radar screen about five hundred kilometres due east of the mainland. It was a perfect night for the patrol. Earth's sky was virtually cloudless and the first vestiges of sun painted the horizon with a dull ochre glow. Not that that sun would reach New Bzadia for a few hours, but here, east of the mainland, high in the sky, the embryonic sunrise was the promise of a good day to come.

The cool night air was smooth, with not a trace of turbulence. It was like gliding on ice. To the north, far below and in the distance, a dull glow was the tiny settlement of Lord Howe island, as yet untouched by the war.

Out of the corners of his eyes, Zane was aware of the narrow angular shape of Nikoz's fighter to his left and Shelz'zah's to his right. All three planes were Razers, the smallest and fastest craft in the Bzadian air fleet.

They were on increased patrols. Longer hours, greater frequency.

The previous day, human stealth fighter/bombers had attacked Bzadian patrol boats up and down the coast, surely the precursor to some kind of attack on the mainland.

"You seeing this?" Nikoz's voice sounded casual, almost amused by the blip that had appeared on the 3D scope.

"I'm seeing what you're seeing," Zane said. A boat, in the middle of the ocean, where no boat had a right to be.

"They're either brave or stupid," Nikoz said.

"Crazy, if they think they can avoid our patrols," Zane said.

"There's more than one."

The voice came from Shelz'ah, the youngest on his patrol team, but her skills with the Razer were quite extraordinary. She had just returned from Chukchi where she had earned the Bzadian sash, the air force's third highest honour, during the abortive crossing of the Bering Strait.

Shelz'ah was right about the ships. A vague blur behind the first vessel, right on the edge of Zane's radar screen, solidified into a solid contact.

"Scumbugz are up to something," Nikoz said.

"We'd better check it out," Zane said. "Alter course to zero four seven."

The three Razers, as if a single craft, banked slightly as they turned onto the new heading. They were running about seven hundred miles per hour, just below the speed of sound, to conserve fuel.

Within a few minutes a third signal was tickling at the edge of the scope. "We got another..." Nikoz's voice broke off.

"What the hell is that?" Shelz'ah asked.

More blips were coming onto the scope now. A ring of ships with a large one at its centre.

"Nikoz, you're the expert on Scumbugz navies," Zane said. "What are we looking at?

"Carrier strike group," Nikoz said. "The one in the middle is an aircraft carrier."

"That has to be where the stealth fighters came from yesterday," Zane said.

"I thought all their ships were stuck in port," Shelz'ah said.

"They are. They were," Nikoz said.

"They haven't risked them out on the open ocean," Zane said. "Not since the early days of the war. They can't afford to lose them."

"They're heading for New Zealand, if they stay on this course," Shelz'ah said.

"Let's get in a little closer and get a visual to confirm," Zane said. "Accelerate to Mach one."

* * *

Sharp thunder, far distant, like the cracking of a whip, made Price turn her head, although there was nothing to be seen, not even stars. The expanse of the sail, black against the night sky, blocked everything in that direction.

There was nothing to see, yet she couldn't stop herself looking. The sound brought her back to reality. This was not a pleasure cruise. This was war, and they were about to sail into the middle of it.

"Ours?" she asked.

"Who knows," Barnard said. "One sonic boom sounds just like another. Could be scream-jets."

"Why they call scream-jets?" Monster asked. "Make noise like bang, not like scream." He imitated the sound of the planes, "Bang, bang, bang."

"Because Pukes are gonna scream when they hear 'em coming," The Tsar said.

"It's the sound the engine makes as the plane approaches ignition speed," Barnard said.

"I like The Tsar's answer better," Wall said.

"Somehow that doesn't surprise me," Barnard said.

"So explain to us dumb-asses how a plane can approach ignition speed before its engine starts," Wall said.

"I don't think you'd understand it if I did," Barnard said.

"Don't let her intimidate you," The Tsar said. "It can't be easy being smarter than everybody else in the world."

"Do I intimidate you, Tsar?" Barnard asked.

"Not anymore," The Tsar said. "I got you figured out."

"Don't be so sure," Barnard said.

"Just tell me about the scream-jets," Wall said, smacking a hand into his forehead in mock exasperation.

"It's magic," Barnard said. "You need two elves and a unicorn."

Price laughed. "Tell him, Barnard. I'd like to know too."

"Come on, I'll buy you an ice cream," The Tsar said.

"Carrier jets," Barnard said, with a roll of her eyes. "They lift the scream-jets high, real high, then launch them at supersonic speeds. Rocket boosters kick in and they dive until they reach Mach four, then the scramjet engine fires and they go hypersonic."

"How do they land?" The Tsar asked. "And don't tell us fairies lower them gently back to earth."

"I don't know," Barnard said.

"You don't know what?" The Tsar asked.

"How they land," Barnard said. "I'm not an aeronautical engineer."

"Mark this day in your diaries, kids," The Tsar said. "This was the day we found something that Barnard didn't know the answer to."

"Tsar, you're so stupid you could fail a DNA test," Barnard said.

"However they land, it's still a helluva way to fly," Wall said.

"Helluva way to fly," Monster agreed.

"And the Pukes don't have anything that fast?" Wall asked.

"Not even close," Barnard said.

"Boo-yah," Monster said.

"Unless they can come up with a way of countering the Screamers, the air war is about to turn in our favour," Price said. "And who controls the air, controls the battlefield.

There was silence from her team as the implications of that began to sink in. For the first time in over a decade there was a possibility of not just surviving, but of actually winning the war. It would be too late though for Emile. And Hunter. And Wilton.

Price turned her face away from the breeze. The cool sea air was making her eyes water.

The Tsar was manning the scope. He handed it to Wall and came to sit by Price. He put his arm around her shoulders.

She turned and stared at him until he took his arm away.

"You looked cold, Big Dog," he said.

"I'm your commanding officer," Price said. "You salute me, you don't hug me."

"Aye aye captain," The Tsar said, saluting comically.

"Monster's the captain," Price said.

After a moment she reached over and put his arm back around her shoulders. She was cold. She moved slightly, nestling her back into him.

"What's going on over there?" Monster called out from the back of the boat. "Hands off my girl."

"I was cold," Price called back, smiling. "And I didn't know The Tsar was your girlfriend."

The Tsar elbowed her in the ribs and Monster laughed.

"Anyway," Price said. "At least I'm not lying naked in a bed with an Inupiat woman."

Monster was silent and she felt The Tsar draw away a little.

"Bit harsh," Wall said.

Price regretted saying it as soon as the words left her mouth. In the wilds of the Bering Strait, a native Inupiat woman named Corazon had saved Monster's life by bringing up his body temperature when he had hypothermia. But her husband, Nukilik, had died helping the Angels, and thinking of her brought back memories of him.

The moment stretched uncomfortably and she was almost glad of the distraction when the Bzadian patrol boat appeared. Almost.

* * *

The group of ships was coming into visual range, and the high definition cameras in the nose of Zane's craft zoomed in.

A grey blur on the surface of the ocean gradually resolved into the distinct outlines of warships, sleek and fast, cutting through the dark surface of the ocean, leaving long white gashes on the black backcloth behind them. There was something quite majestic about the way the bows rose into the air before crashing down into thundering furrows of spray.

"Can you identify them?" Zane asked.

"The two at the front are missile cruisers," Nikoz said. "The smaller ships to the sides of the carrier are destroyers."

"What about that larger ship next to the carrier?" Shelz'ah asked.

"Supply ship," Nikoz said. "Whatever they're doing here, they're planning on staying a while."

Zane's craft shuddered as it struck an invisible patch of turbulence. Wild air. An unexpected bump in what had been an otherwise clear and smooth flight. He barely noticed it. His focus was on the ships.

"That's ... a concern," Zane said.

"I agree," Nikoz said and all the earlier amusement was gone from his voice.

"Why?" Shelz'ah asked. "Their defences are no match for our dragons."

"Of course," Zane said. "But they know that too, and they must know we'd be looking for them, after the attacks yesterday. So what are they doing here?"

"And why aren't they turning and running for safety now they've been spotted?" Nikoz asked. "They would have seen us about the same time we saw them."

As he spoke, a smaller blip detached itself from the carrier. Zane's enemy aircraft warning indicator went off almost simultaneously.

"They're putting their birds in the air," he said.

"Time we were gone," Shelz'ah said.

"They have nothing that we can't outrun," Nikoz said.

"Let's try and figure out what they're up to," Zane said. "We'll disappear long before they get within missile range."

The blip was followed by another, and another, until there were six enemy aircraft rising in a wide circular pattern over the carrier group.

"Just trying to scare us off," Zane said. "They wouldn't dare come near us. And it's not the planes I'm worried about, it's the destroyers. If we get within range they'll start throwing SAMs at us."

"The aircraft aren't coming this way, they're just circling and climbing," Nikoz said.

These were not normal tactics, Zane thought. Whatever the humans were up to it they were doing it in a way that they had not done before. He seriously considered turning back. That would probably be the sensible choice. His patrol group were lightly armed and they were heading into something that they didn't understand. Or was that the whole point of the human tactics? To confuse him? To force him to withdraw before he got too close?

The whole situation was strange, but also intriguing. More than that, it was his duty to find out what was going on. In any case there was no danger. The human planes were too far away and too slow to pose any kind of threat.

"Just a few more minutes," he said, "Let's get some high-res shots of the ships, maybe that'll help Coastal Defence Command figure out what they are up to."

The human planes continued to climb, higher than he had seen any go before, almost to the stratosphere. What was the point of that? They were burning fuel at a massive rate just to gain altitude.

"I think we should get out of here," Shelz'ah said.

She seemed nervous for someone who was about to be decorated with the Bzadian Sash.

"Just a few more kilometres," Zane said. "We…"

He stopped speaking. The six planes, in formation, had put their noses down and were now heading towards Zane and his patrol.

"Okay, let's head back and call this in," Zane said, still not particularly worried. "Maybe that was what the height was about, to help boost their speed. It won't be enough though."

The fast little Razer had a top speed of more than Mach 3. The fastest human fighters were less than half that fast.

He banked his plane around then punched up the power. As they regained supersonic speed after the turn he saw a vapour cone appear like a fuzzy circular disc around Nikoz's and Shelz'ah's tail fins, and he knew the same was around his own. There was no sound though. When you were travelling faster than sound you could not hear the sonic boom you created. He kept increasing the power until his airspeed indicator hit Mach 2. Nikoz and Shelz'ah stayed in formation at his wingtips.

* * *

"Picking up something on the scope," Wall, said. "A boat. Heading in our direction."

"Azoh!" Price swore. The name of the Bzadian spiritual leader had become a popular profanity.

"I thought ACOG was supposed to have sunk all the patrol boats up and down the coast," The Tsar said.

"They were," Barnard said.

"Check it out, Tsar," Price said. She was immediately conscious of the lack of The Tsar's warmth against her as he moved to take back the scope from Wall.

He nodded. "Wall's right. There's something there. To the North. Odd engine signature, but definitely a small ship."

"Ok, go silent," Price said.

Monster turned the bow into the wind and Price ducked instinctively as the boom swung towards her, although she knew it would not reach her. The sheets snapped taut as the boom reached the centreline of the yacht. Barnard and Wall lowered the sails. The boat went quiet, the dark canvas no longer straining against the ocean air, the bow no longer rising and falling. They drifted, a cork bobbing restlessly but noiselessly on the ocean.

"Still coming our way," The Tsar said. "Maybe half a klick."

The yacht was made of wood and fibreglass, virtually invisible to radar. The hull, the mast and the sails were all black. The yacht would be hard to see, even with night vision goggles, and it made almost no underwater sounds for sonar to detect. The chances of being spotted were small, but they could take no risks. Their lives depended on it. More importantly, the mission depended on it. Maybe so too did the life of the person they were going to meet.

Lieutenant Ryan Chisnall.

"How close is it going to get?" Price asked, her voice a whisper, although the Bzadian patrol boat was still distant.

"Going to pass in front of us … I'm not sure how close," The Tsar said. "It's going very slowly, minimal engine noise, might be a sonar boat."

"I need to pee," Wall said.

"Dude, you're been peeing like it's the world champs and you got a chance at the gold," The Tsar said.

"Must be the sound of all that water around us." Wall said.

"Well hold it until that boat passes," Price said.

It wasn't the sound of the water. She knew that. It was nerves. She felt the same way. There was something about this stage of the mission, waiting for the danger, the action, that was more nerve wracking than when they were actually in the middle of battle.

The ship was getting close. Voices carried a long way over water at night. Lookouts on the patrol ship might well miss a black mast bobbing in the water a hundred metres from the ship, but if they heard voices they would be sure to investigate. "What's the range?" she asked.

"Three hundred metres," The Tsar said.

There was complete silence except for the light wash of waves against the side of the boat. It seemed odd, yet fitting somehow, that on their third infiltration of New Bzadia they were not using high-powered technology, but one of the oldest modes of travel known to man. A floating hull, pushed by air currents across the sea. It was very low tech in a world of high tech.

Another series of supersonic booms came distantly from the north. A rippling series of explosions, high above and far away.

* * *

"Something's going on," Shelz'ah said. "I've got double blips on the radar, as if the Scumbugz planes have just split in two."

"It could be some kind of long-range missile," Zane said, studying the radar, but the blips were too big for that and his threat detectors were silent.

The original radar contacts were turning, heading back towards the aircraft carrier, but the smaller ones were now streaking towards his patrol, and their speed was climbing.

"They're gaining," Shelz'ah said.

Zane checked his instruments. When the human planes had split into two, they had been over fifty miles away. Now they were closing in on forty.

"Must have been the dive," he said. "Gave them a real speed boost. But they can't sustain it, they'll level off at our altitude and that will slow them down."

He thought about that, then said, "Just to be sure, we'll get the hell out of here. Stay with me."

He punched his power up further, watching as his airspeed rose well above Mach Two.

That speed would use up their fuel cells quickly, but it was early in the patrol and they could afford to waste a little.

"Still gaining," Nikoz said after a few seconds. "And... What just happened?"

It was as if the little human planes had just found a new gear. In unison they had suddenly, and rapidly accelerated.

"Mach Four point five and climbing," Shelz'ah sounded frightened.

Zane didn't blame her. He was starting to get a little uneasy himself. This was not what was supposed to happen on patrol flights. There was a plan. If they encountered larger forces of human planes they turned, outran them and called for backup.

"Scope is not identifying the type either," Nikoz said. "It's not an F-35, or any of their known planes."

"It's something new," Shelz'ah said in a hushed voice. "Hypersonic."

Speeds approaching Mach Five were considered hypersonic, and Bzadian ramjet engines were no use at that speed, no longer producing thrust.

"Go to maximum power," Zane said. He keyed his command radio. "Coastal Defence Command, this is Patrol Echo Three Four."

"Go ahead Patrol Echo Three Four."

"We are under attack by unknown human aircraft. Something new. Travelling at hypersonic speeds. We are inbound at max speed but would appreciate a little help here."

"Understood Echo Three Four, routing an air defence wing in your direction immediately."

Zane breathed a small sigh of relief. Their backup was on its way. All they had to do was stay out of reach of the humans for a few more minutes and the six on three odds would be turned on their head. His airspeed passed Mach Three.

"Thirty kilometres and closing," Shelz'ah said. Her voice was not steady. "Mach Five and still climbing."

Mach Five and climbing! Zane checked his scope. These new human planes were catching up as if the patrol was standing still.

"Twenty-five kilometres," Shelz'ah said.

"We're not going to outrun them," Nikoz said. "We're going to have to turn and fight."

He was right. They wouldn't reach the safety of their air cover in time. Not by a long shot. Still, the Razer was more than a match for any human plane, even at six to three odds.

"We're not going to turn," Zane said. "On my mark, switch power to your reverse thrusters, we'll slow right down, launch countermeasures and let them zip right by. See if they can outrun a rocket."

"They're coming right at us!" Nikoz yelled. "Ten kilometres. Eight!"

"Why aren't they firing?" Shelz'ah asked. Zane didn't have an answer; the enemy jets were well within missile range.

"We just need to keep them off us until the backup gets here," Zane said. "Get ready to slam on the brakes. On my mark. In three, two, one ... now!"

He cut all power to his rear engines and simultaneously engaged his reverse thrusters. His craft shuddered as its speed dropped away, Mach Three, Mach Two...

He saw the human planes flash past overhead. They were small, with wings both above and below the fuselage. Biplanes. There were four tailfins like a rocket, shrouded in the mist of a supersonic vapour cone. Whatever they were, they were like no other human craft he had ever seen.

Even as he saw them the sky went crazy in front of him. The clear air suddenly exploded with the violent energy of multiple, overlapping sonic booms, close by. His plane was wrenched ferociously from side to side and up and down. His windscreen cracked in two places. His instruments went haywire.

As he fought for control of his craft he heard Shelz'ah yell, "Incoming! Six missiles! Breaking right!"

The human planes must have dropped the missiles just before they flashed overhead and in the wake of their multiple sonic booms he had little control.

Shelz'ah's plane turned to the right, deploying countermeasures. Zane launched his own and forced his unresponsive craft to go with her. Nikoz had broken left, he saw on his radar screen.

He started to call instructions to Nikoz and Shelz'ah, but realized with a horrible certainty that there was nothing he could do and no time to do it in. The human planes had fired their missiles at point blank range.

All this he realized in little more than a second because that was how long he had to live.

He opened his mouth to say something, but it became a scream as Shelz'ah's Razer turned from a sleek predator of the sky into a jagged ball of flame. Half a second later so did Zane's.

* * *

There were more explosions to the north, but these sounded different and followed flickers of light in the sky, the way that thunder follows lightning.

"Two hundred metres," The Tsar called softly.

Now they could clearly hear the surge of water against the ship's bows and the low rhythmic knocking of a large diesel engine.

"Absolute silence," Price said. Even as she uttered the words a gust of wind caught the rigging and a pulley knocked against the mast, a sudden loud clanging. Wall moved quickly to tighten a sheet.

Price said nothing. She didn't need to. Everyone on board understood the need for silence. She dialled her night vision lenses to maximum but could only make out a vague black shape advancing slowly towards them.

They drifted. Less than a hundred metres away, the larger, armed craft, advanced steadily through the water in front of them. If it was anything like the last patrol boat they had encountered, it would have a crew of at least twenty, heavy machine guns, high intensity radar and a towed sonar array.

The yacht had no armour and no weapons.

"It's going to hit us," Wall said in a whisper. "Raise the sail, we gotta move."

"No it's not," The Tsar said. "It'll pass in front."

"How can they not have seen us?" Barnard asked.

Price stared at the hull of the oncoming ship, looming larger and larger, green in her NV. It certainly looked as though it was on a collision course, it seemed to be coming directly at them.

"Absolute quiet," she said. "We might get really lucky."

"And if not?" Wall asked. "You may have an invisibility cloak, but I forgot to bring mine."

"Then we're just a bunch of Pukes learning how to sail who got blown out to sea," Price said.

Price held her breath as the ship moved within shooting distance. There was no sign of movement on the ship, no shouts, no alarms or sirens. Could it really be going to pass them by, so closely, and somehow not detect them?

All of them were completely motionless, crouched down in the yacht, as if that would somehow help. There were minor sounds of movement from the cabin. Stay put, Price mentally willed Angel Six. Now would be a bad time to emerge. The Tsar must have been thinking the same thing as he moved silently to the small staircase, blocking the cabin door with his body.

The ship seemed so close that she could almost reach out and touch it. It was certainly within spitting distance, a large black hull, unlit, blotting out the stars, the water splitting into two dense swells as the vee of the bow passed through them.

"Holy Azoh!" Barnard said loudly. Too loudly.

Price shushed her with a hiss.

"Nobody's going to hear me," Barnard said. "Look up."

Price lifted her gaze from the waterline of the ship to the top deck. Barnard was right. There was no need for quiet.

The superstructure of the ship was gone. What was left of it was a twisted, smoking skeleton. The hull was scorched but intact. Somehow the engine was still turning over, keeping the ship moving just enough to maintain steerage. It was a ghost ship, haunting the eastern coast of Australia until it ran out of fuel or ran aground. The way it was heading that would be on Antarctica, Price thought.

As the ship moved upwind of them the clean ocean breeze was engulfed by an acrid stench of burning oil and metal, and something else that Price didn't want to think about.

"Azoh," she said.

"Poor bastards," Wall said.

"Really?" The Tsar asked. "You sound a bit sentimental about a bunch of stinking aliens. Is that because you used to be one?"

Wall shook his head and did not respond.

"I'm with Wall," Price said pinching her nostrils together to block the smell of charred flesh. "I wouldn't wish that on anyone."

"It's just good to see them coming off worst for a change," The Tsar said.

"Tide beginning to turn," Monster said.

"Damn right," Price said. "They've had it all their way for far too long. Now the shoe's on the other foot."

"No. I mean tide beginning to turn," Monster said. "Need to raise up sail. We must getting into bay before low tide."

The wind turned with the tide, in their favour, flicking around behind them, filling the sails and skimming them across the wave tops like a pebble across a river. The smouldering hulk of the patrol ship slipped quickly away behind them, plodding its mindless way towards its rendezvous with Antarctica, if it made it that far.

Within minutes, it seemed, the headlands of the bay slipped past and they entered the sheltered waters within, cocooned from the onshore winds by encircling rocky arms.

The bay was wide at the entrance but narrowed rapidly. They docked at a small jetty, the only one still standing, although the remains of many more were scattered along the shoreline.

Barnard looked at Price. She raised an eyebrow. "Do you want me to …?"

"No, I'll do it," Price said. The boat rocked slightly as she took the narrow, steep stairs that led down to the cabin and she had to hold the handrail for support.

She stopped a moment and took a deep breath before rapping twice on the closed door.

"Rise and shine, Brogan," she said. "It's time to go."

SALT

[Mission Day 1, July 1st, 2033. 0510 hours local time]
[Bzadian Congress, Canberra]

The kitchen smelled like vomit. It always smelled that way, even now, at five in the morning, when nothing had yet started cooking.

The smell came from the huge leaves of the nuguz plant, a Bzadian delicacy. Humans called it pukeweed. Once, on a mission, Ryan Chisnall had found himself in a field of the plants and the stench had almost made him pass out.

Cooked, the smell was less pungent but even so it had taken Chisnall a week to accustom himself to the odour so that he could work in a Bzadian kitchen without tossing his cookies into the nearest pot.

Not that the Bzadians might notice the difference if he did, Chisnall thought. And really the pukeweed was no stranger than some human delicacies. Chinese 'stinky' tofu was said to smell like rotten garbage, and the Swedes had a fermented herring dish that smelt so bad it had to be eaten outdoors.

As a child Chisnall had dreamed of being a chef. His mother had been a wonderful, and creative cook (not a professional chef although Chisnall thought in a different world she might have been) and he had loved watching her make things in the kitchen, helping out when he could. It was a source of fascination for him how a chef could create something out of almost nothing. Mixing together a few dry powders and sauces, adding heat, and suddenly a miracle happened. It was a kind of magic.

He had studied recipe books at a time when other boys his age studied baseball stats or read books about kings and dragons.

Then his parents had died. His father in the war, fighting Bzadians. His mother a year later of a disease that would have been easily treated twenty years earlier. But there were too many people and too little medicine.

Or perhaps she had wanted to die. She had grieved endlessly after the loss of his father. Chisnall had felt forgotten in the aftermath, an afterthought, a spectator to her grief, but that didn't stop him grieving himself when she died. Then the Angels had come along.

The induction programme had been harsh, unforgiving, even cruel, but it took his mind off the death of his parents. When they had offered him the officers' course, he had said yes without question.

And in the cyclic nature of the universe, that had led him, eventually, to here. A chef. He was working for the enemy, but it was a position that gave him access to information that no other human would have access to.

A chef. A spy.

He moved quietly among the highest circles of the Bzadian military, organising their meals, listening to their conversations. Nobody noticed a chef.

As a junior chef, and a new one, Chisnall was very aware of his place, but he was also aware that more and more he was being requested as chef for meetings and formal dinners.

It was all about the salt.

Salt was virtually unknown on Bzadian, a desert planet, lacking the huge, saline oceans of earth. Bzadian chefs who had experimented with it since their arrival on Earth had generally used far too much, resulting in overly salty dishes that had the diners reaching for their water bulbs.

Chisnall had added salt gradually, knowing how it enhanced the flavours of certain foods. It had worked, and his star was rising in the Bzadian kitchen.

It was no accident that had placed Chisnall, with a little training in the ways of Bzadian cooking, in the kitchen at the Congress, the former Australian Parliament House, now the seat of Bzadian Government. His security credentials were genuine and impeccable and completely false. His references and work history was just as false, and just as outstanding.

He had started as a kitchenhand, but invisible hands manipulated the system, and within a month he was cooking meals, a junior chef. Those hands eased his path into a position that no human being should have gotten close to. Yet he was.

The group behind those invisible hands called themselves the Peacemakers. Bzadians who were opposed to the war. They had saved his life after Operation Magnum, hidden his identity, healed him, and eased him into this position in the kitchen in Canberra.

The Peacemakers said they had a different vision of a future for Earth. Instead of one where humans were eradicated, or subjugated, they foresaw a world in which humans and Bzadians co-existed peacefully. For the most part he believed them, but he couldn't shake off a nagging feeling that they had a hidden agenda of their own.

The head chef, Farzo, was standing at one end of the long kitchen space waiting for all the chefs to stumble in, bleary-eyed, from their sleeping quarters. He had roused them for an announcement. There was to be an unscheduled meeting of the High Council. Many high level regional commanders would be attending. The kitchen would be providing food.

Chisnall kept his face neutral, but his thoughts were churning. An unscheduled council meeting? The Bzadian High Council didn't hold unscheduled meetings. That meant it was an emergency meeting, and that meant that something major had happened.

Farzo doled out assignments for the meeting, reluctantly assigning Chisnall an important role.

An emergency meeting. Chisnall's mind was racing, and it had nothing to do with food.

Could it be about the Angels?

Had the Bzadian military learned of the Angels' mission? It was possible. ACOG security had more holes than a golf course.

But he couldn't imagine the Bzadians calling a major, emergency meeting over an Angels' mission. It had to be more than that.

He put the thought out of his mind. In a few hours he would be inside the room of that meeting. He would find out then.

In the meantime, he had ingredients to prepare.

CHESHIRE MOON

[Mission Day 1, July 1st, 2033. 0530 hours local time]
[Batemans Bay, New Bzadia]

The moon had risen now. A quarter moon. A Cheshire Cat moon, Price thought. It smirked from low above the horizon as the six Angels eased their way through the darkened streets of the once thriving beach resort of Batemans Bay.

The aliens had no love of the ocean. On their desert planet there were no seas, no beaches, and few boats. For them, here on Earth, the seaside was a line where water met land, nothing more. As a consequence the town was deserted, unwanted by the Bzadian invaders. There was an eerie feeling to it, a ghost town quality as though the spirits of the former inhabitants remained. Price felt it and she could tell that the other Angels did too, from the way they moved, the way they scanned the hollow eyes of the buildings around them.

On occasion, at an unexplained sound, or a sudden stirring of the breeze, a coil-gun would fly from its back-mount holster, springing over a shoulder into waiting hands. That would set off a chain reaction and suddenly all of the Angels would be gripping their weapons; scanning around them; wondering who had seen what; wondering what they had missed.

Almost all the Angels.

Brogan didn't have a weapon.

Price didn't trust her that much.

The debris of the town's past littered the area, fungal-green in the glow of the night vision lenses. Masts of yachts protruded from the bay: watery tombstones for what lay beneath. Derelict cars rusted in parking lots. In a playground along the foreshore the tattered remains of a children's swing lurched unsteadily in the fitful breeze.

It unsettled Price, skulking along the waterfront here. It unsettled her more than tabbing through the night-time desert in the Australian outback, more than clambering over ice ridges and inching across crevasses in the frozen sub-arctic. It unsettled her because she had grown up in a town just like this. A small beach town.

She associated that town, on the east coast of New Zealand, with the happiest times in her life. Before her parents died. Before what came next.

Here, the darkened buildings, the staring Cyclops eyes of the deserted tourist booths and fast food stands, were like a horror movie version of her childhood, things that she had known and loved, now black and twisted and evil.

They passed a luxury launch, a rich man's toy, built for floating cocktail parties, moonlight cruises and bikini beauties sunbathing on the back deck. It had embedded itself in the sand of the beach, and somehow stuck there through years of tides and storms, slowly rotting.

"Hey Big Dog," The Tsar said. "I might be picking up something."

He had stopped walking and was completely focussed on the screen of his hand-held scope.

"What is it?" Price asked.

"Don't know," The Tsar said. "Just a little tickle. Might be nothing."

Price quickly scouted their location for a hiding place.

On the seaward side of the road, the large overhanging balcony of a shopping arcade seemed to offer the best protection. She led the way to it and squatted against the wall underneath, where they would be out of sight of any prying, flying eyes.

The Tsar stared tensely at the scope for a moment then seemed to relax. He looked at her and shook his head. "It was low and small, might have been a large bird, something like that. Whatever it was, it's gone now."

"No it hasn't," the voice came from Brogan. Price glanced at her, surprised to hear her speak.

"How do you know?" Price asked.

Brogan shrugged. Price watched her for a moment, evaluating her, evaluating what she had said. Brogan sat quietly and closed her eyes.

"Keep moving," Price said. "We can't afford any delays."

"That's a mistake," Brogan said.

"Yeah, well it's my mistake," Price said. "We are Oscar Mike, now."

She stood and led the team back out onto the road that led towards the bridge.

"Imagine this never happened," The Tsar said. "Imagine the aliens never invaded."

"Sure, we'll wake up and find out that this was all just a dream," Barnard said.

"Nightmare," Wall said.

"Seriously. Look at this place," The Tsar said. "Can't you just see it? Sunny little seaside town. Sailing races in the bay, kids playing in the sand, teenagers on jet-skis getting yelled at by the fishermen."

Yes, Price could see it. That was the problem. This dark, twisted, empty version of it.

The Tsar's mind held a different image. "This time of night the bars and nightclubs would still be open. People would be out partying, laughing, dancing in the street – "

That got a snort from Barnard.

"Not into dancing, huh Barnard," The Tsar said. "What's wrong with it?"

"Nothing's wrong with it," Barnard said. "It just doesn't make any sense."

"Oh, well let me explain it to you," The Tsar said. "You play some music and you…"

"You're so funny," Barnard said. "Why do perfectly normal people gather in groups and jerk their bodies around in random ways while listening to music so loud they can't hear their own brain cells exploding."

"It's called having fun," The Tsar said, "But I guess you wouldn't know much about that."

"What's fun about it?" Barnard asked. "I mean really. In what way is that fun?"

"More fun than being here," Wall said.

"You know, Barnard," The Tsar said, "You may be human, but some days I think you're more alien than the aliens."

"Come on you two," Price said. "Play nice, or I'll send you to your rooms."

"She started it," The Tsar said.

"You are so immature," Barnard said.

"Am not, you are," The Tsar said.

The funny thing was, Price thought, that the petty squabbling between those two had increased as they had got closer. Not romantically, there was little likelihood of that happening, more like a brother and sister whose constant bickering hid a deep affection for each other.

A sudden sound intruded, a rattle of a loose roof tile in the wind, nothing more, it made her jump and her coil-gun was in her hands before she even realised it.

She slotted it back into its holster, forcing herself to smile, commanding her breathing to steady. It made her look nervous and she did not want to look nervous. Especially in front of Brogan.

Imagine the war hadn't happened, the Tsar had said. But the war had happened.

The war had been a disaster for the human race and a blight on the planet Earth. But in the depths of the blackness there were pinpricks of light. The Bzadian war had saved her, or more accurately, Recon Team Angel had saved her, taking her away from... what came next. Those were memories that did not bear thinking about.

And if she ever went back... well... she was not the person she was before. Lil Pup they used to call her, but Lil Pup had grown up.

Lil Pup was the big dog now. She was no longer someone who could be kicked around.

"Would be in bed, big sleeping, if not for war," Monster said, wrenching her back into the here and now. That made her laugh. Monster always made her laugh. For a long time she had kept Monster at a distance, unwilling to commit to a relationship where one or the other of them could be killed at any time. But as Barnard had once pointed out to her, that was exactly the reason to commit.

"Not likely," Barnard said. "Now'd be the middle of the afternoon in Hungary."

"Big sleeping," Monster laughed. "Big lunch then afternoon for sleeping."

"I know what I'd be doing, bro," Wall said.

Barnard cut him off. "You wouldn't be doing anything, 'bro'. If the Pukes hadn't come, you wouldn't even exist. You or your girlfriend over there."

Wall and Brogan exchanged a look but said nothing.

What could they say? Barnard was right. Wall and Brogan were Ferzerkers, products of the top secret Bzadian programme to infiltrate human society. They had been birthed by Bzadians in the depths of Uluru. Both now claimed to be fighting on the human side of the war, but Price couldn't forget the treachery. Brogan's actions had jeopardised their first mission. A close friend of hers had paid with his life, and so, nearly, had the rest of them.

Brogan looked different now. The time in jail had done that to her. Maybe it was the solitary confinement. Part of it was the prison buzz cut hairstyle, but it was more than that. There was an edge to her jawline, and an intensity in her gaze that had not been there when Price had last known her. A thin scar disrupted the line of her otherwise perfect lips. She looked hard. More than that, she looked cruel.

But it wouldn't help any of them, or the mission to dwell on the past. And whatever she felt about Brogan it was her job to keep the team focused, and operating as one unit.

"Barnard keep your opinions to yourself," Price said. "They're here now, and they're on our side."

"You sure about that?" The Tsar asked.

"I'm sure," Price said, with a confidence that she didn't feel.

"Why are you here?" Brogan asked, abruptly, that intense gaze fixed on The Tsar.

"What do you mean?" The Tsar asked.

"Why are you here, fighting Bzadians?" Brogan asked.

"They invaded my planet. I'm helping kick their butts," The Tsar said. "I am a lean, mean, alien butt-kicking machine."

"Boo-yah," Monster said and held out a fist. The Tsar bumped it vigorously.

"You're here by an accident of birth," Brogan said. "By chance you happened to be born a human. I was born Bzadian. I made a choice to be here."

"Same goes for me," Wall said.

"I guess you must have done something to convince ACOG that you deserved to be here," The Tsar smiled. "I know I damn well wouldn't have let you come."

"They must have liked my pretty blue eyes," Brogan said.

The Tsar turned to Price. "How did she talk herself onto this team?"

Price hesitated before answering. She really didn't know the answer. She knew the role Brogan had to play in their mission, but she did not know, and could not really understand, why ACOG had decided to trust her. It was Daniel Bilal, the secretive Military Intelligence officer from the Pentagon, who had briefed Price personally on this mission. He had given nothing away about Brogan, other than what her role was to be.

A sound from the other side of the road almost had her reaching for her weapon again, but she controlled the urge.

A moment later a large snake emerged from a drainpipe and darted off down an alley, an oily black wriggle amidst the leaves.

"Just take my word for it," Barnard said. "Chisnall asked for her to be included on this mission, and ACOG agreed. That's all you need to know."

Price pressed her lips tightly together. So Barnard knew what Brogan had done to earn Bilal's trust. Yes, Barnard was the intelligence officer but she was not in charge of the mission. It irked Price not to have the full information about who was on her team.

"What you know that we not know?" Monster asked.

"That's classified," Barnard said.

"Chisnall asked for Brogan?" The Tsar asked. "I thought it was Bilal's idea."

"That's what you were supposed to think," Price said. "That's what everybody was supposed to think."

"Why he ask for her?" Monster asked.

"That's classified," Price and Barnard said, almost simultaneously.

"Enemy soldiers up ahead," Brogan said.

The team scattered, dropping to the ground, or pressing themselves against the corner of a building, finding whatever cover they could.

"What have you got on the scope?" Price hissed.

"Nothing," The Tsar said. "All clear."

Price released her weapon from its holster and brought the scope to her eye. She flicked from Night Vision to Thermal Imaging and back.

The road ahead looked clear.

A wild bush growing up through cracked pavement offered a better viewpoint so she dropped and crawled across to it, easing her weapon between the branches and leaves until the scope was clear.

Still nothing visible.

"Are you sure?" she asked. "What would they be doing here, now?"

"There's nothing there," The Tsar said. "Brogan's just freaking out. She hasn't been on a mission for a long time."

"Hold your position," Price said. Brogan was not the type to freak out, no matter what. "Brogan, what have you seen?"

"Nothing." Brogan's voice sounded calm, but intense. "I heard something. Two Pukes talking and a weapon release."

"Why is nothing showing on the scope?" Price asked.

"Scopes don't work well around a lot of buildings," Brogan said. "Too much interference."

"She's right," The Tsar said.

"Okay, I'm going to recce forward a couple of streets," Price said. "See if she's not just imagining it."

"I'm not," Brogan said. "And hold your position. They're coming this way."

Price waited. She was almost ready to move anyway when her thermal imaging scope showed a vague blur at the far end of the road. It solidified into three shapes, then another two. Five soldiers, clear now in the sights of her weapon.

What the hell were they doing here?

It was too late to back away. The soldiers would pick them up if they broke cover.

"Everybody seeing what I'm seeing?" she asked softly.

She got a chorus of grunts in reply.

"Okay, if they keep coming, we're going to have to take them out," she said. "Number them left to right. I'll take one, Monster you're two. Barnard, three, Tsar, four, and Wall five."

"If you miss, I'll throw nutrition bars at them," Brogan said.

Price ignored the barb. "Let me know if you haven't got a clear shot, and fire only on my mark. We need to take them down simultaneously."

"How do you know there aren't others?" Barnard said.

"I don't. But these ones we have to deal with first," Price said.

The five enemy soldiers continued towards them, spaced out. A patrol. Why here? Why now?

Price put her sights on the leftmost soldier. She flicked onto Night Vision, which was clearer than the thermal.

She could see the soldier's face. Not enough to make out features, but enough to know that it was a female. She centred the crosshairs on the soldier's nose.

"Wait for my mark," she said.

Still the soldiers drew nearer.

Now it was a fine balance. The closer they got, the easier the shot and the better chance of taking them all down cleanly. But it also increased the chances of the Angels being sighted, and the alarm being raised.

The Bzadians were now just over a block away, no more than fifty metres, approaching an intersection.

"As soon as they cross the road, we'll take them," Price said. "Anybody unsighted, let me know now."

The patrol reached the cross road and Price flicked off her safety catch.

Her finger found the cold metal of the trigger and she breathed in and held it, for a more accurate shot.

The soldiers stopped. Still Price held her breath, the crosshairs still centred on the nose of the female she was targeting. The group appeared to be having some kind of discussion. Price released her breath and slowly drew another. The soldiers began to move. Sideways. They turned into the cross street and were quickly out of sight, heading towards the water.

Price let her breath out slowly.

"Everybody hold," she said. "In case they come back."

They didn't come back.

A few minutes later there came the rising whine of a rotorcraft engine starting up and shortly after that the round metal shape of a Bzadian troop ship rose up in a cloud of dust from behind a large building just a couple of blocks away. Its disc-like shape dipped as it took off towards the South.

"Azoh!" The Tsar said. "We just about walked into that."

"We would have, if not for Brogan," Barnard said.

"What the hell was that doing here?" Wall asked.

"Just a patrol," Price said. "Just sweeping the town."

"They'll be on extra high alert after ACOG blew up all their coastal ships," Barnard said.

"Let me know when the scope is clear," Price said.

Five minutes later, with nothing showing on the scope, and no more warnings from Brogan, they were on the move.

Monster was on point. Behind him The Tsar was walking in odd, jerky movements. He was making sounds which might have been singing. "Chicka chicka chicka chicka whacka whacka wow wow."

Just his way of releasing the tension, Price thought.

"What's wrong with The Tsar?" Barnard asked.

Price stifled a smile. "I think it's called the clown walk."

"Oh. Dancing," Barnard said.

"Oh no, now he's twerking," Wall said, clutching at his eyes.

"You can't un-see that," Barnard said.

"Cut it out, Tsar," Price laughed. "And keep your eyes on that scope."

* * *

[Mission Day 1, July 1st, 2033. 0630 hours local time]
[Bzadian Congress, Canberra]

Chisnall moved through the High Council chamber setting up platters of food for the meeting.

Bzadian meetings could go on for hours, even days. That could create a problem. The Angels were due to arrive in Canberra at nine. He had to be free by then, no matter what. For now he concentrated on what he was doing.

A continuous supply of food and beverages was maintained on the meeting tables. Typical Bzadian meals were served in a style that the Spanish would call Tapas, and the Chinese would call Dim Sum: small portions of different dishes on shared plates.

The meeting room consisted of a series of concentric oval-shaped rings. In the centre sat the High Council, the seat of Bzadian government. High ranked military leaders sat in a larger ring around that, and lower ranked officers in an outer ring. At one end of the oval was a raised circular speakers' platform. At the other end was a small circle of chairs for Azoh's closest advisors, surrounding a single chair that Chisnall had never seen filled. A ceremonial chair that represented Azoh.

In the air above the oval a 3D globe rotated slowly, created by concealed projectors. It showed Bzadian and Human territories, Bzadian in blue, Human in red. Hotspots, where active fighting continued, were shown in white. There was not much red.

Some of the councillors and military officials had already arrived. They congregated in small groups or sat in their places at the tables. Chisnall made himself as unobtrusive as possible. This was the time when they would be least guarded, chatting informally before the meeting started. This was the time he would learn the most.

Already he was picking up conversations. Mostly in the high language. A language reserved for high level officials and Azoh himself. It had taken six months of intensive study to become even passable in the language. Fortunately he had had little else to do while they had rebuilt his shattered spine.

Most of the conversations seemed to be about a new kind of weapon, a revolutionary new human weapon. It had them worried. Although it was not mentioned specifically, by inference he was able to deduce that it was some kind of aeroplane.

He picked up other conversations also, about New Zealand. He was not close enough to hear the details, but from the tone, it was clear that the small country to Australia's east had just become a threat.

As he passed by the main doorway to the room an officer

entered. Not just any officer, Field Marshall Leozii, the Supreme Military Commander and Leader of the High Council. He was talking quietly to an aide. The conversation seemed to be to do with the meeting, and Chisnall clearly heard the name Azoh.

Time stood still for a moment.

If he had interpreted that scrap of conversation correctly, Azoh himself was due to attend this meeting. That was unprecedented. The Bzadian spiritual leader did not attend military strategy meetings. As far as he knew, Azoh did not venture out of the inner sanctum on the lower levels.

What could be so important that Azoh himself would attend the meeting?

Could that be good news for the Angel mission?

In what was surely the most daring and audacious move of the entire war, he, with the Angels' help, was planning to infiltrate the very heart of Bzadia. Azoh's private chambers. ACOG approved of the plan. And no wonder. The insight they would get into the Bzadian military machine was worth almost any price. His ACOG contact, Daniel Bilal, had personally fought to get the mission approved, including the re-activation of Recon Team Angel to do it.

Chisnall ran through the implications of Azoh being here, instead of there, as he carried on with his work.

He had almost finished setting out the food platters when the strangeness came on him. He froze, one hand hovering over a plate of salted sierfruit.

Something was wrong. The feeling was that of coldness, but not of the physical body. He had had it ever since he could remember. Like ice in his soul, his mother had said. The strangeness always meant danger. Like the night the army men, in their bright, shiny dress uniforms and white gloves, had knocked on the door to give them the news about his father. Or the night Hunter had died.

The strangeness was on him.

Something was wrong.

He willed his hands back into motion, setting out dishes of sauce for the sierfruit.

Something had just changed in the room. Someone had just entered. He didn't know how he knew that. Perhaps it was the momentary quieting, a hush that rolled around the room before conversation quickly resumed, as though they didn't want the person to realise the reaction their entry had caused.

Chisnall continued setting out the fruit platters. It would be too suspicious if he turned to see.

Could it be Azoh? Surely not. The entrance of the supreme leader of all Bzadians would surely be a grand affair.

Whoever it was, it was someone that even these people were afraid of.

He picked up an empty platter and glanced around casually as he left, trying to spot any new faces. He saw no one he recognized, but that meant nothing. There were many faces here he didn't know. And he could not scan everyone in the room without seeming obvious.

But he could not ignore that feeling. It had never been wrong before.

* * *

Price stared at a long dark bridge that spanned the mouth of the river that fed into the bay. Satellite scans had showed it to be intact, although they would not know for sure until they tried to cross it. A decade of neglect could do bad things to a bridge. It was also the point at which they were the most vulnerable.

A low, boxy lift-bridge, with criss-crossed metal beams, it spanned three hundred metres. For each of those metres they had nowhere to go, nowhere to hide.

In the centre, a span of the bridge could be raised vertically on two metal towers to allow boats to pass below. One of the towers looked intact. The other was starting to crumble. No boats would be going under this bridge any time soon.

They were crouched in one of the food kiosks along the waterfront. It was 0540 hours. If ACOG information was right, a Bzadian air patrol would pass this area at exactly 0543. The Angels remained in hiding. Price wanted to keep moving, but she did not want to get caught on the bridge. If they had been here ten minutes earlier they could have crossed the bridge before the patrol.

A few minutes. A small delay, leading to a bigger delay. That's how missions got off schedule. That was how missions failed. But right now there was nothing she could do about that.

She eased from her squatting position into a sit, with her back against the wall for comfort. She sipped slowly from her water tube. The water was warm from her body heat and slightly sweet, dosed with nutrients and glucose for energy. She took a nutrient bar from her belt pack and peeled back the plastic wrapper. It tasted like a grass clippings. From a lawn that was popular with dogs.

She noticed Barnard take a nutrient bar out as well, examine it, then replace it in her belt pack, taking out a different bar. Barnard caught her eye. Price nodded just once. It was not a nutrient bar. Far from it. It was the key element of the most secret part of their mission. Only she and Barnard knew about the bar, because they were the only ones privy to the real reason they were here. The others had been told they would rendezvous with their former lieutenant. After that, they had been deliberately kept in the dark, for a very good reason.

"We're all orphans, right," Wall was saying.

"I guess," The Tsar said. "Except for you two test tube babies who never had real parents in the first place."

"I think that still counts as orphans," Barnard said.

"So how come you never talk about it?" Wall asked.

"Who wants to talk about something like that?" The Tsar asked.

"Wouldn't it help?" Wall asked. "Instead of locking it all up inside?"

"Some things are better left locked up inside," Barnard said. "Like stupid questions."

"Did your parents all die in the war?" Wall asked.

"Wall, take a hint. I don't think they want to talk about it," Brogan said.

Price glared at her. The last thing she wanted to talk about were her parents, let alone how they died. But whatever Brogan said, she found herself determined to do the opposite.

"My folks died from IBS," she said.

"What's IBS?" The Tsar asked.

"Irritable Bowel Syndrome," Barnard said.

"That's like when you get pain in your guts, right?" The Tsar asked.

"That's it," Price said.

"You can't die from that," Barnard said. "It's not life threatening."

"My parents did," Price said.

"Bull," Barnard said. "Both of them?"

"Yup. My dad was taking mum to see my nana. He got a real bad attack. Got dizzy from the pain. Drove into an eighteen-wheeler. Burst into flames. Cooked them up good. Police had to identify them by DNA."

"That's just awful," Wall said. "I'm not sure I wanted to know that."

"You asked," Price said.

"What about you, Monster," Wall asked. "What happened to your parents?"

"War," Monster said, and refused to be drawn further.

"Okay, Barnard then," Wall said.

"What is this, the Spanish inquisition?" Barnard asked.

"Like The Tsar said," Wall said. "I never had parents. So I don't know what it feels like to lose them."

"Me either," Barnard said.

"Did they die when you were really young?" Wall asked.

"Nope. I was ten."

"Then you must have felt something," Wall said.

"No as a matter of fact I didn't," Barnard said.

"I don't believe you," Wall said.

"You know what, Wall?" Barnard said tiredly. "I wish I did. I wish that something twisted inside my chest and made me feel sick and all those other movie clichés. But it didn't. Am I proud of this? Hell no. When my father died, you know what I felt? Inconvenienced. That's it. And I hate myself for not feeling anything else and I cried at his funeral, but I was just acting. Are you happy now?"

There was an uncomfortable silence. The Tsar moved over and put a hand on her arm, but she shook him off.

"Your turn, Tsar," Brogan said. "How did your parents die?"

"Time we changed the subject," Price said.

"Just when it was getting interesting," Brogan smiled.

Price had to fight an urge to get up and punch her in the face.

"It doesn't matter how my parents died," The Tsar said. "Ask me how they lived."

"Good idea," Price said. "How did they live?"

"They were good parents. They were loving. They were happy. They were successful. They were good people," The Tsar said. "That's what I want to remember about them. Not how they died."

"Successful, what does that mean?" Price asked, just happy to be off the topic of death.

"We were quite well off," The Tsar said.

"So you were a spoilt rich kid," Barnard said. "That explains a lot."

"Bite me," The Tsar said.

"I have too much respect for my taste buds," Barnard said.

"Was your father in the Russian mafia," Wall asked.

"Nah, manufacturing," The Tsar said. "Nothing exciting."

"Manufacturing, yeah right," Wall said. "That's like those American mobsters saying they're in the waste disposal business."

"How rich you were?" Monster asked.

"Well we lived in a big house, had nice cars, that kind of thing."

"Sounds pretty average to me," Barnard said.

"We had the latest model Mercedes and Lamborghini," The Tsar said. "Plus a Rolls Royce convertible that never got driven. We had a housekeeper, a gardener, perfume in the toilet and a dacha – a holiday house – by a lake."

"Russian mafia," Wall said. "No question."

"You had perfume in the toilet?" Price asked.

"For when you take a crap," The Tsar said. "Stuff you spray around to cover the smell."

"Not Monster," Monster said. "Smell is natural."

"I'm with Monster on that one," Wall said. "All that pot pourri and floral bouquet stuff, mixed with the smell of the crap, it makes me wanna gag."

"Just open a window," Price said, "Or light a candle. It burns away the methane gas."

"No it doesn't," Barnard said. "That's a myth."

"Thank you, professor Barnard," Price said.

"It's not my fault if you believe everything you read on the internet," Barnard said.

"Well anyway, we didn't have that cheap stuff in our bathrooms," The Tsar said. "We had real perfume. Expensive stuff, hundreds of dollars a bottle. Big names, like Chanel and Givenchy, stuff like that."

"Oh how very posh," Barnard said.

The Tsar laughed loudly and abruptly. "Once when I was young we went out for dinner to a fancy restaurant. This man walked in with his wife. He was the local mayor. She was this elegant lady in a long flowing gown, manicured everything, diamond earrings and pearls up to here. My dad knew him, so they came over to say hello. And the wife was being all cute and smiling at me and saying how adorable I was and I turned to my mom and said, 'that lady smells just like our toilet.' "

"Always the charmer," Price said, amidst the laughter.

"Here they come," The Tsar said. "Two fast movers, travelling south to north."

"Right on time," Price said.

They moved out as soon as the jets had passed out of range, staying in the darkest shadows, out of the pools of light scavenged from the moon.

Price motioned for the others to stay hidden while she stole quickly across to the bridge. The roadway looked solid and was strong under her first tentative footstep. A few cars had been abandoned here and there along the span, but they did not block the bridge, and could provide a little cover, should it be needed.

"Anything on the scope?" she asked.

"All clear," The Tsar replied.

"Ok, we are Oscar Mike," she said, glad to be away from the town with the memories and feelings it brought.

She waited till they caught up with her, then led the way across. Low wooden fences on either side gave way to tall girders.

All seemed clear. It all seemed easy.

They were travelling light, for which Price was glad. They carried only small belt-packs containing a minimum of ammunition, explosives, medical supplies and rations. Enough for two days. The mission was supposed to take only one.

Price She let Wall take point, and dropped back next to Barnard, switching off her com. Barnard saw the movement and did the same without being asked.

"What do you know about Brogan?" she asked.

"What's that skipper?" Barnard asked.

"You know how she got Bilal to trust her, don't you?"

"Even if I did, I wouldn't be able to tell you," Barnard said. "That information is not essential to the mission."

"It's essential to me," Price said. "I'm team leader. I have to know if I can trust her."

"Price," Barnard said. "We've been through hell together. You're the closest thing I have to a sister. But I have orders from ACOG not to talk about what Brogan did. Trust me, she did something to prove herself. But I can't tell you what."

"That's not an acceptable answer," Price said.

"Deal with it," Barnard said.

Price walked alongside her for a few more paces. They passed a car, just a wreck, sitting on rusted rims, the tyres perished long ago.

"I rang Chisnall, you know," Price said. "On that secret number that nobody was supposed to know."

It was true. She had broken the rules out of a desperate desire to speak to her former team leader. Their bond was a close one. She had been through things with him that Barnard would never know. She had almost died for him. Twice.

"You were told not to," Barnard said.

"I wanted to hear his voice," Price said.

"But nobody answered, right."

"How'd you know?"

"It's too risky for him. He can only answer that phone at certain times," Barnard said. "You could have put his life in danger, calling him like that."

Price's fists were clenched. She forced her fingers to relax, breathing in and out slowly, pushing back the anger. She was upset because she knew it was probably true. Angry that she might have endangered Chisnall's life. Furious at the unfairness of it all.

"What did Brogan do?" Price asked.

"I told you that's classified," Barnard said.

"Jeez Barnard, you're hard," Price exploded. "You don't trust me? What if I order you to tell me?"

"I'll refuse," Barnard said.

"Easy," Monster's voice came from behind them. "Fight is for enemy."

"Don't take it personally, Price," Barnard said. "It's ACOG security, not a popularity contest."

"Look at you two," it was Brogan's voice. "Like children fighting over toys."

"Stay out of it," Price said. "You don't even belong here."

"Tell that to Ryan Chisnall," Brogan said.

"You smug witch," Price said. "We don't need you."

"Yes you do," Brogan smiled.

A combination of tension, fatigue and frustration erupted inside Price. She marched back to Brogan, and grabbed the other girl, shoving her backwards into a metal railing.

Brogan did nothing to resist, nothing to stop herself overbalancing into the water below.

"Don't be so sure," Price said, her hands white knuckled on Brogan's equipment straps. "You're a dirty traitor and I don't need anyone on this team that I don't fully trust."

Brogan seemed indifferent to the onslaught. Her eyes moved slowly from Price's face down to her hands. She started to smile again but stopped and her eyes suddenly shifted to the north.

"Something's coming," she said.

"Don't try and—"

"Contact on the scope," The Tsar hissed. "Solid signal. Air mobile. Slow mover. Half a klick, dead ahead. Same signal I picked up earlier. Whatever it was, it's back."

"Everybody freeze," Price said.

That was a dumb thing to say. Everybody was frozen. What they needed now was to do something.

"Across or back, LT?" Brogan asked, casually removing Price's hands from her equipment straps.

"How'd it get so close before you picked it up, Tsar?" Price asked.

"It's small," The Tsar said. "Very small."

"You're sure it's Bzadian?" Price asked.

"It's giving off all the right signals," The Tsar said. "Seems to be some kind of rotorcraft."

"Rotorbot," Wall said immediately.

"Azoh!" Price swore.

A rotorbot was a Bzadian drone. A small, unmanned, autonomous rotorcraft. Bzadians used them for patrolling far flung areas.

"Four hundred metres," The Tsar said.

"Across or back?" Brogan asked again. "Can't stay here."

They were way too exposed, out here in the middle of the river with nothing but the thin framework of the bridge as cover. On the other side of the river a group of buildings offered them good concealment. But moving forward was moving towards the rotorbot.

Price briefly considered ordering the team over the side of the bridge into the river, where the cold water would hide them, and their heat signatures. But the movement, and the splashes were sure to attract the electronic eyes of the creature.

"Three hundred fifty metres," The Tsar said.

"Across or back?" It was Wall who asked this time and Price was acutely aware of her own hesitation.

"Gotta move, LT," Barnard said, "Gotta do something."

"We stay here. Camo down," Price ordered, pulling her own camo sheet out of her backpack.

"We're going to stick out like skid-marks on a wedding dress," The Tsar said.

"You sure you want to do this?" Brogan asked.

"Shut your mouth and follow orders," Price said.

"Just asking," Brogan said with another infuriating smile.

Price ignored her. She laid her camo-sheet on the roadway and activated it so that it picked up an image of the tar seal. She slid underneath, lying flat on her back to keep the lowest possible profile. She put her eye to one of the spyholes but could see nothing.

"It's coming right at us," The Tsar said.

"Everybody stay real frosty," Price said.

* * *

The route back to the kitchen took Chisnall past the wall of heroes. A long curving corridor covered on both sides with photos of Bzadian soldiers.

There were two requirements for a soldier to have his or her photo on the wall of heroes. Firstly, they had to have done something heroic. Secondly, they had to be dead.

The twenty-seventh picture from the right, on the third row, was one he avoided looking at. It was the only face among them that he knew. It belonged to a Bzadian soldier that he had met, on more than one occasion. Each time they had fought, and each time Chisnall had won. But he had got to know the soldier, and he respected and admired him. In a different world they might have been friends.

His name was Yozi.

A female stood in the corridor, staring at the photos. She wore the white robes of the administration staff.

She glanced up as he emerged from the meeting room, an empty platter in his hands. He didn't recognize her, but neither should he. Outside of the kitchen staff, the only Bzadians he knew by sight were the various high commanders. He had studied their faces until they were ingrained on his memory. Anything overheard was only as important as the person who said it.

He caught his breath slightly as he realised where the female was standing. She was standing at the place he avoided. Twenty-seventh picture from the right. Third row. She was tall for a Bzadian, probably a bobblehead like Yozi.

He looked straight ahead and held the platter high. Just a chef, going about his business.

It didn't work. She looked up as he approached and caught his eye.

"I knew him," she said, her head bobbing slightly as she talked, confirming his guess.

Chisnall used one hand to briefly cover his face. A Bzadian gesture for 'I beg your pardon.'

"We were paired for fifteen years," she said.

Chisnall stopped walking. To continue would be considered rude. It would attract attention he did not want to attract.

"It is unusual in our culture," she said.

Chisnall said nothing but could not help the widening of his eyes.

Our culture, she had said. In a society where people did not form lasting relationships it was unusual for paired couples to stay together longer than a few years. But why had she used the words 'our culture' to another Bzadian.

"He would never admit it to anyone," she said. "For fear of ridicule. But it was true."

A highly ranked General rounded the corner of the corridor ahead of them, talking in a low voice with his Vaza: a tall, misshapen female who was his bodyguard, among other things.

The general glanced at Chisnall.

"I must return," Chisnall said, shuffling the empty platter around on his arm.

She was silent for a moment, then, as the general and his Vaza approached within earshot, said, a little more loudly, "The other members of the group wanted me to pass on our appreciation of your appetizers. They were delightful."

Chisnall smiled and nodded.

"Thank you," he said, "It is a pleasure to serve, and I will pass your compliments on to the others involved."

The pair passed with a sideways glance.

The woman looked back at the photograph and lowered her voice again. "He was a hero long before Uluru," she said. "Ask any of those who served with him. But it was Uluru that made him famous."

"Of course," Chisnall said, wishing he had something more significant to say and desperate to get back to the kitchen.

"Nobody knows what happened at Wivenhoe," she said. "His body was never found."

"That is sad," Chisnall said. "But I must excuse myself. My head chef will be wondering where–"

"Some people did not want his photo on this wall," she said. "They think he was somehow responsible for the disaster, or didn't do enough to stop it. But I knew him. I know he would have done everything he could, and more."

For a moment Chisnall's mind flooded with images of Yozi diving into the waters of the dam, disappearing below the water as he disarmed the bomb Chisnall had placed there. Then that faded and all that remained was the look of calm, acceptance, as a giant snakehead of water rose above Yozi and prepared to strike.

"I'm sure... he was a hero... at Wivenhoe," Chisnall said.

"Yes," the woman mused. "I'm sure he was. But only Chizna would be able to tell us that."

A fist suddenly clenched around his heart. A panic, and urge to run that welled up from deep within him, spreading icy fingers throughout his body.

But panic was the killer. The unclean beast. That thought had been beaten into him until it was ingrained in his psyche and that gave him the strength to stay where he was, and even to smile a little as he shook his head. "Chizna? I don't know this name."

For the first time she turned to face him, glancing quickly both ways along the corridor first.

"It is not safe to talk here," she said. "I will meet you in the art gallery. I will be there in an hour."

She whirled, her cloaks flowing out around her like a sandstorm, then was gone.

* * *

Price could hear it now, a soft humming from above them. Scanning the sky carefully she finally caught a glimpse of it, a black disc blotting out stars. It was incredibly bad luck to have been caught by one of these things in such an exposed place.

It flew well above the girders of the bridge, not slowing.

Thank God!

The beating of Price's heart began to ease as the sound receded and the rotorbot, just a vague dark blur now, drifted across towards the far shore.

"Are we clear?" she asked The Tsar, when the disc had moved out of sight.

"I think so," The Tsar said.

"It's coming back," Brogan said. "Nobody move."

How she knew, Price had no idea. Brogan had slid under the rusting wreck of the car they had passed.

That plus her camo sheet, gave her good protection from the hovering bot.

"No it's not," The Tsar said. "It's continuing to move over the town."

"It's coming back," Brogan said again.

"What do you know about rotorbots, Barnard?" Price asked.

"Not much," Barnard said.

"I know a bit," Wall said.

"Then talk, and quickly," Price said.

"Okay," Wall said. "They're primarily designed for surveillance, with Hi-Res and thermal cameras, plus sensitive microphones."

"Any armaments?" Price asked.

Wall nodded. "Twin needle guns and a short range, anti-personnel rocket, all mounted underneath. And Brogan's right. If a rotorbot thinks it has a contact it moves away. Lulls the enemy into a false sense of security. Then it comes back and compare the images before and after, to see if anything has changed."

"You're sure about all this?" Price asked.

"Basic training at Uluru," Wall said.

"Who's the moron now, Barnard?" The Tsar said and Price could hear the grin in his voice.

"Knowledge does not equate to intelligence," Barnard said.

"Everybody hold where you are," Price said. "Let's give it a minute or two."

She shifted just slightly on the rough surface of the road. A stone that she hadn't noticed when she lay down, now seemed to be burrowing its way into her back.

"It's coming back," Brogan said for the third time.

Price scanned the sky above them through the pinhole in her camo-sheet, but all she could see was the boxy grid of the girders of the bridge and the faceless smirk of the moon.

"Oh crap," The Tsar said. "It's heading back in our direction."

"Oh now there's a surprise," Brogan said.

ROTORBOT

The rotorbot hovered just above them, so close that Price felt she could hear every swish of its rotor blades.

It had passed over the top of the bridge the first time, but then had returned much lower, inside the box girder construction of the main span of the bridge. It had passed over once, then returned.

Clearly something had disturbed it. Perhaps the odd lumps on the otherwise flat surface of the road.

"Think it knows we're here?" The Tsar asked, his voice little more than a murmur.

"It knows something's here," Wall said. "It just isn't sure what."

"If it knew it would have blown us all to hell by now," Brogan said.

"It will be relaying pictures to its base for analysis," Wall added.

"So we can expect company anytime soon," Price said. "We need to get out of here."

"You move a muscle and the rotorbot will chew you to bits," Wall said.

"Any chance it will get bored and go away?" The Tsar asked.

"Poor to none," Wall said. "Once it has detected a possible threat it will stick with it. Unless it detects a more direct threat somewhere else."

"How do we kill it?" The Tsar asked.

"Not easy," Wall said. "They're well armoured underneath. The brains are on top, in the middle, where you can't get a shot at them."

The rotorbot moved lower, hovering barely a metre or so above Price. She stopped talking. She stopped breathing, not wanting the slightest movement to be noticed by the killing machine above her. But there was movement. The downwash of the rotorbot was rippling the fabric of the camo sheet. She gripped the hand and footholds in each corner, stretching the sheet as tautly as she could.

Even lower, the rotorbot came, caressing her body with cold hands of air. One of its needle guns turned slightly, aiming right at her head. Could it see her eye through the tiny pinhole spyhole? Price doubted it, but still had to fight an overwhelming panic, the urge to cut and run.

To the East end of the bridge she saw a slight movement.

The Tsar had taken advantage of the rotorbot's focus on Price and had crawled out from under his camo sheet. What was he doing? It would see him for sure.

It started to turn in his direction and without really thinking what she was doing she let go of one of the corners of her camo-sheet.

It rustled and flapped in the breeze from the rotor, and the rotorbot immediately turned back.

She snapped the sheet tight and froze as the rotorbot prowled around her like a dog sniffing out a bone.

The Tsar climbed onto the railing of the bridge. It was rusting and brown flakes crumbled under his touch, but there was no sound as they drifted to the ground. Above him towered the tall girders of the lift tower, easily wide enough for him to hide behind, if he could reach it before the rotorbot turned again.

Price herself did not dare move, the rotorbot was already way too interested in her little patch of the roadway.

Even as she thought that, the rotorbot jumped up, as if startled and shot back to the southern end of the bridge. Someone else had had the same idea, Price realised. A slight movement. Enough to catch the machine's interest without attracting fire.

She looked back to the tower. The Tsar was gone, hidden behind the girder.

What was he thinking? She could not figure out his plan, if he had one. She looked up.

In the centre of the tower hung a massive concrete weight, a counterbalance for the weight of the centre span. A matching weight hung in the tower at the other end of the lift-bridge. That one looked straight and solid, however the one at this end was lopsided and appeared to be on the verge of falling. Parts of the tower had fallen away, but an enclosed ladder remained. It led up to the top of the span, where there were the remains of the bridge's control cabin. Now she saw it. His plan was to get above the rotorbot.

The rotorbot spun around in her direction and she froze again. Unmoving. Part of the bridge.

It drifted back to where The Tsar had been, to where his camo-sheet now lay flat on the road. It seemed agitated, if a hovering automated rotorcraft could seem agitated.

She realised what it was doing. Exactly what Wall had said it would do. It was comparing before and after shots of the same area of the bridge. One of the lumps in the roadway was gone. It probably wasn't smart enough to work out what was wrong, but it knew something was different.

It stayed in that location, but spun around to face the southern end of the bridge. The moment its cameras were facing away, The Tsar was moving again. She saw him put a foot on the first rung of the ladder, testing it. It held, and there were no creaks, squeaks, clangs or other noises. He took a firm hold of one of the higher rungs and swung himself onto the ladder. Still he had not attracted the attention of the bot.

He went up a few rungs quickly then froze as the bot again rotated in his direction, needle-guns probing the darkness. It began to move in Price's direction and she willed it back. Somehow it worked. The bot reversed its course.

A few more rungs, then a few more, and now The Tsar was level with the machine. Still it faced away from him. He reached the top of the span, where a narrow walkway led across to the control cabin. He was above the rotorbot now, and out of view of its camera, as long as the rotorbot remained in the enclosed centre span of the bridge.

The Tsar drew his sidearm. His coil-gun would be more accurate, Price thought, but the sound of the back holster spring release would be far too loud. The Tsar knelt down to steady his aim and reduce the distance. The rotorbot moved, he aimed again, and fired. The needle gun hissed.

The rotorbot moved just slightly as he pulled the trigger, changing position just a matter of millimetres. It was enough. Price heard the shot hit the metal hull of the craft and ricocheted out over the side of the bridge.

The rotorbot reacted instantly, sensing that it was under attack. From the sound of the shot it must have worked out exactly where its attacker was. It rose up, trying to get above The Tsar, but quickly realised that it was constrained by the top span of the bridge. It was only a metre below him now and The Tsar tried to line up on it again. Before he could fire, the rotorbot's brain figured out what it had to do.

It swept back along the bridge, towards clear air, where it could rise up higher and bring its cameras, and its guns, to bear.

The Tsar whirled, trying to get off another shot, but with such a small target, moving so rapidly, he had no chance.

It reached the end of the enclosed section but before it could rise up, there was a shout, and movement on the bridge below.

Price looked down in horror to see Brogan running back along the bridge, yelling at the top of her voice. She had panicked, and lost it, was Price's first thought. But surely not. Not Brogan. She was as tough as nails. Was she trying to alert the rotorbot to their presence?

The rotorbot swivelled and fired once, then began to chase after her. It again passed right below where The Tsar was crouching on the rusted metal walkway.

He twisted around and over the side of the walkway, dropping down between two of the metal girders. His left arm rasped against one of the girders with a metallic shriek but there was no longer any need to be quiet.

His timing had to be perfect and it was, perhaps because he had reacted without thinking, without trying to work out speeds and angles. His subconscious mind did instantly what his conscious mind could never have done. The Tsar landed square on top of the rotorbot as it flew underneath. Price heard the hissing of its needle guns as man and machine fell from the sky, the combined weight far too much for the small rotor-blade engine.

For a moment it recovered, slightly, lifting up a little as its rotors went to maximum power. But only for a moment. The machine wobbled as it dropped and The Tsar slipped sideways, desperately grabbing at the edges of the machine. The machine bucked in the air like a rodeo bull. Its needle-guns began to fire, a constant staccato hiss, some kind of automatic defence mechanism, spinning and firing at random.

It skidded sideways in the air, slamming into the girders of the bridge. Was it an attempt to knock him off? Was the brain of the machine that smart? Probably not, but intentional or not, the impact with the bridge flung The Tsar sideways and off the edge of the disc. The only reason he hadn't fallen was one hand, fingers clenched like a steel claw, which had latched onto the glass dome in the centre.

And it was a creature. A creature of metal not flesh, with a brain of circuits instead of synapses, but a creature that did not want to die, and somehow it sensed that The Tsar's one goal was to kill it.

The crash into the side of the bridge set the rotorcraft spinning, dropping at the same time, they were crashing, the Tsar and the machine and it seemed to go on forever but it was barely more than a second before the rotorbot hit the roadway with a crunching sound. With one last burst of energy the machine whirred, jolted and lifted, throwing The

Tsar to one side but Price was already there, throwing her weight on top of the rotorbot. Wall was there too, coil-gun in hand, his combat boot trapping one edge. The three of them held the injured beast down, but still it tried to rise until the stock of Wall's coil-gun came down on a glass dome in the centre, shattering it. He reversed his weapon, inserted the muzzle and fired. There were sparks and a flash from inside the rotorbot and it crumpled back to the ground. Its rotors slowly wailing to a halt.

"Good work," Price managed, gasping for air.

"Now let's get the hell out of here before the Pukes come to find their missing toy," Wall said.

"Is everybody ok?" Price asked. "Angel Team, check in."

Everybody was not ok. The Tsar lay where he had fallen, half across the side of the rotorbot. A dark pool was spreading slowly under his head.

"Oh no. Oh God no," Barnard said.

110-RKH

In 2012 in the midst of the Bzadian migration to Earth, before it turned into an invasion, one of the great transporters failed to make atmospheric entry.

Statistically the loss of the ship was insignificant, a very small percentage of the thousands of huge spaceships that made the voyage to Earth.

And the loss of just one ship was especially surprising when you considered that the transporters had never been tested. They had been built in space and launched in space for a one-way trip to earth.

Yet the crash of the ship designated as 110-RKH was a devastating blow for the aliens. Far greater than they were prepared to admit at the time, at least to their new human landlords. Of all the transporters that made the great journey, that was the one they could least afford to lose.

An equipment malfunction caused the spaceship to miscalculate its entry and damage its wings, eventually falling to earth under the eyes of every television channel on Earth. It was a slow-motion disaster that happened over the course of a day, with Bzadians and humans alike helpless to stop it. Three thousand souls extinguished before they even had a chance to wake from stasis.

It changed world opinion. The outpouring of compassion over the loss of so many lives softened humanity's wariness of the aliens and paved the way for the greatest humanitarian disaster in Earth's history.

110-RKH, like all the transporters, had as its destination

the country then known as Australia. It may not have made it, but the others did. More than six thousand transporters dotted the great red desert of the Australian outback before Earth governments began to sense that something was wrong.

These first Bzadians were not mere settlers. They were assembling an army.

Even if human governments had understood the significance of the loss of 110-RKH, there was nothing that anyone on Earth could have done.

ALIENS DON'T DANCE

[Mission Day 1, July 1st, 2033. 0610 hours local time]
[Batemans Bay, New Bzadia]

"Tsar? Tsar!" Barnard was the first to The Tsar's side.

Monster pushed her out of the way, pulling at The Tsar's armour, examining the wound. He removed the Tsar's helmet and checked his neck. The others quickly gathered around. The Tsar seemed to be unconscious, and that surely was not a good sign.

"Status?" Price asked, dropping to a knee beside him.

"Not so good," Monster said. "Unlucky. Armour is soft at neck. Needle got through. Now stuck in throat. He bleeding very badly. Maybe artery."

He pulled a mediscope from his belt-pack and began to scan The Tsar's neck.

"What can I do?" Barnard asked. "What can I do?"

"Will ask if need," Monster said.

"Give him room to work," Price said and Barnard reluctantly eased backwards.

Price straightened also, standing with the others as Monster attended to The Tsar.

"We need to get out of here," Wall said. "The Pukes just lost a rotorbot. They're already on their way."

"Are you suggesting that we just leave The Tsar to die?" Barnard snapped.

"We'll all die if they get here and we're still here," Wall said.

"Barnard, what are we looking at?" Price asked.

She already had a pretty good idea, but wanted Barnard focusing on something other than The Tsar.

Barnard stared at her for a moment, then took a deep breath.

"There's a ready reaction force in Canberra, they're the closest," she said. "But they're part of the capital's defences, I doubt they'd send those. We'll probably get a couple of scout ships real soon, or they may just redirect other rotorbots, if they have them in the area."

"What about regular forces?" Price asked.

"They'll send teams from Melbourne, or Brisbane, or maybe both," Barnard said. "That'll take them a little longer. But Wall's right. We have to get out of here. It's going to be touch and go, even if we leave right now."

"Can you move him?" Price asked.

Monster looked up and nodded. "Too dangerous to extract needle. Will tape needle in place and bandage. Can move."

"How are you going to move him?" Barnard asked. "You can't…"

Monster could and did.

He reached down and hoisted The Tsar up in a fireman's lift.

"Jeez Monster," Price said. "That can't be good for him."

"Worse is staying here," Monster said. He lurched into a run, doing his best to give The Tsar a steady ride.

"Okay Angels, we are Oscar Mike," Price said. "And hustle."

Wall had picked up something off the road, it had been lying under The Tsar's body. His scope. He showed it to Price.

The screen was cracked and dead. Without it they had lost their best defence against prying Bzadian eyes in the form of rotorcraft or fast movers.

"Damn," Price said as they ran after Monster.

She reached the dead rotorbot about the same time Wall did, and said, "Give me a hand with this mother."

Wall took one side, lifting it easily. Price struggled with her end, but managed to raise it and together they eased it over the side railing. It hit the water on one edge and sank with little splash, and only a stream of bubble indicating the location.

"Left or right, LT?" Brogan called, she was first off the bridge.

Ahead of them to the right a road led into a residential area. To the left was a small, overgrown park and parking lot. Behind it was an area of forest.

"Left," Price said. "Better cover in the trees."

"Everybody down!" Brogan yelled.

Price had heard and seen nothing, but dived into a nearby bush, wrapping her camo sheet around her. A second later two fast movers roared overhead, low and fast. Almost certainly the same air patrol they had seen earlier.

"That'll be just an initial recon," she said. "As soon as they are out of range, get moving. We have to get to that forest before the slow movers get here."

The jets made a second sweep before disappearing off to the north in a blaze of noise and afterburners.

A narrow dirt track through the park led up a rise towards the wooded area, it was densely overgrown, and they had to push through it.

Although only minutes, it seemed like hours before they reached the comparative safety of the trees. Price found a fallen tree branch and went back to erase their tracks, scratching out boot-steps and straightening stalks of grass. She caught up with the other Angels and. She found them gathered around The Tsar, lying on the ground at the base of a large tree. Its heavy branches and leafy foliage gave good cover from any overhead watchers.

Barnard was holding an IV bag, which was dripping clear fluid into an opening on the arm of The Tsar's combat suit. Bzadian suits had automatic IV tubes at the elbow for exactly this kind of situation.

Monster was using the mediscope to examine The Tsar's neck. He clearly didn't like what he saw.

"Monster?" Price asked.

Monster shook his head. "Needle has nicked carotid artery. He's losing a lot of blood. If I leave it there, he die."

"And if you pull it out?"

"He die quicker," Monster said. "Needle is stemming the blood flow."

There was a long silence as the team considered the implications of that.

"Gotta leave him," Brogan said.

"Get puked, Brogan," Barnard said. "You and the horse you rode in on."

"We leave no one behind," Price said. "Unless they're dead. And The Tsar ain't dead."

"He's going to be," Brogan said, and as Barnard clenched her fists and moved towards her, added, "Just telling it like it is."

Price took a deep breath, forcing herself to be calm, to act like a leader. Brogan was probably right, but that didn't make it any easier.

"What to do, LT?" Monster asked.

"We must…" Price started but trailed off.

"Leave him here," Brogan said after another silence.

"No," Barnard said.

"It's your choice, LT," Brogan said. "Either we carry on with our mission, and he dies, or we give up on our mission. And he still dies."

"You'd leave him here to die?" Barnard asked.

"Here's as good as anywhere," Brogan said.

"You'd leave a fellow Angel to die alone in a forest?" Barnard said. "You really are a cold-hearted witch."

"He's not conscious," Brogan said. "He doesn't know he's alone."

"We know he's alone," Barnard said.

"Take him with us," Wall said. "When we get to Canberra we can leave him at a Puke hospital or something."

"Like that wouldn't jeopardise the mission," Brogan said.

"It would save his life," Barnard said.

"It makes for no matter," Monster said. "He would no survive journey."

Barnard stepped right in front of Brogan, eyeballing her. "We're not leaving him," she said.

"I know he's your special friend," Brogan said, with that infuriating smile, "But he's going to die and there's nothing you can do about it."

Barnard's arm drew back, to strike, but Price, behind her, saw it as it happened and reflexively caught her elbow.

"Wait a sec," Price said. "There's nothing we can do about it. But you can?"

"Maybe," Brogan shrugged.

They all stared at her.

"If you trust me," she said.

* * *

[Mission Day 1, July 1st, 2033. 0630 hours local time]
[Government Building, Canberra, Central Meeting Room]

The war had been good to Colonel Nokz'z. Mostly.

Had it not been for the war he would have had nothing. He would have been nothing. He was under no illusion of that. At first they had said there would be no war, but there was war and when the war started they needed Nokz'z, or at least people like Nokz'z.

Brutality did not come naturally to the Bzadian species. It had once, but that was a very long time ago. War, violence, bloodshed, it had all disappeared over the centuries as their world had evolved. It had become a safer, gentler place. A dull, boring place, in Nokz'z opinion. Without death, or the threat of death, what was life? Just a meaningless cycle of the same day over and over again.

Weapons had gradually rusted or been dismantled, existing only as curiosities in Museums. Discussion was preferred over argument. Diplomacy over fighting. But to prepare for migration to a savage, violent world, Bzadians had been forced to rediscover their history. Warrior-personalities, once reviled, were now revered.

Nokz'z considered himself a throwback to a glorious time. If not for people like him, they would have no chance against the barbarians that inhabited this planet called Earth.

Bzadia needed people who could do what he could do. Who would do what he was prepared to do. He was not like the others, Nokz'z knew that. He took pleasure in things that would horrify most of his kind. He knew that he was despised by many of his associates. But they tolerated him. They needed him. He told himself they secretly admired him and what he did, although he was too smart to really believe that.

Some of his compatriots felt sympathy for the humans, considering them noble savages who would eventually come to accept and tolerate Bzadian rule. But to Nokz'z they were vermin, pests, and he was the exterminator.

But he did not tolerate failure, especially not in himself. Nor did his masters. And what had happened in the Bering Strait could be called nothing less. A small team of scumbugz, disguised as Bzadians, had disrupted their carefully laid plan for the invasion of the Americas. On the precipice of success, their million-strong army had been stopped in its tracks by four or five, humans. Not just humans, children!

Had those children survived? He could not know. He was lucky to get out with his own life as the humans had cut huge trenches in the ice-floes and the vital core of his army had slid to a frozen, watery grave. A disaster, his masters had called it, and his punishment was to lose command of the invasion force. Those weak bureaucrats and soft politicians had had him reposted, to the Coastal Defence of New Bzadia.

True, it was an important posting, they were too afraid of him to give him anything less, and the defence of the motherland could not be considered inconsequential, but when the invasion of the Americas finally took place, it would not be his name that would be on the flags of victory. It would not be Nokz'z that children read about in history classes, the conqueror of Earth.

There was nothing he could do about that, for now.

His quarters were in the east wing of the Congress building. Earlier that morning he had been shaken out of a pleasant dream and called to an emergency meeting. No information had been given, but for a meeting to be called so urgently and on such a large scale, it had to be something major.

He entered the meeting room to find it humming. Delegates chatting in small groups, chefs placing platters of food on the tables. He cursed himself for being late. He preferred to be early so he could watch others as they arrived. Observe their demeanour, see who they were talking to.

Commandant Goezlin, the head of the secret police, the dreaded PGZ, was in a huddle with two or three others. He must have flown in from Uluru very early that morning. Or perhaps he was already in Canberra on other business. He looked up when he saw Nokz'z enter, and after a moment or two broke off the conversation, walking, seemingly casually in Nokz'z direction. But nothing Goezlin did was ever casual.

"Colonel."

"Commandant."

"I hear you have lost a rotorbot," Goezlin said.

Nokz'z took his glasses off and polished the lenses. How typical that Goezlin knew this before he had even learned of it. He replaced his glasses and nodded. "I am waiting for details to come through as we speak."

Someone would be severely punished for this.

"Am I correct that it was lost on the coast, almost due east from here?" Goezlin asked, not really a question. "Batemans Bay?"

Nokz'z considered that. The bay was regularly patrolled because of its proximity to Canberra.

"Your information sources are impressive," he said, noncommittally. "But a lost rotorbot could be a malfunction. We have lost them before for this reason and I am not going to jump into any rash action before I have full details."

Goezlin shook his head. "But as you undoubtedly know, it was operating in alert mode, tracking something, before it was lost."

Did Goezlin know everything?

"My people are on it," Nokz'z said, trying to salvage some dignity from the situation.

"Yes they are," Goezlin said, but the small upturning of the corners of his lips said a shame you were not. He seemed momentarily distracted, Nokz'z thought, his attention taken by one of the chefs working on the tables around the room.

The chef finished what he was doing and turned, walking past them and out of the room. His eyes flicked over both Nokz'z and Goezlin as he passed. He had no reaction to Nokz'z, but when he saw Goezlin there was a slight widening of his eyes, a momentary hitch in his stride. This chef recognised Goezlin. That was unusual. Very few would know Goezlin's face. He was a man of the shadows, a dark creature of the night.

Unless of course this poor chef had once been unfortunate enough to register on Goezlin's radar.

Goezlin turned back to Nokz'z as the chef left. "What are your plans to deal with this possible intrusion?"

"I have no plans, as I am awaiting further information," Nokz'z said. "We do not even know if it is an intrusion, and if it is, we do not know their target."

"I think the target is obvious," Goezlin said. "The same day we call an emergency meeting, we lose a rotorbot close to the capital. Most of our top military leaders will be congregated in one building, in one room. Azoh will be attending. A small team of assassins, or saboteurs, could cause irreparable damage to our military leadership."

Nokz'z had to fight to keep the surprise and annoyance off his face. Azoh would attend the meeting? That was almost unprecedented. But as head of Coastal Defence, his responsibilities included the defence of the capital and the government building. Why had he not been informed of this?

"This meeting was only called a few hours ago," he said. "The scumbugz could not have known about it in time to send it a team of assassins. Such an attack would be weeks in the planning."

"They might not have known about the meeting," Goezlin said. "But they may have known that we would call such a meeting in response to a major threat. They may have planned the first use of their new jets deliberately to provoke the meeting."

New jets?

"I will create a perimeter around the Congress," Nokz'z said. "Nobody will get through."

"And Batemans Bay?" Goezlin asked.

"I will saturate the area with patrol craft and rotorbots," Nokz'z said. "If necessary I will raze it to the ground.

"I am glad to see that you are well on top of this situation," Goezlin said.

Damn him!

Goezlin moved off without speaking further. He left the room via the same door the chef had just taken, Nokz'z noticed. It seemed casual.

But nothing Goezlin did was ever casual.

* * *

The Tsar, unconscious, rode on the tray of a small garden truck. A utility vehicle built on a golf cart chassis, it was battery powered and almost silent. Wall had found it in a work shed at the motel.

Monster rode with The Tsar, tending to his wound as best as he could. The bandages were dark green in the NV lenses and the colour was spreading slowly in a pool around his neck. Barnard was next to him, holding the IV bag, dripping what little plasma they had into his veins.

The Tsar was a concern, but distance was a greater concern. The further away from Batemans Bay the better.

Price, riding shotgun, turned and looked back at The Tsar. It was strange how such a little thing, a slender length of steel, could turn a person from a big, vivacious, fun-loving show-off into a small, grey thing. Gone was the ready smile that oozed a genuine charm. Gone was the raw energy that sparkled from his eyes. The Tsar had always been larger than life. Now the life was gone from the body and without it he looked older, shrivelled and dull. The bright star that was The Tsar had been dimmed.

An overgrown but passable track through the trees led them to a long-abandoned highway. You never realised how clean highways were until you saw an abandoned one, Price thought. Street-sweeper and the tyres of thousands of cars kept them clear. But not this road. It was papered with leaves, studded with rocks and crinkled by broken branches. Even so the going was easy, Mother Nature had so far left only a light coating of her skin on this man-made thing, although twice they had to veer around fallen trees. If left alone, the highway would gradually sink back into the earth it was built on, a relic for some future civilisation to dig up and wonder at.

But would that civilisation be Human or Bzadian.

About three very nervous kilometres they found a wide open area of forest, clear-felled. A firebreak, although after years of neglect, it too was well overgrown. The Bzadians wouldn't call it neglect. They didn't believe in cutting and slashing at the natural world around them. They lived amidst and amongst the flora and fauna and shook their heads in mild disbelief at the human obsession with shaping and prettifying their environment.

After a brief discussion the Angels turned into the firebreak. The going would be slower, but they would be less likely to run into Bzadian patrols. Even so they stayed as close as possible to the tree line, ready to duck back under cover at the slightest sign of trouble. Brogan's eyes scanned the sky constantly and she often seemed to be listening to things that nobody else could hear. Her sight and hearing abilities were extra-ordinary, Price thought. Wall too seemed beyond human. For his size he was immensely strong. Price had seen that in the Bering Strait. But his endurance was a surprise. He had been running along behind the garden truck the entire way, wielding a long rake, smoothing the grass back into position after the truck had passed. Yet he showed no trace of strain or exhaustion. When they bred humans in the bowels of Uluru, they bred them good. Not quite super-humans, but something in between.

The side-track was a blemish on the otherwise unbroken wall of the forest. A dark intrusion into the trees, just wide enough for the little truck.

Price slowed to a stop and got out to investigate. It turned out to be a dead-end, but it was almost perfect for their needs. Somewhere to hide, not too close to the town. She eased the little truck in between two trees and stopped again in a wide space, well concealed by dense overhanging foliage.

She turned and stared at Brogan, sitting quietly in the passenger seat. Brogan returned her stare without blinking.

"Do you really think you could do something for The Tsar," Price said.

"It's a possibility," Brogan said. "But as I said, you'll have to trust me."

"Trust doesn't come easy around here," Price said. "Especially not for you."

"It's your call," Brogan said.

"Monster, what do you think?" Price asked.

"Do anything will kill him," Monster said. "We no can remove the needle without he bleed to death."

"But do you trust Brogan?" Price asked.

Monster shrugged and did not answer.

"Barnard?" Price asked.

"You can trust her," Barnard said.

"Give me a reason," Price said.

"Can't do that," Barnard said. "It's classified."

"I'm not prepared to let her touch him unless I am convinced," Price said.

"Take my word for it," Barnard said.

"I can't do that," Price said. "What do you know?"

"I can't…" Barnard was wiping The Tsar's forehead with a cool cloth. She dropped it and looked up at Price for a moment. Without warning she exploded. "Jeez Price, is this some kind of control thing? Because this is The Tsar's life we're talking about!"

"Keep your voice down," Price said, looking around at the silent forest. "This is not about you and me, it's about The Tsar. I'm the one who has to make the decision, and I'm the one who has to live with the consequences. Don't ask me to do that without giving me the facts."

Barnard stared at her a moment longer then went back to wiping The Tsar's forehead. Without looking at either Price or Brogan, she said, "Brogan gave up the other Ferzerkers."

"Is that true?" Wall asked. There was a mixture of emotions in his voice, and Price couldn't help but think that he was one of those Ferzerkers. If he hadn't already switched sides, he too would have been betrayed by Brogan.

"It's what she does best, isn't it?" Barnard said. "Betraying people. Chisnall asked for her to be on the mission but ACOG wouldn't agree. They ended up making a deal. She gave up everyone from Uluru that she knew of, and she gave them some good leads on a lot of others, especially those that have infiltrated the military. She was the one who identified Lieutenant-Colonel Reid."

Price caught her breath. The court-martial of Colonel Thomas Reid had been headline news for weeks. He had turned out to be the one responsible for putting a Ferzerker onto Little Diomede Island, which had nearly allowed the Bzadians to catch ACOG napping in the recent ice war.

Brogan sat unmoving, unmoved, it seemed, by Barnard's revelation. "Now you know," she said. "I chose to be here, even though it meant betraying people that I had known since birth. People that I had sworn to protect."

"Can't have been too hard," Monster said. "You have plenty practice."

"Get over it, big fella," Brogan said. "That's in the past. Let it go. And learn to speak English."

Price saw Monster's shoulders begin to rise and she quickly held up a hand to stop him, shaking her head. Monster took a deep breath and sat back down.

"You know what I can't stomach, Brogan?" Price said. "It's not that you murdered a friend of mine and nearly got us all killed. It's not even that you betrayed someone who trusted you. What gets on my wick is when you hung out that big sob story to Chisnall about your parents dying in a shipwreck."

"He told you about that?"

"Of course he did. Poor little orphan Brogan. But the joke is that the rest of us are orphans. All of us know what it feels like to lose the two people who love us the most. To be alone. But you... you just feed us a story. It was all a fraud. You're a fraud Brogan."

"It was the cover story they gave me," Brogan said.

"Is that supposed to make it better?" Price asked.

"I know about your foster parents," Brogan said.

Price, who had risen to her feet, sat back down with a thump on the seat of the truck, rocking it a little on its suspension. "That's none of your goddamn business."

"Maybe," Brogan shrugged. "But I know what they did to you."

"What that got to do with anything?" Monster asked.

"Until I was five I was raised by a Bzadian couple," Brogan said. "Closest thing I'll ever have to a mum and dad. They treated me really well, which can't have been easy, considering that I looked like the enemy." She shrugged again. "It's sad the way humans treat their young."

"Don't try to turn this around," Price said.

"I'm just saying," Brogan said. "You didn't deserve what they did to you. What's wrong with the human race? Bzadians don't do that stuff."

"Nothing's wrong with the human race," Barnard said. "Don't judge an entire species by a few psychos."

"Yeah? Then what are you doing here?" Brogan asked. "All of you. You're child soldiers. Think about it. This ain't some paintball game." She nodded towards The Tsar. "Your society cares for its children by sending them out to die in some muddy ditch. Now do you want me to help him or not?"

There was silence.

Price twisted around in her seat and leaned over The Tsar, listening to his breathing, low and ragged, noting the pallid colour of his cheeks. She touched his forehead, recoiling from the clammy coldness of his skin.

Brogan had been the team's medic long before Monster. Plus she had Ferzerker training. And really what choice was there? Without her, The Tsar would die anyway.

"Do what you can," Price said.

"You kill him if remove needle," Monster said.

"Thanks for the advice," Brogan said.

Monster shook his head but stretched out an arm, handing her his mediscope.

Barnard climbed down from the tray of the truck to give Brogan room, but not before her lips accidentally brushed against The Tsar's forehead. She clearly thought nobody noticed, and when she glanced up, Price quickly looked away as if she had not seen.

Brogan climbed over and examined the injury carefully before sitting back on her haunches, pursing her lips.

"What's your plan, Brogan?" Price asked.

"Monster's right about the needle," Brogan said. "It has pierced the right carotid artery. He's leaking like a cheap umbrella, but the needle itself is partly blocking the hole. Pull it out and we turn a trickle into a flood. However…" She took a deep breath. "If we were able to cauterise the wound then we might be able to save him."

"How to cauterise wound?" Monster asked. "To do this must remove needle. Remove needle, he die."

"We might be able to do it with the needle," Brogan said. "If we can heat up the needle, then withdraw it, and if we're really lucky, we might be able to cauterise the flesh as we pull it out. It'll have to be quick though."

"Is this really possible?" Price asked.

"Possible, yes," Brogan said. "Chances of success, slim."

"Is it our best option?" Price asked.

"No. A hospital would be our best option, but I forgot to bring one of those," Brogan said.

"How to heat needle?" Monster asked.

"Electrical current," Brogan said. "I was thinking of using one of our combat suit batteries, but the car batteries that power this truck would be much better. Wire them in parallel to increase the voltage and pray like…" She broke off abruptly and looked at the sky. "Incoming, fast movers!"

"Everybody stay where you are," Price said. "We're well covered here."

She strained her ears but could not hear whatever it was that Brogan had heard.

"Are you sure?" She asked. "There's…"

She broke off as the high-pitched whine of fast moving jets came from overhead.

A moment later the ground and the trees around them shook from thunderous explosions to the east.

"They're hitting Batemans Bay," Barnard said.

"That's good," Price said. "It means they don't know where we are."

"They're not just hitting it," Wall said, as the explosions continued. "They're annihilating it."

"As long as they focus on the town, we'll be okay," Price said.

"I wouldn't count on it," Barnard said.

She had barely finished speaking when a much closer wave of explosions rolled up through the forest behind them.

"Everybody get down," Price yelled. "Find what cover you can. Get The Tsar off the truck."

Monster and Barnard together lifted The Tsar and placed him on the ground next to the truck, taking advantage of what little protection it offered. Price found a depression in the ground and pressed herself into it.

More blasts, flame and smoke, rippled through the forest, closer and closer.

The ground was moving like an earthquake now, rolling shudders making it difficult to even breathe. Barnard spread herself over The Tsar, protecting him from the debris that began to rain down on them. Earth, rock fragments, tree shards. Whole branches, sheared off, were flying through the air like spears. The heat and pressure waves smashed through the forest, bending back tall gums and stripping them of their leaves. The little truck got shunted sideways by one blast, rolling onto its side, slamming into a tree, where it wedged tight.

For a few moments the barrage seemed to stop, but it was only a respite, the eye of the storm. Through a momentary gap in the trees, waving like prairie grass in the wind, Price saw the menacing, bug-like shape of a Bzadian dragon, rocket ports alive with fire. It was a creature from hell, and it brought hell with it. In an awesome display of fire-power the dragon began to take the forest apart. Whole trees, on fire, were flying through the air, the earth erupting like a thousand volcanoes.

"We gotta get out of here," Wall shouted over the noise of the explosions. "It's getting closer!"

"No!" Price yelled back. "Stay down. Stand up and you'll die!"

As if to make her point a tree trunk came crashing through

the forest around them, smashing into the ground and rolling over and over, ending up on top of Price's dip in the ground. A heavy branch, smoking, but not burning, embedded itself into the dirt between her legs.

"Listen to your LT," Brogan yelled. "There'll be rotorcraft and rotorbots hovering overhead, just waiting for us to break cover. We have to ride it out."

A tree at the edge of their clearing suffered a direct hit, about midway up. It shattered into thousands of splinters and shards, raining down all around them, splattering off their combat armour, but not penetrating.

There was screaming now on the com, pain, fear, Price could not tell, and still the earth heaved and trees danced their awful dance, still the fists of smoke and jagged teeth of red and yellow flames punched and chewed their way through the forest.

Price could hear more screaming, some of it hers, although it was drowned out by wave after wave of crashing thunder and bone shaking rumbles.

And then it was over.

Just as quickly as it started, it stopped. The only sounds were the diminishing whine of the jets overhead, the fading echoes of the explosions, and the intense and painful ringing in Price's ears.

"Azoh," Monster said.

"Is anybody hurt?" Price asked. "Is everyone okay?"

Amazingly there were no injuries.

"We need to get the heck out of here," Wall said.

"We're not going anywhere until Brogan operates on The Tsar," Price said.

"I don't know if we have time," Brogan said. "Look."

Price looked back to the east through the blackened, broken and upturned trees of what had been a thriving forest. The sky was glowing like a second sunrise, orange and red boiling into the sky. The world was ablaze.

"It'll spread, and quickly," Barnard said. "It hasn't rained in this region since February. This place is a tinderbox."

"Do what you need to do, Brogan," Price said. "But do it quickly."

* * *

[Mission Day 1, July 1st, 2033. 0630 hours local time]
[USS Apple, Hauraki Gulf, Auckland]

Flight Commander Molly Shaw was glad to be back in the action. The USS Apple, on which her jet was based, had been sheltering in its home base at Naval Base San Diego since the sinking of the USS Galaxy and her entire strike group early in the war. Human ships were just too vulnerable to the incredible firepower of the alien warplanes.

But not anymore.

Scream-jets had changed all that. Faster than any Bzadian jet, much faster, able to outrun any Bzadian missile, they were about to change the face of the war.

They had their drawbacks though. Launching them was a long-complicated procedure. They had to be attached to a carrier jet, which would then take off and climb almost to the stratosphere before releasing the jet. That took time.

Landing was impossible. The scream-jets could not fly at speeds slow enough to land. Instead they ditched. They would cut engines and go vertical, letting gravity suck away all their speed. When they reached the apex of the climb they would begin to fall, parachutes would deploy and they would ditch in the ocean as close to the carrier as possible. Recovery helicopters would pick them up and bring them back to the ship for re-deployment.

Shaw was glad to be on the leading edge. The sharp end of the knife. Bringing the fight to the Bzadians with a direct attack on their soil. Showing the aliens that humans could now strike where and when they pleased. The scream-jets had already had their first encounter with Bzadian jets, and it had proved decisive.

The one thing she wished they had was an AEW plane, Airborne Early Warning. All of those had been lost in the early years of the war and priority had been put on producing new warplanes, not surveillance planes.

There was little point in having an AEW plane aloft, when you knew it was going to be the first plane targeted by the Bzadians.

In any case, the USS Apple had twelve fighters permanently aloft, flying in concentric circles, actively looking for any intruders. They had permanent links to radar stations all along the western coastline of New Zealand. The defensive ring of ships that surrounded the USS Apple was on high alert, and would remain so permanently.

Even so Shaw would be happy once she was in the air and on her way to her target: Canberra, New Bzadia. The centre of Bzadian government. They were about to learn a lesson they would not easily forget.

The smoke from the explosions had been black, or dark grey. The smoke that was starting to eddy around them now was white. Smoke from the forest, which was well ablaze.

Wall, obeying Brogan's instructions, jury rigged some wiring from the truck. Brogan borrowed a medical marker pen from Monsters medikit and examining the wound carefully with the scope, made a series of careful markings on the bandages, and the skin of The Tsar's neck.

She wound a tight coil of wire around the protruding end of the needle in The Tsar's neck and inspected it carefully. Another wire was connected to a metal pad. She stripped off The Tsar's armour and taped the pad to his thigh.

"What's that for?" Price asked.

"Grounding pad," Brogan said, but didn't explain further. She took a small flashlight from a utility pocket and hooded it, making a pencil thin beam, then handed it to Price. Price flicked off her NV and without needing to be told, aimed the flashlight at the wound on The Tsar's neck. She didn't like what she saw. The bandages were weeping blood. She had seen that in the NV, but somehow the dark green colour had not seemed as bad as the bright red that showed in the glow of the flashlight.

Brogan stopped moving, listening. "Everybody freeze!"

Price heard it almost immediately. The quiet whop whop whop of small rotorblades. It faded in and out, just at the limit of her hearing. Rotorbots were quiet, so it was somewhere close by. Having unleashed hell, the Bzadians were coming back to survey the results of their work.

A gust of air from the east brought a plume of dense smoke, and with it a fist of hot air. Branches trembled. Leaves shook. Smoke eddied around them, filtering through the trees, dancing in the pencil thin beam of the flashlight. The flashlight! She flicked it off. Even the tiny beam of the hooded bulb risked detection by the sensitive cameras of the rotorbot.

"We gotta get out of here," Wall said. "Or we're going to be crispy fried critters."

"Not while that rotorbot is sniffing around us," Price said.

"Not until Tsar is fixed," Monster said.

Price almost smiled. But 'fixed' seemed like the right word somehow. The Tsar was broken. Badly broken and it surprised her how much she wanted him 'fixed'. When he had first come on the team he had seemed so full of himself, but that easy charm and ultra-confidence had grown on her, on all of them. Brogan's plan had to work. It just had to.

The smoke around them trembled and the sound of rotorblades grew louder. It was closer now, much closer. Maybe even at the end of the short track they had found. She rested a hand on her sidearm as she thought through her options. There were none. They couldn't risk the operation while the rotorbot was there, but it was clear that the fire was spreading, and heading in their direction.

It was a race against time, and any way she thought it through, it was a race they lost.

If the rotorbot found them, it was all over anyway, they wouldn't be so lucky twice. Lucky. Price smiled bitterly to herself as she watched The Tsar's chest fluttering in light, shallow breaths.

The rotorbot moved past them, a flickering shadow in the thickening smoke through the trees. An insect with a deadly sting in its tail. It must have been barely a few metres away and Price was very aware that any second it could decide to turn in their direction. They waited. Gradually the sound receded.

But as it did, so the smoke intensified. Any thicker and Brogan wouldn't be able to see enough to operate.

"Do it," Price whispered. "Forget the rotorbot. Do it now, as quietly as you can."

Brogan nodded, a half-seen gesture in the darkness. "When I say, connect the battery," she said. Then after a moment's longer examination of the needle, she said, "Ok, now."

The coil of wire began to glow red, Price could not tear her eyes off it. Brogan also watched it intently, only looking away after the needle had reached a dull orange glow, warming to red. Then she turned to the mediscope, completely focused on the small screen as she clamped the end of the needle with a utility tool.

After a moment the flesh of The Tsar's neck began to smoke and there came the terrible smell of burning flesh.

"Okay, shut it off," Brogan said, and Wall disconnected the battery.

Slowly, desperately gently, Brogan eased the needle out of The Tsar's neck, watching every millimetre minutely on the mediscope. At one point she pressed the needle back into his neck before withdrawing it again, agonizingly slowly.

When the needle was fully out, she dropped into onto the ground as if it were a foul, evil thing.

There was silence for a moment.

"Well," Price asked.

"I think I got it," Brogan said. She examined the wound a moment longer, then applied some antiseptic cream and started to bandage The Tsar's neck.

"How will we know?" Barnard asked. The intellectual ice queen of the team seemed pale and shaken.

"If he lives," Brogan said. "Then we'll know. Get some plasma into him."

"Last bag," Monster said, opening his medikit.

Price checked the time.

They were already well behind schedule.

SUBTERFUGE

[Mission Day 1, July 1st, 2033. 0700 hours local time]
[Bzadian Congress, Canberra]

"Who are you?" Chisnall asked.

The art exhibition area was a large, open gallery situated at the rear of the main entrance to the Congress, through a wide set of double doors. Remodelled by Bzadian architects in the Bzadian style, the walls were undulating curves like ocean waves. The floor was a maze of circular columns, each adorned on every surface with Bzadian paintings. You could get lost in this vast hall, a forest of art. Lighting was low, with spotlights illuminating each painting. They stood and walked in shadows. It was the perfect place for a clandestine meeting.

When Chisnall had arrived, the woman had been standing near the entrance, admiring a landscape, that judging by its content matter, had to have been painted on Bzadia. It showed endless deserts and two moons. The woman had ignored him and Chisnall had taken that cue, walking straight past her and into the gallery itself, stopping to examine some works not far from the entrance.

It had taken him longer than he had planned to reach the gallery. There had been a moment in the meeting room when he had almost lost it.

The face, the thin high cheekbones, the high, strained voice. It was a vision from his nightmares, from his first ever Angel mission. Goezlin had been at Uluru. He was the chief of the Bzadian Secret Police, the PGZ, and as such, technically a member of the High Council, although this was the first time Chisnall had ever seen him at a meeting.

Goezlin was the cause of the strangeness that had come over him earlier in the meeting room, he had no doubt about it.

Had Goezlin recognised Chisnall? Chisnall couldn't be sure. His appearance had been changed. Not dramatically, but enough. The colour pattern of your skin was a major identification feature to Bzadians, as were the shape of your skull. To human eyes the odd 'corn-kernel' shape of the Bzadian skull all looked the same, but to Bzadian eyes minute differences were extremely important. The shape of the eyes and nose were secondary. He had fooled facial recognition software to gain a position in the kitchen at Government house, but would it be enough to fool Goezlin?

When he had left the meeting hall he had avoided going back to the kitchen, instead finding an unlocked janitors closet. He had ducked inside, and left the door open a crack. After a moment, footsteps had sounded outside and Goezlin had walked past.

Why? Had he recognized Chisnall? Was he following him? Or was it just a coincidence?

If his cover was blown, then he would have to make his escape, and as quickly as possible. But he was on the verge of something momentous, something that could change the course of the war. He would leave only if there was no other choice.

He had waited until Goezlin was well past before exiting the closet and returning the way he had come, taking a roundabout route to the gallery.

It took a few minutes for Kozi to make her way inside. A cautious approach, ensuring she was not being watched, and that no one would connect her to the person who just entered.

He had used the time to examine some of the works.

There was a fundamental difference between Bzadian and Human art, he decided. Bzadian art was very literal. Accurate representations of people and scenes, at times almost photographic in quality. Yet somehow lacking soul.

The woman had moved a little past him, close enough for them to talk quietly, but far enough that they did not appear to be standing together. She did not look up at his question, but continued to gaze at a large portrait.

"I am your contact," the woman said. "I am Kozi."

That was almost certainly not her birthname, Chisnall thought. Yozi and Kozi. They would have changed their names when they became 'paired'.

Chisnall turned his gaze to a different painting, although in truth he barely saw it. His mind was fully occupied with what he had just learned.

"I have been here for nearly six months," Chisnall said. "I have been waiting for a contact since that time. Why now?"

"Until now your job was to lay low. To become accepted. To gain the trust of those around you," Kozi said. "You always knew the time would come when we would call on you. Now we have a specific task for you to perform."

Now, Chisnall thought. On the day of the most vital Angel mission ever. In the middle of an emergency Bzadian government meeting. Perhaps because of the meeting.

The timing could not have been worse.

Chisnall almost asked Kozi how he knew he could trust her, but the question was really unnecessary. Just by her presence here, he could trust her. If not, then he would be in a PGZ prison cell by now. Besides, she was a bobble-head. All of the Peacemakers he had met so far had been bobble-heads.

"What is this task?" Chisnall asked.

"We will get to that," Kozi said. She moved off, walking casually, admiring works as she walked. After a moment Chisnall followed after her. She had moved to a different section of the gallery.

The section was labelled as Indigenous Art. In it were paintings that he knew well. The Mona Lisa; The Starry Night; The Scream. These were works by the great art masters through human history. Da Vinci, Van Gogh, Munch. The Bzadians had assembled them here from all around the world. Works from the indigenous peoples of Earth. Humans.

Kozi stopped in front of the Mona Lisa. Chisnall turned to face the other direction, finding a series of paintings of Native Americans, wild, untamed, riding horses through the wild American west. The artist was George Catlin, and it struck him, looking at the artworks, that it was a depiction of a lost time, a time before settlers had come to America. It was a way of life that was gone forever. The way human civilisation would be gone forever if the Bzadians won the war.

Chisnall examined the paintings, saying nothing, waiting for Kozi to speak. After a moment, she did.

"Do you think it a coincidence that the wife of your enemy is now your contact?"

"A little," Chisnall said.

"It is no coincidence," Kozi said. "I asked for this role. I wanted to meet you face, to face, the man who killed my pairling. I wanted to find out the truth of what happened."

"You hold me responsible for his death, yet you hold no grudge?" Chisnall asked.

"You were both soldiers," Kozi said. "I had, and still have, great sadness, but no anger. At least not toward you. To those who started, and who prolong this war, yes. But we will get to that in good time. Tell me about Yozi. For many months I held out the hope that he had been captured by human forces after Wivenhoe, that this was why his body was never found. I no longer believe that to be true, but still, I must know."

Chisnall thought of the mighty snakehead of water that smashed into the dam where Yozi was standing. There wouldn't have been anything to find. His body would have been pulverised.

He began to speak, slowly, deliberately, at times with his eyes shut, discussing, for the first time ever, the events of that day.

He told Kozi about Yozi diving into the lake at the base of the dam to disarm the bomb. He told her of the other bombs that sent an enormous wall of water smashing into the dam, powerful enough to smash through the massive steel gates, and concrete walls of the dam.

"Yozi could not swim," Kozi said when he stopped. She said it as a fact, not as an accusation that Chisnall was lying.

"That did not stop him," Chisnall said. "He was a true hero."

"It may surprise you to know that Yozi wanted the war to end, as I do," Kozi said. "Although he would never let that interfere with his duty."

"I am sorry for your loss," Chisnall said. The words sounded trite and meaningless.

"You had the chance to kill him earlier," Yozi said. "In the deserts at Uluru. But you did not. Yozi could not understand why you did not do your duty that day."

"It did not feel right," Chisnall said.

"And your feelings were more important than your duty," Kozi said. "Perhaps this was why Yozi respected you."

There was silence and she walked on to another painting. Chisnall did not move.

"We believe there is a way to end this war," Kozi said. "Quickly and with little further loss of life on either side. It will not be easy, and it will involve some difficult decisions. The question is, whether you are prepared to do what it takes."

"I have been asked that question before," Chisnall said. "To stop this war, I believe I would do almost anything."

"I hoped you would say that," Kozi said. "Now we must find out if it is true. I have left a package for you near the front entrance, in a corner beneath a painting of Uluru. There are instructions in the package. There is also a phone. If you need to talk to me again, press the talk button. It will connect directly to me."

Chisnall studied the paintings for a little longer.

When he turned, she was gone.

* * *

The filters on the Bzadian combat suit removed the fact of the smoke, but not the smell of it. An acrid, bitter smell that seemed to permeate itself throughout Price's body as if it had got into her bloodstream. They had replaced The Tsar's helmet too. Brogan was worried about the wound, but right now breathing was the bigger of the two problems.

Besides, if the artery in The Tsar's neck wasn't sealed, then it wouldn't matter, Price thought, but didn't say that out loud.

The rotorbot had not left, in fact now there were two of them, maybe more, the beat of their rotors corrugating the smoke around them.

The Angels had left their little hiding hole in the wall of the forest. They had had to. But the smoke, although unpleasant, was helping them. It was so thick now that visibility was just a few metres.

They huddled under camo-sheets, to hide their heat signatures, the only way the rotorbots could find them in this thickening smoke. Barnard lay on the back of the truck with The Tsar, holding her camo-sheet over both of them. Monster had offered, but Barnard had insisted.

Tsar's camo-sheet was spread over the hood of the truck, to obscure any heat given off by its electrical engine.

The glow of the fire lit the smoke behind them, and from the wide area, Price was sure that it had already jumped the firebreak. Perhaps the Bzadians had not yet learned about Australian wildfires, she thought. If they had, they would have kept the firebreaks clear despite their cultural leanings. If fire took hold here, and was not kept in check by firebreaks, it could spread all the way to Canberra.

Several times they stopped when the sound of the rotorbots grew louder. Waiting in frozen fear until the sound moved off.

They came to a crossroad, where a highway intersected the firebreak. This road was much cleaner than the last one.

"Take it," Monster said.

"We can't risk the roads," Price said. "We'd be too easy to spot."

"We'd make better time," Barnard said. "And the smoke is still giving us good cover. I think it's worth the risk."

Price wondered if her concern for The Tsar was colouring her thinking.

"Nothing is worth the risk," Brogan said. "Stick to the firebreak."

"Take road," Monster said.

"Why?" Price asked in exasperation.

"Just feeling," Monster said.

"Monster…" Price began but Barnard cut her off.

"Take the road," she said. "We're going too slowly. These wildfires can travel at the speed of a car in a strong wind."

Price couldn't argue with that, but she still wasn't sure if Barnard was offering the right advice for the right reasons. She eventually nodded. Not so much because of Barnard. It might have been silly, but she trusted Monster's 'feelings'.

She just hoped she wouldn't be proved wrong.

The highway was faster, much faster, than the rough, undulating earth of the firebreak. It was also noisier, which worried Price more than she was going to tell the others. The engine was louder at speed, and the knobbly off-road tyres made a constant buzz on the tarseal.

"Any sign of rotorcraft?" Price asked.

"No sign of anything," Brogan said. Her eyes and ears seemed to be almost as good as The Tsar's now defunct scope.

"Great," Price said.

"I'm not so sure," Barnard said. "They've been buzzing around everywhere, searching for us. Why have they suddenly bugged out."

"Because they've given up," Wall said.

"Why would they suddenly give up," Barnard said. "If they've gone, it's for a reason."

The easterly wind, that had given them such a boost in the yacht, had increased in strength. Strong gusts were buffeting the truck, bringing with them squalls of black smoke, reducing visibility at times to barely a metre.

"Must go faster," Monster said, glancing backwards.

"I'm going as fast as I can," Wall said.

"Not fast enough," Monster said.

Looking back Price saw what he saw. A huge flickering glow behind them, consuming the sky, turning night into day. Her semi-informed guess had been right. The fire was catching them up, and it was catching them up fast.

"That's why the rotorbots have disappeared," she said. "They can see this coming and they've got out of harm's way."

"They'll send them back to search for our bodies later," Wall said.

"Any other happy thoughts, keep them to yourself," Price said.

Barnard was studying the GPS map on her wrist computer.

"There's water ahead," she said. "Not much more than a stream though. Looks like a tributary to a river. It's very narrow, but it might be enough."

"Enough for what?" Price asked.

"We get in the water, let the fire burn past us," Barnard

said. "It's our best chance."

"How far ahead," Price asked, watching the rapidly grown glow behind them. The air was filled with burning embers, swirling and dancing on the wind currents. It looked like a scene from someone's version of hell.

"About a klick," Barnard said. "Don't spare the horses, Wall."

"I got a bad feeling about this," Wall said.

"Try and cheer up," Price said. "Things could be worse."

"How could things possibly get any worse," Wall said.

Things got worse.

BOOK TWO: WORLD ON FIRE

More inhumanity has been done by man himself than
any other of nature's causes.
Samuel von Pufendorf

KOZI

[Mission Day 1, July 1st, 2033. 0745 hours local time]
[Bzadian Congress, Canberra]

Kozi did not answer. He tried the phone she had given him three times, but each time it just clicked through to a messaging system and he had no intention of leaving a message. Not about this.

He stood at the window of his tiny apartment and stared at the rising pall of smoke to the east. The entire horizon seemed to be on fire. But really the whole world was on fire and had been for over a decade.

Right now, fires, literal or figurative, were not his problem.

In the box had been a salt shaker.

But this container did not contain salt. That was obvious. Why go to all that trouble to give him a container of salt. Or perhaps it did contain salt, but it would be mixed with something else.

Apart from the salt shaker, and the phone, the box had contained one other thing, a brief message written on a flimsy type of paper. When Chisnall tried to pick up the paper, the mere touch of his hand caused the paper to dissolve, turning to a small pile of ash-like dust in the bottom of the box.

But he had already read the message. It confirmed something that he had already suspected.

Azoh, the Bzadian spiritual leader, would be attending the meeting today. The message had even given the time Azoh was expected to arrive.

The message said nothing else. But it didn't have to.

Like everyone else at the meeting, Azoh would require food.

When the phone finally rang he snatched it up on the first ring. The video was dark, and she was standing in shadows, but it was her. She said nothing, but waited for him to speak.

"What's in the container?" Chisnall asked.

"What do you think is in it?"

"Poison," Chisnall said.

"Then why did you ask?" Kozi asked.

"You want me to kill Azoh," Chisnall said and the words, uttered out loud, hung heavily in the air, as if something rotten, a foul stench, had just solidified in front of them.

Kozi said nothing.

"Why?" Chisnall asked.

"I asked you if you would do whatever it took to stop the war," Kozi said. Her eyes glinted like hard diamonds, sparks amidst in the shadows.

"How will this stop the war?" Chisnall asked.

"It will," she said. "That's all you need to know."

"You're asking me to commit murder," Chisnall said. "I'd like to know why."

She moved forward, bringing her face into the light.

"Bzadian politics are very complicated," she said. "There are many races, and many divisions within those races. But at the top there is Azoh. When Azoh becomes, the successor is chosen, so that should Azoh fall ill or die, the new Azoh, Azoh-zu, is ready to replace them."

Chisnall waited patiently.

"It is a great honour for us when Azoh-zu is chosen from our race," Kozi said. "When Azoh dies and Azoh-zu becomes, that confers great power onto the leaders from that race. You could say that they control the government. Our current Azoh is from the Corziz people. They are the most warlike and hostile of our people. Goezlin, the head of our secret police, is Corziz."

She paused, letting the information sink in.

"Azoh-zu, the successor to Azoh, is Yzeyze. I also am Yzeyze."

Bobble-heads, Chisnall thought.

"You want me to kill your leader, so you can take over the government," Chisnall said.

"We must replace Azoh, to stop the war," Kozi said. "Our last Azoh, a great and strong leader, from the Hezar race, was on 110-RKH."

Chisnall stared at the phone. Everyone knew the story of the great spaceship that had crashed on entering the Earth's atmosphere. It had been a slow motion disaster that had played out over several days and was a key factor in gaining sympathy for the Bzadians.

"The Azoh-zu was very young, and not ready, but still had to become," Kozi said. "But our new Azoh proved ineffectual, manipulated by advisors and generals."

"Why now?" Chisnall asked.

"Because the war has turned against us," Kozi said. "That is what today's meeting is about. Humans have developed new fighter planes. The tide of the war is turning."

"Good," Chisnall said.

"You do not understand," Kozi said. "Up until now we have held back our major weapons. We do not wish to destroy what you call the free territories. We want to live in it. But rather than face defeat, our High Council will vote to destroy the Americas. That will be decided in this meeting."

"So if Azoh lives, then the Human Race dies," Chisnall said.

"But if Azoh dies, and the Yzeyze assume control of the High Council, then we will negotiate for peace," Kozi said.

"Bzadia would not dare to use their nukes," Chisnall said.

"Not nukes," Kozi said. "Positronium weapons."

"What are they?" Chisnall asked.

"Just understand this," Kozi said. "They make nuclear weapons look like firecrackers."

"Whatever they are, it makes no sense," Chisnall said. "You know that we have nukes. Thousands of them, many on submarines that you cannot detect, within a few minutes flight of your coast."

"Your leaders would never give the order to fire," Kozi said. "They would be dead, Washington destroyed, the Pentagon vaporised, before a single nuclear missile could be fired."

"How can you be so certain of this?" Chisnall asked.

"Because one of our weapons is already there," Kozi said.

* * *

Bright headlights illuminated the smoke ahead of them, turning the dark night into a strange murky twilight.

"Crap!" Price said.

"Take the road he said," Brogan muttered, "I got a feeling."

"Pull over," Price said.

"Where?" Wall asked.

On one side was a heavy median barrier, and on the other, a high dirt bank. They were trapped.

"Just stop," Price said, but unnecessarily, the truck was already coming to a halt.

"Get out and camo-down on the berm," Price said. "Hurry. Everyone but Barnard. You stay with The Tsar."

The others had barely rolled off their positions on the truck when Price, sliding across into the driver's seat, flicked the truck into reverse and floored the go pedal, backing up twenty metres down the road, stopping only as the front of the oncoming vehicle emerged through a swirl of smoke.

Headlights caught them in a smoky blaze and the on-coming vehicle immediately began to slow.

It wasn't a Bzadian vehicle. That was clear even as it pulled to a stop. It was a human vehicle, but that was not unusual. The Bzadians had appropriated many human vehicles since they had taken over Australia. This one was yellow, at least the small part of it she could make out behind the blaze of the headlights was.

It was Barnard who realised first. "Fire truck," she said.

Before she really had a chance to think through what she was doing, or formulate a plan, operating only on instinct and inspiration, Price jumped down and ran towards them, waving her hands wildly.

"Help!" she cried, flipping up her face-mask.

She got a mouthful of smoke and ended up coughing and choking, but that only seemed to add authenticity.

One of the firefighters swung himself down from the truck. The leader of the team.

"Fire coming this way," she shouted. Surely that would be the last thing the enemy would say.

Perhaps if she had been The Tsar they might have believed him. The Tsar had a way of making people believe him. But the Tsar was lying unconscious (dying?) on the back of the garden truck. And even Price's best efforts were not convincing enough.

A needle-gun appeared in the hand of the firefighter.

"These have got to be the ones they're all looking for," the firefighter called back to the truck. "Call it in."

"No, don't," Price said. "Not if you want to live."

The firefighter looked around at a tap on his shoulder and his gun drifted away from Price's face. Monster reached over and relieved him of it, his own gun steady on the back of the firefighter's head. Brogan and Wall were already up in the cab of the truck, covering the others.

"They'll have a medikit," Brogan said. "It'll have a plasma kit in it. Get it, The Tsar needs all he can get."

"Puke plasma," Price said.

"Same same," Monster said.

"He's right. Plasma is plasma," Brogan said. "And without it I don't think The Tsar will make it. He's lost too much blood already.

Brogan and Wall ushered the remaining firefighters out of the fire truck at the point of her coil-gun. There were two in the rear seats, four of them altogether.

"What now, LT?" Wall asked.

"Isn't it obvious?" Price asked. "We take the truck. Try and outrun the fire."

"What about the firefighters," Barnard asked.

"They're not our problem," Price said.

"You're just going to leave them here?" Wall asked.

"Show them where the river is. If they stay in the water they should survive," Price said.

"Bzadians no can swim," Monster said.

"You're right. Let's just shoot them. It will be quicker and less painful," Price said, then immediately regretted it when she saw the disappointment in Monster's eyes. She turned to the head firefighter. "Strip off your uniforms."

He shook his head.

"I'm trying to save your lives," Price said. "Do you understand that? But I'm running out of time. That fire is heading this way, fast. I don't want to kill you, but you need to give me another option here."

She raised her coil-gun towards his face.

With a reluctant glance around at his team, the leader began to strip off the outer layer of his uniform, a loose-fitting fire-proof coat. The other firefighters quickly followed suit. Next they handed over their helmets.

Monster collected the uniforms while the others covered him.

"There's a river about three hundred metres back the way you came," Price said. "Get to it. Use our little truck if you want. Get in the water, follow the river as far as you can, it gets wider and deeper the further you go. When the fire comes, get your heads under water as long and as often as you can."

* * *

Hiding beneath a thermocline, in the deepest shadows of the ocean, the USS Oracle was silent, invisible and deadly.

Only active sonar would be able to detect her, and if any surface vessel did start pinging, the USS Oracle would gently move in another direction.

But for now she lay still, just off the coast of Australia, maintaining her depth, holding her position with long lazy slow turns of her screws, her sonar operators and automated systems constantly scanning for any threat. Doing what she did best. Hiding in the deep.

The other thing the USS Oracle did well was to fight. Sleek and elegant, she was the ultimate predator with a real sting in her tail. Twenty-four stings to be exact, in the form of Trident III ballistic missiles. Fast, accurate, and devastating. Each one of the missiles contained eight MIRVs, Multiple Independently Targetable Re-Entry Vehicles. That made a total of 192 warheads, each with the power of twenty-five Hiroshimas.

The USS Oracle was a kick ass boat.

Captain Aidan 'A-Sam' Weiss was in the Command and Control Centre, known as the CACC. He too was quiet, sitting, apparently relaxed, in the captain's chair, which was really no more than a round stool. Space on board even a modern submarine, was strictly limited.

"Surface contact, airborne, bearing nine zero degrees," a voice called into the quiet hum of the control centre. Weiss turned to see Josh Allan, their sensor buoy operator, intent on his screen.

"Confirm contact," Executive Officer Leon Setefano, A-Sam's 2IC, called back.

"Confirming contact, airborne, fast movers, appears to be six of them," Allan said. "One larger signal, that's got to be a Dragon class, sir, and the rest are either type one or type twos. I'll have better data shortly sir."

"Any chance they are heading for our position?" A-Sam asked.

"Not on the current course," Allan said. "They'll miss us by about twenty klicks."

"Even so," A-Sam said. "XO, bring the crew to Alert Three."

"Aye skipper," Setefano said, pressing buttons on the control panel that would silently sound the alert throughout the boat.

They all knew what he was thinking. They had been together as a crew for far too long not to know. The current heading of the enemy fast-movers would bypass the USS Oracle. But it could be a feint. At the last minute they could wheel around onto a new course, giving the submarine very little time to react.

But if they did that, A-Sam was ready. The submarine was ready.

"Confirm now one Dragon class jet, and five type ones," Allan said. "No change in course, I don't think they know we're here. Flying low, real low, staying below radar."

A-Sam glanced at a chart on his electronic console. He didn't need to, it was just habit. On the course they were on there was only one possible target. The small island nation of New Zealand.

And sheltering in Auckland Harbour was Carrier Strike Group Nine. The USS Apple and six other ships. The base of operations for the upcoming raid on the Bzadian homeland.

"Do we alert them skipper?" Setefano asked, as usual reading his mind.

A-Sam took off his cap and massaged his temples with his thumbs, a habit of his when he was thinking.

"What's your opinion, XO?" he asked.

"Got to let them know," Setefano said. "Give them time to get their birds in the air."

"They'll already have birds in the air," A-Sam said. "They'll be expecting an attack just like this."

"Even so, the more warning they get, the more prepared they'll be," Setefano said.

He was right, A-Sam knew that. A few extra seconds could make the difference between life and death. But his orders were to remain on station unless he was directly attacked.

If he broadcast a warning to the USS Apple, he would have to move. The risk of detection was just too great.

"We'll just sit tight," he said. "They've almost certainly picked those Puke jets up on satellite by now."

"Aye skipper," Setefano said. He knew not to argue. When the captain made a decision, his mind was already made up.

* * *

"The bomb is smaller than a shoebox," Kozi said. "Hidden by a Ferzerker within sight of the Pentagon."

"Who?" Chisnall asked. The Ferzerkers, humans, bred in a secret project by Bzadians inside Uluru, had infiltrated many levels of human society, including the government and the military.

"That is not important," Kozi said.

"Who?" Chisnall asked again. "I am not sure I believe you."

"His name is Colonel Reid," Kozi said after a moment. "But that knowledge will do you no good."

Chisnall was silent for a while. If what she said was true, and he had no doubt it was, then the human race was closer to extinction that he had ever imagined.

"Why me?" he asked at last.

"Because you are not Bzadian," Kozi said. "Azoh cannot see into your mind. No Bzadian could ever get close enough to Azoh to carry out this task. But you can. You look like a Bzadian, but are not one. Your thoughts are your own."

"You are sure of this?" he asked.

"I believe this to be true," she said. "And there is something else. As we speak, defence forces are cordoning off the Congress."

"Why?" Chisnall asked, suddenly cautious.

"I don't know," Kozi said. "It would seem they are expecting some kind of attack."

The Angels. Somehow the Bzadians had learnt of their mission. What were they walking into?

"I need to warn you," Kozi said. "If your people were to attack the seat of our government, it would almost certainly precipitate the use of the positronium weapons."

"Is that a threat?" Chisnall asked.

She shook her head sadly. "It is simply a truth. In the event of an attack on Congress those that oppose the use of the weapons would no longer have a voice."

"If I do this," Chisnall said. "If I poison your Azoh, your people will hunt me down, torture me and kill me."

"They will not find you," Kozi said. "The poison is untraceable. They will know she has been poisoned, but not when, or by whom. If any suspicion does fall on you, we will protect you."

After she hung up, Chisnall sat thinking for a long time.

The Angel mission to infiltrate Azoh's chamber was in serious jeopardy. Was it even necessary? Perhaps even more so now than before. A new Azoh, a new government, could change the course of the war. Understanding their thinking could be vital to ACOG. But every move they made had so many permutations that it seemed like walking through a minefield, blindfolded.

KILLING AZOH

The first firefighting rotorcraft they saw flew right overhead as they approached the outer suburbs of Canberra. A monsoon bucket swung underneath, trailing a thin line of water that glinted through the haze of smoke in the unnatural and sinister twilight. The rotorcraft was followed by three others.

"We made it," Wall said, almost disbelievingly.

"Be thankful that it's midwinter," Barnard said. "Or we'd be toast by now."

The highway between Batemans Bay and Canberra was a winding and hilly one. The fire that was chasing them was not restricted to roads, it roamed where it pleased. Several times the fire had threatened to cut them off, and they had driven through showers of sparks, flames reaching out at them from both sides of the road, protected only by a thin shower of water from specially designed nozzles on the top of the truck.

"I wonder how the firefighters got on," Price said.

"Who cares," Brogan said.

The Tsar lay on the floor in the rear of the cab. His eyes were open, Barnard sat with him, giving him measured sips of water.

"What happened?" he asked.

"Cut yourself shaving," Barnard said.

"Nice to have you back with us," Price said, looking around from the front seat.

"Damn," The Tsar said, weakly. "I was having a really nice dream."

His voice was scratchy and hoarse.

"What about?" Barnard asked, gently stroking his forehead. It was an uncharacteristic gesture for her. Unusually soft. Unusually feminine.

"I don't remember," he said. "But I think you were in it."

"Was she naked?" Wall asked, earning himself a weak fist bump from The Tsar but a flying wad of blood-soaked dressings from Barnard.

The strange, ghostly sunrise poured into the cab through the side windows colouring The Tsar's face to a dusky red. His eyes were fixed on the orb of the sun.

"Whenever I see a sunrise," he said. "I am reminded that I live on a humongous spinning ball of rock hurtling around a giant ball of fire."

"What's your point?" Barnard asked.

"How insignificant we are in the scheme of things," The Tsar said.

"That's bull. It's all relative," Barnard said.

"What's relative?" Price asked.

"The scheme of things," Barnard said. "You may think you're insignificant in terms of the solar system, but to some ants' nest you just stood on, you're pretty freaking major. You're a force of nature, an act of God. It's all relative."

The Tsar tried to laugh, but managed only a single hiccupping sound. His eyes closed again and he was silent for a while.

"I realised something, Barnard," he said. "You really are an alien."

"Me? Why?" Barnard asked.

"Aliens don't dance," The Tsar said. "Their art sucks, they don't do music, except for simple kids' songs. And they don't dance."

"Hang in there, Tsar," Barnard said.

"I'll try," The Tsar grimaced, an almost-grin. "But only if you promise to prove me wrong."

"Prove you wrong, how?" Barnard asked.

"Prove you're not an alien. We'll go out dancing," The Tsar said.

"Sure," Barnard said, surprising them all. "When all this is over."

"Yeah, now I remember. That was my dream," The Tsar said, his voice trailing off into nothingness. His eyes closed and his breathing was shallow and quick, like that of a child.

"When we get to Canberra we should go to the hospital," Brogan said. "Leave The Tsar there. He's lost too much blood. At least in a hospital he'd have a fighting chance."

"Not going to happen," Price said. "The Puke disguise won't fool a doctor, and once they realise there's one fox loose in the farmyard, they'll pull out all stops to find the rest of us."

"If they haven't already," Wall said.

"So The Tsar is expendable, is that what you are saying?" Barnard asked, rounding suddenly on Price.

"We all are," Price said quietly.

Barnard glared at her for a moment, then lowered her eyes and nodded.

"So where to?" Wall asked. "Time you filled us in on the plan."

"We'll rendezvous with Chisnall in Canberra," Price said. "From that point on, it's still classified."

If not for Brogan she would have been happy to fill the team in on the details.

"Where is meeting place?" Monster asked.

"At the Congress," Barnard said.

"The Congress?" Brogan asked. "What is he doing there?"

Barnard stared at her without saying anything.

Brogan rolled her eyes and rested her head on the seat.

"What time is meeting?" Monster asked.

"Oh nine hundred hours," Price said.

"We're going to be late," Barnard said. "We'll miss the rendezvous."

"Then we'll arrange a new one," Price said.

"How do we get out?" Wall asked.

"Under cover of an air-raid," Price said. "We'll call it in when we reach the safe house. While the Pukes are dealing with that, we get to the extraction point and a rotorcraft will take us out, just like at Uluru."

"So in the meantime we just hang around waiting for Chisnall to make contact?" Brogan asked.

"No, we have a way to contact him, once we get there," Price said. "All we have to do is remain inconspicuous until then."

"Inconspicuous," Wall laughed. "In a bright yellow fire truck."

Price watched Brogan carefully. One question that had never been answered was why Brogan had agreed to come on the mission. Brogan had been close to Chisnall, very close. But she had betrayed him. How was she feeling about seeing him again? Brogan caught Price's gaze, staring back at her.

"He's not going to have you back," Price said. "If that's what you're thinking."

"Oh, really? Brogan said. "Because that's why I'm really here. To kiss and make up with an old boyfriend."

"Whatever you think, it's not going to be easy," Price said.

"Sure. Life's hard. And then you die," Brogan said. "There's a rat-trap at the end of the mouse-maze."

* * *

Kozi had said Azoh was young, but she hadn't said how young. And Kozi had also neglected to tell him one other fact. Azoh was a girl.

Her entrance was a grand affair. Surrounded by her personal guard, the Azaykin, she entered in a procession, led by her most senior advisors.

She wore bright blue robes, flowing like the sea amidst the desert sand colour of the Azaykin. Her advisors wore a deeper brown.

They made their way slowly through the council chambers, arriving at the ceremonial chair. The leader of the High Council, Field Marshall Leozii, formally offered her his hand, which she accepted. He then helped her to the chair.

Azoh's eyes were soft, her skin pure. Her face was covered with ornate jewellery attached by piercings through her eyebrows, ears, and nose. Elaborate tattoos covered her cheeks and forehead.

If Chisnall had to guess he would have put her at no more than seventeen or eighteen years old, although he suspected she was older than she looked.

The salt shaker rattled a little on the tray with the other condiments he was carrying. Chisnall had been selected to present Azoh with a tray of appetisers, another formal part of the ceremony.

There was no doubt in Chisnall's mind that the Peacemakers had played a hand in that. It could be no coincidence that he had been chosen for this tremendous honour.

But Azoh was a girl.

Had Kozi deliberately withheld that information from him, worried that it might affect his decision. Or had she simply not deemed it important enough to tell him.

After all why should it matter? Killing Azoh would stop the war. It didn't matter what gender, age or colour hair Azoh had, this was not about her. She was a pawn. A piece to be played in an interplanetary game of chess. No, more than a pawn, a queen, who had to be taken.

And yet for some reason it did matter.

Azoh sat and as she did, her gaze swept around the room. It took in everyone, one by one, only for a second, but when her gaze passed across his eyes, Chisnall felt that she was indeed seeing inside his brain, into his soul, as if she knew his every secret. Her eyes seemed to probe his, only for a millisecond, then it was gone.

No wonder Bzadians thought Azoh could read their minds, Chisnall thought. He was human, and supposedly safe from her prying mind, but even so he felt like he had just been through an MRI scanner.

He approached, exactly as he had been instructed, pausing and bowing his head as he neared.

Then she spoke. Her voice was soft and young, a pure sound, like cool spring water bubbling up through rocks, like the first quiet murmurs of a spring shower.

"Do what you must do," Azoh said, and unbelievably, she was talking to him.

He almost went through with it. Almost. But her words seemed stuck in his brain, circling around and around like a line from a song you cannot get out of your head.

Do what you must do.

He placed the tray of condiments on the table by her side, and keeping his gaze averted, anything to avoid those probing eyes, he backed away, the salt shaker now palmed and secreted in a pocket of his uniform.

"Chef, stop," a voice commanded next to him.

Chisnall froze, every instinct telling him to run.

"Where is the salt?" the voice asked, gesturing at the tray.

The silence seemed overwhelming and to go on for hours, although in reality it was only for a moment.

"It…. has been overlooked," Chisnall said. "I will return to the kitchen and get some."

"No need, there is some here," Field Marshall Leozii said. He took a shaker from his own table. He placed it on Azoh's food table with a disparaging look at Chisnall. If nothing else, Chisnall thought, his career as a chef was over.

But that could be the least of his problems. He was dismissed with a subtle hand signal from one of Azoh's advisors. He turned, to find Goezlin staring at him, and began the long walk down through the council benches, away from Azoh's chair. He forced himself to walk slowly but his mind and heart were racing. Had Goezlin identified him?

He reached the door and only then increased his pace. He had reached the hall of heroes when he saw Goezlin, flanked by two PGZ agents, emerge from the meeting room behind him.

Chisnall turned a corner and increased the length of his stride, quickening his pace even more without appearing to hurry. A curve in the corridor hid the PGZ agents from sight and only then did he start to run. But there was little point. He had nowhere to run to.

* * *

"Looks like they're expecting us," Wall said.

"They're expecting something," Price said.

A kilometre away, two rotorcraft, one a surveillance craft the other a gunship, were slowly circling, maintaining a constant vigil over the Congress.

In a different life, in a former world, this had been the seat of the Australian Government, Parliament House. At the time it was built, the most expensive building in the world. Price wondered if the aliens knew that, or if they would care. Closer towards the river sat the old Parliament House, now a Bzadian museum.

The Angels watched from a vantage point on the other side of the river, on top of an unfinished high-rise building, a luxury hotel, according to the dilapidated signs that were erected on both sides of the construction site.

Rusted scaffolding and tattered tarpaulins encased the building like a decomposing, peeling skin. The building had been under construction when the Bzadians had invaded. They hadn't completed it, nor had they bothered to tear it down. It stood tall, silent and slowly decaying, a monument to a way of life that was gone forever.

They had found a place to hide the fire truck amidst the empty containers and deserted site offices at the rear of the building. Barnard had stayed to guard the truck and tend to The Tsar. The rest of them had trekked up the concrete fire staircase in the centre of the building.

From below a parapet on the second-to-top floor they looked out across the waters of Lake Burley Griffin to the Congress on the other side. A rectangular complex in the middle of two concentric ring roads, it had been largely dug out of the hill it was built on. Two curving shapes, like boomerangs, outlined a huge grassy lawn that rose above the buildings, and was topped by the massive metal flagpole.

To the east, a blanket of grey smoke suffocated the horizon, making a mockery of the sunrise. The low sun lit the top layer of smoke.

It would have been a serene, pleasant view, particularly with the lake in the foreground, if not for the tanks that were slowly rumbling into position on all the roads that led into the Congress. Crash barriers and barbed wire fences were being erected in a circle on the outer ring road.

"So much for meeting Chisnall," Wall said. "They've locked the place down. Looks like nobody is getting in or out."

"We might as well turn around and go home," Brogan said, and smiled before anyone could say anything. "Just telling it like it is."

* * *

Chisnall looked around desperately. He had a few seconds at most before Goezlin and his goons arrived. The kitchen was almost deserted, the chefs were all at the formal greeting of Azoh in the meeting room.

His eye fell on an industrial size spray can of cooking oil. Footsteps sounded in the corridor behind him. He snatched up the can and placed it on top of one of the gas elements on the cooking hob and spun the knob around. The electronic igniter clicked a few times and he could smell the gas, then it lit with a small whoosh. Flames lapped at the base of the spray can.

He upended a large cooking pot and placed it over the can and the clawing flames, concealing them. He moved away from the stove and opened a cupboard, intending to hide the salt shaker, just as Goezlin entered behind him.

Goezlin wasted no time.

"Search him," he said.

"What are you doing?" Chisnall asked, as the two large PGZ men grabbed him by the arms and started searching his clothing.

Goezlin said nothing.

"I am just a chef," Chisnall protested. "All I did was to forget the salt!"

"Really," Goezlin said as one of the PGZ agents showed him the salt shaker he had just taken from Chisnall's pocket.

"A simple mistake," Chisnall said. It sounded incredibly lame.

"Have it tested," Goezlin said to one of his goons. "And be careful with it. I doubt that it contains salt."

"What are you talking about?" Chisnall said.

"You were at Uluru and Wivenhoe," Goezlin said. "Your name is Chizna."

"You are mistaken," Chisnall said. He carefully avoided looking at the pot on the stove-top.

"I did not recognise you at first," Goezlin said, "Because you have changed your appearance. It will be very interesting to see what is in that salt shaker. Perhaps we have just witnessed a human plot to murder Azoh."

"No!" Chisnall cried.

"I must get back to the meeting," Goezlin said. "Take him to headquarters. Isolate him. He is extremely dangerous. No one starts the interrogation until I get there."

Rough hands grabbed Chisnall's wrists and hauled them to his neck, where a neck cuff secured them in place.

As he was dragged out of the kitchen, Chisnall allowed himself one last, desperate glance backwards at the stove.

Goezlin disappeared back towards the meeting room. Chisnall stumbled along between the two large PGZ agents, wondering how everything could have gone so suddenly, spectacularly wrong.

And then the oil bomb exploded.

Heating the aerosol can of oil beyond its limits, the can burst, releasing a mist of highly inflammable oil onto the flames of the stove.

Chisnall didn't have to see the pot hit the ceiling, he heard it, just as a sheet of flame erupted out through the kitchen door behind them.

Then he was running, taking advantage of the shock that temporarily loosened the grip on his arms.

The sprinklers had immediately kicked in.

Water was cascading down his face and the floor was slippery. Fire alarms were blaring.

He skidded around a corner and burst through a door, not knowing or caring what it was or where it went. An office, it led into a series of larger offices, and he could see another entrance door on the far side. He slammed into the door, but it would not open. The door he had just come through crashed open again as the PGZ men reached it. Chisnall ducked down, below the level of the desks, desperately searching for another way out. A door, a window, anything!

He could see nothing, and slid under a desk, hoping against hope that they would somehow miss him. Footsteps sounded just metres away. He crawled into a corner, bunching himself up in the shadows. It didn't help.

The desk above him was suddenly no longer there, tipped over on its side. What replaced it was the large shape of two PGZ agents.

He barely saw the guns. All he could think about was the salt shaker.

Goezlin would test it. He would find the poison. In his eyes this would be a plot by humans to kill the Bzadian spiritual leader.

The Bzadians were teetering on the brink of all out nuclear war with humans.

Chisnall had a horrible feeling that he had just pushed them over the edge.

But perhaps that had been Kozi's plan all along.

* * *

A large black bird, a crow, was watching Price, pausing only to peck at something under its feet. Price watched it back. Crows made her uncomfortable. There was something sinister about them. This one watched her for a moment longer, turning its head from side to side, then went back to its meal.

Looking at its claws, Price saw what it was eating. The carcass of another bird, a fledgling. The sight made her uncomfortable and she shook a hand at the crow to scare it away. It ignored her and carried on eating.

"What the hell?" Wall's voice dragged her eyes back to the front.

Across the grassy fields of the Congress, people were pouring out of the doorways of the building. The sound of sirens came clearly through the air, already hazy with the smoke from the bushfires.

A thin plume of smoke was rising, somewhere near the centre of the building.

"Chisnall," Brogan said.

"You don't know that," Wall said.

"She is right," Monster said. "Is Chisnall."

"Whether it is or not, it's our ticket in," Price said. "We are Oscar Mike, right now."

The crow watched them leave.

The Tsar was still unconscious when they got back down to the fire truck. Barnard had already started the engine, but slid out of the driver's seat as the others arrived. Monster swung himself up and slammed the door shut.

"Is The Tsar okay?" Price asked as the others climbed on board.

"Breathing's steady, pulse is strong, I think he's going to be okay," Barnard said, unable to keep the light from her eyes or the song from her voice.

"Hit the sirens," Price said as Monster gunned the engine.

He swerved the machine out of the construction site, around a corner and onto the main road leading towards the capitol building. The road was lined with trees, as was the median strip in the centre of the road. They crossed an intersection and through a small forested area. Although she had seen aerial photos, Price was still amazed at the amount of greenery and foliage surrounding the building. If the bushfire made it this far, it would find plenty of fuel, she thought.

The soldiers on the barricades saw them coming and wasted no time, pulling back the barricades that blocked the roads, waving the fire truck through. Their truck was yellow, not red, a bushfire truck not a city fire-engine, but in the heat, the panic of a fire in the heart of their government, no questions were asked. The soldiers left the gates open, and behind them Price heard the wail of more sirens.

"What now?" Wall asked.

"I don't know," Price said. "Keep an eye out for Chisnall. If they are evacuating the building then he will be somewhere outside."

She had barely finished speaking when Brogan said, "There."

"Where?" Price asked.

"That's him, that's Ryan Chisnall, straight ahead of us.

There was a catch in her voice but this was no time for emotions. Price followed her outstretched hand and saw three figures emerging from a side entrance. One of them with his hands to his neck, the other two holding him, one to each arm.

"Bull," Barnard said. "You couldn't make out his face at this distance."

"Yes I can," Brogan said.

"I'd believe her," Wall said. "I think she's right, and my eyesight is not as good as hers."

"Damn," Price said. Chisnall's captors wore the blood red uniform of the PGZ.

The truck was approaching a bridge across an inner ring road as the PGZ car pulled away from the curb. It turned into an exit road, heading directly towards the Angels.

"Gotta do something, Monster," Price said. "Gotta stop them."

"No problem," Monster said.

The truck reached the bridge a little before the car did. Monster waited until they were just metres apart, then veered right into the car's path.

The PGZ driver either had good reactions, or was well trained. He flung the car to the right, onto a grassy berm, out of the way of the truck, swerving around, aiming for a gap between the truck and the bridge railing.

Monster went with him, spinning the wheel back, the truck leaning, almost to the point of tipping as it swung back in the other direction. The car almost made it. Half a second more and it would have been through and clear.

The truck hit the side of the car at speed, just behind the door pillar, spinning it sideways, then slamming it into the concrete side railings of the bridge in a tangle of bent metal, rubber and broken glass and a shower of concrete shards. The car teetered for a moment on the edge of the bridge then it was gone.

There was a terrifying silence that seemed to go on forever. Then came the crash as the car hit the roadway below.

DRAGON STRIKE

[Mission Day 1, July 1st, 2033. 0920 hours local time]
[Tasman Sea, off the coast of New Zealand]

Flying low above the water, the dragon and its attendant razers were hidden from radar by the curvature of the Earth. Nor were they picked up on satellite. They were flying in a dead zone. Satellite coverage in this part of the world was not overlapping, and there was a thin strip where coverage from one satellite finished, before the next started.

The planes were finally picked up by coastal radar stations less than fifty kilometres from the coast of New Zealand.

On board the USS Apple, already on high alert, alarms sounded, people ran. Weapons turrets went from passive alert to active seeking. The first scream-jets, waiting on the runway, were immediately launched, and others lined up behind them. With four catapults operating, each launch took less than a minute, and the massive elevators were already bringing more planes up to the flight deck. Launching the carrier jets was not the problem, however. To launch the scream-jets the carrier jets had to climb almost to the stratosphere, and that took time.

The circling F-35 fighter jets went to afterburners, racing to the west to try and engage the Bzadian planes before they could get within striking distance of the ships.

On board the USS Apple Super-ARBOC systems went to work, throwing a curtain of chaff and countermeasures into the air, concealing the ship from radar or radio-guided missiles.

On the missile frigates and destroyers that screened the USS Apple, covers slid off missile silos and the moment a solid radar target was achieved, a porcupine forest of smoke trails sprouted.

Ground based SAM stations added their sound to the massed shriek of indignation.

Witnesses would later say that it was as if the air had turned black, such was the volume of ordnance that was being hurled at the incoming alien fighters.

It wasn't enough. The Bzadians weren't here to fight a pitched battle. The moment the USS Apple came within range, the dragon fired its full complement of air-ground missiles then, as if a single craft, the entire wing of fighters wheeled around and headed for home chased by a swarm of stinging insects.

The Bzadian countermeasures were awesome, the dragon was equipped with thousands of anti-missile missiles and the protective cover of the five razers added further firepower.

In a seething mass of yellow and orange explosions that lit up the early morning Auckland skies the human missiles were swatted from the skies. Most of them.

One slipped through the defences and a Razer disintegrated in a sheet of flame. Another missed by metres but that was close enough. It exploded just below the left wing of the Bzadian craft, peppering it with shrapnel. The wing, straining to cope with the stress of the rapid banking turn, snapped, setting up a vibration that shook the plane to pieces even before it crashed in a spiral to the earth.

Two more Razers disappeared in blinding flashes before the superior speed of the Bzadian planes began to make a difference.

On board the USS Apple, alert boards were screaming at over a hundred and sixty incoming Bzadian missiles.

Now the missile boats that surrounded the ship were no longer firing at the Bzadian planes. Instead they were hurling a curtain of metal hail at the incoming missiles.

All of the ships in the fleet were equipped with 'R2D2' Phalanx auto-cannons, each capable of throwing up an astounding five thousand rounds per minute, a wall of lead through which the Bzadian missiles had to penetrate.

Most of the Bzadian missiles were destroyed by ground-air missiles before they got anywhere near their target. Others were misled by the chaff and decoys thrown up by the S-ARBOC systems.

Less than thirty penetrated the screen of destroyers and the Phalanx systems on board those ships continued to knock them down even as they passed overhead.

The USS Apple's own phalanx guns were its last line of defence and missile after missile fell to them, it all happening in a matter of microseconds.

But there were too many incoming missiles and the last of the Bzadian missiles was destroyed less than ten metres from the flight deck.

It was too close. Far too close. The heat flash and shock wave of the explosion hurled jet aircraft around like toys, fuel tanks exploded, men and women were blown overboard, or jumped into the ocean, on fire, screaming.

In the aftermath, there was no permanent structural damage. Nothing that could not be repaired. But the flight deck was littered with debris and burning wreckage. Until it could be cleared, the carrier was out of action.

In the sky above the carrier, the first scream-jet to take off finally reached its launch altitude.

Flight Commander Molly Shaw, looked down at the glow that was the USS Apple, far below.

The pukes were not going to get away with that, she thought.

Travelling already at supersonic speeds, she hit the rocket boosters the moment the carrier detached. The rising scream of the engine echoed the anguished wail of the ship below.

Mach two passed, Mach three, and the speed continued to climb.

Shaw rammed her hand down on the ignition system, and felt the kick as the scramjet engine fired.

She clenched her lips tightly shut against the rapid acceleration and went hunting dragons.

THE PLAN

[Mission Day 1, July 1st, 2033. 0930 hours local time]
[Bzadian Congress, Canberra]

Chisnall opened his eyes as the vehicle he was in lurched to a halt, rocking back and forth on its suspension.

For a moment he couldn't orientate himself. Nothing made sense. Vague memories of a girl in bright blue robes were interspersed with those of a face like a skull and of being hauled through corridors.

But here he was now on the floor of a vehicle, a truck of some kind.

He dimly heard Price's voice barking orders, and through the open doorway he saw members of his old Angel team running to take up defensive positions.

Then Price was back, leaning over him as he sat up, examining his head.

"Monster, come here," she called. "He's coming around."

The next thing the thick, strong arms of his best friend were wrapped around him, as much a hug as a lift, and he was being carried out of the truck.

"It's good to see you, buddy," he managed, gasping in the crushing grasp.

When Monster finally let him go, grinning like a madman, he managed to stand by himself, and Price was the next to embrace him, briefly but emotionally, before returning to direct the other team members, co-ordinating kill-zones and fields of fire.

He watched her work with a sense of satisfaction.

Retha Barnard was crouched behind a pillar. She trotted over and held out a fist for a bump.

Chisnall grinned and pushed her hand aside, wrapping one of his arms around her. The other arm didn't seem to be working. Barnard managed a cursory clasp and awkward pat on the back before returning to her position. She wasn't much of a hugger.

"I can't tell you how good it is to see you all," Chisnall said. And it was. It really was.

"Good to see you too, Ryan," Price said.

"Boo-yah," Monster said.

"Guys," Wall said. "I don't want to interrupt your little Oprah moment but I figure we got about thirty seconds before the Pukes work out that there's only one place you could hide a fire truck around here."

"Who's the new guy?" Chisnall asked.

"That's Wall," Price said. "Hayden Wall. Specialist First Class."

Chisnall stared at him for a moment. He knew the name from somewhere, although he had never seen Wall before. There was an uncomfortable feeling that went along with that name. Somehow he associated it with death.

He stood with his back resting against the side of the truck and looked around, still dazed and feeling more than a little confused. They were in a parking garage. Grey concrete walls, floor and ceiling held up by circular pillars. Bzadian vehicles were scattered around the garage in no particular order. It seemed cavernous and gloomy despite the bright fluorescent strips overhead. The ceilings were low and oppressive. It felt like a trap.

The truck he was leaning on was yellow, a chunky, angular beast with large knobbly tires. It took him a moment to recognise it for what it was: a fire truck. It was parked at the rear of the garage, sandwiched between two heavy concrete walls that concealed it from the front entrance. A small pile of firefighter coats and helmets was stacked against one of the walls.

"Kill the lights," Price said.

Wall dialled his coil-gun down to slow and silent, and took out the overhead florescent tubes around them, leaving them in deep shadow. The sound of the shattered glass tinkling on the ground was louder than the sound of the shots.

"Barnard, take a quick scout around," Price said. "Check for other exits, doorways up into the building, anything like that. We need an escape route. Wall, take a C4 pack and mine the entrance. When they find us we'll blow the front door and escape out the back."

Barnard and Wall disappeared.

Monster had a mini flashlight in his mouth. He was checking Chisnall's arms and legs, feeling for broken bones. When Monster got to his right arm Chisnall had to bite his lip to stop himself from crying out.

"Arm broken," Monster said.

"What happened?" Chisnall asked. "I feel like I was hit by a truck."

"You were," Price said. "Monster was driving."

"Monster, you need to re-sit your licence," Chisnall said.

"Did no your mother tell you not to get in car with strangers." Monster grinned at him, moving a mediscope over his head.

That was when Chisnall noticed the wet warmth trickling down his face. He touched it and his hand came away dark red in the light of Monster's flashlight.

"Good to see you, Monster," Chisnall said, but now it all came flooding back. The girl was Azoh. The skull face was Goezlin. The two goons dragging him through the corridors were PGZ agents.

"Hold arm like this," Monster said, moving Chisnall's left hand onto his right elbow. Another wave of excruciating pain washed over Chisnall.

"Try not to move arm," Monster said.

"No kidding," Chisnall said.

"How is he?" Price asked.

He going to be fine," Monster said, packing the mediscope away. "But head wound is bad bleeding, and also right ulna is broken."

"Can you patch him up?" Price asked.

"Can't fix arm here," Monster said. "Need hospital. And need more dressings for head. Used all ours on Tsar."

"I'm okay, I can wait," Chisnall said. "The Tsar's here too? What happened to him, and how is he?"

"Had an argument with a rotorbot," Price said. "He's up in the truck unconscious. He's not good, but we've done all we can for him for now."

A small sound, like a dog whimpering, came through the open door of the fire truck.

"What he needs is a hospital," a voice said. A voice that he knew all too well. It came from behind a small sedan-like car two pillars away. His former sergeant lifted her head up and looked directly over at him.

"Hello Holly," Chisnall said.

"Lieutenant Chisnall." Brogan acknowledged him with a brief nod.

Chisnall stared at her for a moment before her face disappeared back behind the car.

Just the sight of her gave him goose bumps. The bitter icy kind. It was the same girl, but somehow not the same girl that he had once thought he was in love with. It was as though a storm had blown through and stripped away everything soft and feminine about her. What was left was harsh and coarse and shattered.

"What's your take on Bogan," he asked of Price in a low voice.

She shrugged. "So far so good. She says she's on our side."

"You trust her?"

She shrugged again. "You want my honest opinion?"

"Of course."

"She's been perfect, Price said. "Too perfect, if you know what I mean. Everything she has done has been straight down the line. She gave up the other Ferzerkers to get on the team; she saved The Tsar's life; she's helped us avoid Bzadian patrols. It all seems designed to get her here. With us, with you, right now. Why? What's her end game? That's what I want to know."

"You don't think she could be genuine?" Chisnall asked.

"What do you think?" Price asked.

"Time will tell," Chisnall said.

"That's a crappy answer," Price said. "What if it's too late?"

"Just keep an eye on her," Chisnall said. "Where are we?"

"Underground parking garage in the Congress," Price said. "There was a lot of smoke and confusion and I don't think they've realised what just happened. Not yet anyway."

"Smoke from the fire I started?" Chisnall asked. He had thought the sprinkler system would have taken care of it. Had he burnt the entire building down?

Price smiled. "A little. But the Pukes did this to themselves. They bombed the hell out of a town east of here and stared a massive bush fire. It's heading this way."

Chisnall sat on the steps of the fire truck as another wave of pain from his arm threatened to overwhelm him.

* * *

The emergency mobile command centre was wide and long, but still crowded and bustling with the number of people that were jammed into it. Radar operators, communications specialists, military co-ordinators. Most of them seated at consoles or watching video screens. There was a sense of urgency, but not of panic.

The command centre smelled faintly of smoke, not quite filtered out by the air-conditioning system. The smell made Nokz'z nose itch a little. He had always been oversensitive to smells.

He worked his way down the length of the centre, watching as operators powered up and tested equipment, preparing the truck for use.

A communications officer caught Nokz'z's attention. He was bent over a console with a radio pressed to his ear.

"Yes, Corporal Kazen?" Nokz'z asked.

"Update on the fire sir. Fire teams have now entered the

kitchen and extinguished the seat of the fire. It appears to be under control."

"Have you received confirmation that Azoh is safe?" Nokz'z asked.

Azoh and her team had retreated to the bunkers deep beneath the building as soon as the fire alarms had sounded.

"Yes sir," Kazen said. "The bunker area is secure. Sprinklers contained the fire to just the kitchen and the surrounding corridors."

"Any word on the cause of the fire?" Nokz'z asked.

"Not yet," Kazen said. "The firefighters are currently conducting mopping up operations and building checks. We should be able to return to the building in about thirty minutes. The fire investigators will go in then too."

"I want to know as soon as possible," Nokz'z said.

"It was a kitchen fire," Kazen said. "A lot of fires start in kitchens."

"Not in the Congress they don't," Nokz'z said. "If there was the slightest chance that it was deliberately lit, we need to know who did it and why."

And if it was connected somehow to the loss of the rotorbot at Batemans Bay, he thought.

"Yes sir," Kazen said.

"Goezlin for you, sir," the Vaza said, right at his elbow, where she belonged. She was not a great conversationalist, preferring single word sentences where possible, but her skills in other areas were outstanding.

"Tell him I'll call him back," Nokz'z said.

"He's here," the Vaza said, indicating the door at the rear of the command centre.

Nokz'z exchanged a glance with the Vaza and shook his head. The last thing he needed was the PGZ commandant poking his nose in where it was not wanted. He strode to the rear, opened the door and stepped down, fixing a firm but polite smile to his face. It was a mask, but it was a mask that he was well practiced at. The Vaza followed.

The air was acrid with the smell of smoke. Nokz'z found himself rubbing at his nose, as if to wipe the smell away. He stopped himself doing it. It looked weak.

The Commandant of the PGZ was waiting impatiently on the tarmac outside, flanked by a number of his officers, hard-faced and emotionless.

"Ordinarily, commandant, my time would be yours." Nokz'z said. "But as you can see we are rather preoccupied at the moment. There has been a fire in the building, a bushfire heading in our direction, and there may be some enemy infiltrators coming in from the coast. I trust you will excuse me."

Goezlin smiled thinly, a token show of civility.

"A bushfire that you started," Goezlin said. "A kitchen fire that you failed to prevent, and infiltrators that are already here, inside the secure area."

Nokz'z bowed his head, as much to conceal his expression as a gesture of apology or deference. When he lifted it the mask was back, firmly in place.

"What are you trying to tell me, Commandant? Infiltrators inside the grounds of the Congress? Not possible. No one is able to get in or out."

"Except fire appliances," Goezlin said.

"Of course," Nokz'z said. "There is a fire."

"A few moments ago a fire appliance smashed into one of my cars," Goezlin said. "It was transporting a very important prisoner. That vehicle is now missing, as is my prisoner. Two of my men are in hospital."

Nokz'z held his face emotionless, but his heart was now racing. A bad situation had suddenly got worse. Much worse.

"The fact that they were able to gain access to these grounds so easily makes me wonder if they had help from the inside," Goezlin said.

"You are not suggesting that I—"

"Of course not. But I should warn you, Colonel, that more mistakes like this will not be tolerated."

"Of course, Commandant," Nokz'z said.

This close, one on one, he was suddenly aware of every tiny detail of Goezlin's face. The fine lines around his eyes, not smile lines. Smiling was surely unknown to this creature. The cheekbones, so harshly defined they looked like curved scars. His misshapen tongue, one side of which was noticeably shorter than the other.

How he would like to slow roast this thin faced devil over a hot fire.

"We will find the fire vehicle," Nokz'z said. "You will have your prisoner back. The perimeter is sealed, they cannot have escaped."

"You are sure of that," Goezlin said, and Nokz'z was sure he heard a faint mocking tone.

"We will start the search immediately," Nokz'z said.

* * *

"I'm not kidding, guys," Wall said, running back from the main entrance, punching numbers into a remote detonator. "There are Pukes all over the place like flies at a barbecue."

"Jesus, Wall. Couldn't they have genetically engineered you to be happy?" Price asked.

Wall shook his head and took up a position behind a car.

Barnard arrived back also. "There are no doors leading into the building, probably for security reasons."

"Damn," Price said.

"It's okay," Barnard said. "I checked a schematic of the building and there is a maintenance corridor running along the back wall. The concrete is thin there. We should be able to blow our way through."

"Prepare it," Price said. "Use det cord. We may be heading that way in a hurry."

"Did that already," Barnard said.

Price nodded and turned to Chisnall. "What's going on? We saw you getting arrested."

The memory of that made Chisnall feel sick to his stomach. Not just because of the prospect of interrogation by the dreaded PGZ. All the planning, all the risk. It was all for nothing. His carefully created position in the Congress kitchen. All gone. Because he let himself get recognised.

"Do you remember Goezlin?" Chisnall asked. "The PGZ guy we met at Uluru. He saw me."

"That's bad," Price said. "Real bad."

"Sorry guys," Chisnall said. "I guess that's it. I blew the mission."

"Let me be the judge of that," Price said, and Chisnall looked at her with a raised eyebrow.

This was definitely not the same girl that he had led on the Uluru and Magnum missions.

Price saw his expression and smiled grimly. "We've come through a lot to get here. And I'm guessing this mission was pretty important to start with. So it ain't over till it's over."

Chisnall looked at Barnard. "You have it?"

Barnard nodded, and tapped a finger on her belt-pack. "I nearly ate it once or twice."

That earned her a sharp glance from Price.

"I really don't know how –" Chisnall began.

"Tell us what the mission is," Price said. "Let us decide if we can still pull it off."

"Barnard didn't tell you?" Chisnall asked.

"Wasn't up to me," Barnard said. "Anyway all I really knew was to bring the bugging device."

"Bugging device?" Monster asked.

"Movement by the entrance," Wall called softly.

"What have you got?" Price asked.

"Couple of soldiers, just having a quick scout round," Wall said.

Chisnall peered around the edge of the concrete wall, seeing two dark figures examining the garage through the sights of their guns. He pulled his head back as one of them turned in his direction.

"Everybody stay out of sight, and stay frosty. They don't' know we're here yet," Price said. "Now Chisnall, shoot."

"Ok," Chisnall said, thinking quickly how to tell her in as few words as possible. "I've been undercover in this building for about six months," he said. "But there's one place I can't go, and that's Azoh's quarters."

"Azoh, the leader of the entire Bzadian race," Price said.

"Yeah, that Azoh," Chisnall said.

"Why you want to go see Azoh?" Monster asked.

"I don't," Chisnall said. "That's why Barnard brought the bug."

"You're going to bug Azoh's bedroom?" Price asked.

"Not her bedroom, her meeting chambers," Chisnall said.

"Wait a second, Azoh is a she?" Price asked.

Chisnall nodded. "Not all that much older than us, from the look of her. Every major decision the Bzadians make goes to her for advice and a kind of blessing. If we could bug her meeting room then ACOG would have inside knowledge of everything the Bzadians are planning to do, and when they are planning to do it."

"So where are these quarters?" Price asked.

"Below us," Chisnall said. "There are basements and sub-basements. The deepest levels form a kind of bunker system where Azoh resides."

"And how exactly do you plan to get in?" Price asked. "I'm thinking they are not just going to let you waltz inside."

"That's why Brogan is here," Chisnall said.

* * *

"You're sure the fire truck didn't leave the grounds?" Nokz'z asked.

Kazen nodded. "The perimeter guards saw it enter, but it has not left."

"Then they are here somewhere," Goezlin said.

"It does not show anywhere on the feed from the surveillance craft," Kazen said.

"They have to be in the parking garage," Nokz'z said. "There's nowhere else. Get a team in there right now."

"One team may not be enough," Goezlin said.

"My soldiers are very competent," Nokz'z said.

"Of course they are," Goezlin said. There was just that trace of a mocking tone again, or was it just Nokz'z's imagination? "But I believe we may be dealing with Angels."

Nokz'z forced a smile to cover the grinding of his teeth. Angels. He had a score to settle with them. "Send two teams," he said. "Is there any way from the garage back inside the building?"

"None," the communications officer said. "There is only one way in or out, and that is via the entrance ramp."

"Good," Nokz'z said. He turned to Goezlin. "Who is this prisoner that is so important to you?"

"That is not something that you need to know," Goezlin said.

"I beg to differ," Nokz'z said. "It is my men who are tasked with recapturing the prisoner. We should know who we are dealing with."

"His name is Chizna," Goezlin said.

He had volunteered that information too easily, Nokz'z thought. Why? "This Chizna was at Uluru," he said.

"Now a spy," Goezlin said.

"Inside the Congress?" Nokz'z asked.

Goezlin nodded shortly. "How long has he been there? What secrets has he discovered? I need to talk to him."

There was a slight emphasis on the word 'talk' that completely altered its meaning. Nokz'z felt he would not want to be 'talked' to by Goezlin. A fantasy briefly flitted across his mind where he was the head of the PGZ and Goezlin was strapped to a chair in front of him. He pushed the thought aside.

"Is it not your job to catch spies before they can do us damage?" Nokz'z asked and regretted the words immediately.

Goezlin turned slowly to face him, turning his head to the left and right like a bird eying up a morsel. His pupils were jet black and coldly knowing. He was making Nokz'z nervous, and worse, Goezlin knew it. Nokz'z prided himself on being the king of calm, but this man had the ability to conjure storm clouds in a clear blue sky. Nokz'z felt transparent and fragile, as if his skin had just turned to glass, revealing his vital organs and every aspect of the inner workings of his body.

"It is indeed my job, and I caught him," Goezlin said. "But it was your job to keep spies out, and it is a job you have not done well. Now, again thanks to you, he is on the loose. I want him alive. If he is killed, the consequences for you will not be pleasant."

The sound of gunshots came from the far end of the building.

"I want them all alive," Goezlin said.

"Pull the soldiers back," Nokz'z said to Kazen. "Get me Captain Jazki."

* * *

"We just ran out of time!" Wall shouted over the sound of gunfire, echoing from the hard-concrete surfaces of the garage. The walls around them spat stone chips and puffs of grey dust.

The Angels returned fire, the gunfire from both sides combining into a deafening orchestra of percussion.

"That's it, Price," Chisnall had to shout to be heard above the thunder. "The mission is blown, we just have to try and get out of here."

"Okay. Everybody get ready to move," Price said. "Monster, you grab the Tsar. Barnard, when Wall destroys the main entrance, blow us a back door at the same time, so they don't hear two explosions. We'll hide out until the raid."

"What raid?" Chisnall asked. He didn't get an answer.

"Hide where?" Wall asked, emptying almost a full clip at the entrance. He ducked down as the car that was protecting him shuddered under heavy fire. He held up the detonator control and flipped off the safety switch.

"There's a tunnel system," Price said. "Links up a few of the old buildings. We can get to the former American Embassy building, outside the cordoned off area. We don't think the Pukes know about the tunnels. This was supposed to be our escape route after the mission."

"What is embassy used for now?" Monster asked.

"Communications," Barnard said. "Central communications centre for the Bzadian military."

"Just pen-pushers and powerpoint rangers," Price said. "We should be able to deal with them."

"Before we go anywhere, what's this about a raid," Chisnall asked again. "Bilal didn't say anything about a raid."

"He wouldn't have. It's 'need to know'. But it's our ticket out of here," Price said. "We got some new jets, real fast. They're going to hit Canberra as soon as we're clear. That's gonna send the Pukes a message. From now on we can attack where and when we want. We'll call the raid in as soon as we're clear."

"What if we don't call it in?" Chisnall asked.

"We've got till noon," Price said. "If they don't hear from us by then, they assume we've been compromised or captured, and they launch the raid anyway."

"Ready to rock and roll," Wall said. "On my count, Barnard. Blowing the entrance in three…"

'Everybody get on the ground, take cover," Price called.

"Wait!" Chisnall said.

"Got no time to wait," Wall said. "Two."

"Let me think," Chisnall said.

"Got no time to think," Wall said.

"No, you don't understand," Chisnall said. "The Pukes are a whisker away from blowing us all to hell."

"Wall, wait," Price ordered.

"Nukes?" Monster asked.

"I don't have time to explain it now," Chisnall said. "But they're real close to the edge. An attack on Canberra would nudge them over."

"Then ACOG will retaliate," Price said.

"If they can," Chisnall said. "But any which way the free territories go boom boom bye bye. Good night and thanks for playing."

"Grenade!" Brogan shouted. "Everybody down!"

Chisnall hit the floor, lying in a black pool of old oil as a sharp crack lit up the darkness around them.

"Wall, frags!" Brogan called. She stood, taking cover behind a pillar. Wall took a pair of grenades from his belt and tossed them to her.

"Frag out!" Brogan shouted. She pulled the pins and hurled them, one after the other, at the entrance. The firing from that direction stopped for a moment as the roar of the grenades echoed through the parking garage.

"Can you stop the raid?" Chisnall asked.

"We could try," Price said," but I doubt they'd listen. The ACOG bigwigs think this is what it's going to take to end the war."

"End the war, or end the world," Chisnall asked. "They don't know about the positronium bombs."

"The what?" Barnard asked.

Chisnall did not reply. He was silent, thinking deeply.

"They're pulling back," Wall said.

"Boo-yah," Monster shouted.

"It ain't a good thing," Brogan said. "They'll be back."

"Gotta move, Ryan," Price said. "Whatever you think, we're going to get slaughtered if we stay here."

"Okay. I have an idea," Chisnall said. "It's pretty wild and we're going to have to have real big cojones to pull it off."

"Big cojones we got," Price said. "But they're no use to us if we're dead."

"We gotta go!" Wall shouted.

"Is this a private party or am I invited," a voice said.

SEVEN KINDS OF CRAZY

[Mission Day 1, July 1st, 2033. 0940 hours local time]
[Bzadian Congress, Canberra]

The Republican Guards were regarded as the elite of the Bzadian army, tasked with defending cities and major installations. It was the Republican Guard who defended the capital city of New Bzadia, still known by its human name of Canberra.

If the republican guards were the elite of the army, the Nzgali were the elite of the Republican Guard. The Nzgali were specialists; trouble-shooters; sharp-shooters. The team that were called in when things went wrong. Their equipment, skills, dedication and training were legendary. Their uniforms: jet black.

In this region the republican guard answered directly to Colonel Nokz'z and it was no surprise that it was the Nzgali that he called upon when the Congress was under threat.

Nokz'z watched on the large screens that lined the wall of the mobile command centre as two assault teams converged on the entrance of the parking garage in armoured cars.

Nokz'z was proud of the Nzgali and had taken a personal interest in their selection and training, since he had taken over his post. Everything about them was a step above that of a standard Bzadian soldier. Their weapons were better, their armour was stronger. Their training was more intense. They were selected from the best of the best of the Republican guard, themselves selected from the best of other units. The Angels would not stand a chance.

The armoured cars manoeuvred around a battle tank that Nokz'z had ordered into position on the road directly outside the garage, in case the infiltrators tried to make a run for it.

"Alive," Goezlin said, unnecessarily, Nokz'z thought. He had already made his point a number of times. It was as if Goezlin did not trust the competence of the defence forces.

The armoured cars moved carefully around the tank and accelerated into the driveway, one on each side, the entry and the exit lanes.

The rear lights of the vehicles had just disappeared when there was the sharp crack of an explosion, followed by another and a swirl of dust and smoke filled the entrance. Through it, with the roar of a powerful engine came the large yellow nose of a bushfire truck.

"They were waiting for you," Goezlin said.

The fire truck bounced up the sloping driveway, swerving around the battle tank and hurtled off down the road towards the security perimeter.

The turret of the tank swivelled after them as the fire truck gained speed.

"Do not fire," Nokz'z shouted, "We will stop them at the gates."

The road ahead of them was well blocked by heavy concrete crash barriers.

The two armoured cars now reappeared at the garage entrance, bursting out of the dark underground cavern after the fire truck. They were both just metres from the entrance when it exploded.

A great ball of fire and smoke snorted out of the twin openings, like the nostrils of a dragon.

The force of it lifted both of the armoured cars by the back axles, flipping them over on their sides. Even the mighty battle tank rocked on its suspension.

"I want that truck stopped, and the occupants captured alive!" Nokz'z roared, aware that he was losing his calm, but unable to help himself. Too much was riding on this.

The fire truck turned, along the inner road, keeping away from the perimeter with its concrete and wire defences. It raced around a corner, veering across the lawns, dry and hard from a lack of rain, over onto the forecourt of the building.

Now Nokz'z realised what they were doing. Leaving the roads, sticking to the lawns, racing down the grassy mall that led to Old Parliament House, now a Bzadian museum. There were fences erected across those lawns, but only light ones, no crash barriers. No tanks.

"They're making for the museum," he said, under better control of his voice. "Bring up tanks and cut them off at the entrance."

They tried. They failed. They were simply too slow.

The Angels were already well on their way before any of the Bzadian tanks got moving. They hit the fence at speed, splitting it in two, hurling broken bits of wire and metal into the air.

They reached the road around the museum well before any tanks were close, racing around it, through it, screaming back around onto the main road that led across the lake.

There was an explosion now, just to the left of the truck, rocking it, almost knocking it off course. It went up onto two wheels and Nokz'z thought for a moment that it would go over, and his problems would be solved, but it somehow regained its balance and settled.

"Who fired that?" Goezlin shouted.

"Find out," Nokz'z ordered.

They watched through the eyes of the rotorcraft as the yellow vehicle bounced over a curb and crossed an intersection on the wrong side of the road to avoid a hasty roadblock on the other side. It stayed on that side, narrowly avoiding on-coming traffic, heading for the lake.

More explosions now, left and right of the fire truck, showering it with debris as it hurtled into the built up streets of the city.

"The rockets are coming from the gunship, sir," Kazen said.

"Tell them to stop," Nokz'z said.

"The Angels must know we are tracking them," Goezlin said. "What kind of a game are they playing? What do they hope to achieve?"

The answer to that question became clear as the fire truck spun around corners on the north side of the lake, edging closer to a large complex to the east of the circular park that marked the very heart of the city.

On the screen Nokz'z could see the lights of security cars converging on the truck and on the mall. They blocked the street.

With seemingly no other option, the truck hurtled around into a wide driveway that led into the mall.

The truck disappeared into the car-park entrance and disappeared from sight.

"Seal of the building. Seal off the area!" Nokz'z said. "I am on my way."

"Stay frosty, check your corners," Price called as the team moved down a featureless corridor, somewhere in the bowels of the building.

"Clear," Barnard said, on point, risking a quick glance into a side corridor ahead of them. She checked it again, then motioned the team forward with a hand signal.

"Move, move, move!" Price said.

They reached a cross corridor. In the middle of the intersection was a rest area. Twin sofas facing each other. Brown leather, creased and cracked by years of use.

"Okay, hold here for a moment," Price said. "Barnard, where the hell are we?"

Chisnall sank into one of the sofas. It was not like him, Price thought. The constant pain was making him weak.

The rest of the team automatically spread out into a defensive posture, Price noted, covering all four directions.

"Mainly offices on this level," Barnard said, studying the schematics of the building on her wrist computer. The medical centre is one floor down, south corner."

"Do we have time for this?" Wall asked.

"The skipper's not much use with a broken arm," Price said.

"I'm not the skipper, you are," Chisnall said faintly.

"We can talk about that later," Price said.

"Nothing to talk about," Chisnall said.

"And the Pukes don't know where we are yet," Price said.

"Won't take them long to figure it out," Brogan said.

"We're going to the medical centre," Price said. "Tactical column. Monster, you're on point."

They ignored the elevators, preferring the stairs, and found the centre exactly where Barnard had said it would be. It was deserted.

"All right Brogan," Price said. "Time to earn your keep."

"Again?" Brogan asked with a half-smile.

"You going to help or not?" Price asked.

Brogan nodded. She moved across to Chisnall and examined his arm quickly.

"Lie down, Lieutenant," she said, indicating a treatment bed attached to one wall.

"We can't stay here," Wall said.

"It's a big building, and they don't yet know where we are," Price said. "Will this take long?"

"It's a quick process," Brogan said. "But the skipper can't move until it's finished."

Calling him skipper was deliberate, Price thought. Her way of saying who she thought was really in charge.

"Ouch," Chisnall said, as Brogan eased his arms apart and positioned the broken one on an adjustable rest.

"Grit your teeth," she said. "This ain't gonna take you to your happy place."

"Give him some painkillers," Monster said.

"No," Chisnall said. "There's no time."

Brogan queried Price with a stare, until Price nodded.

Brogan took firm hold of Chisnall's arm and squeezed, manipulating the bone inside. Price didn't need an x-ray to know that she was re-aligning the broken ends of the ulna.

Chisnall's face went white and his forehead glistened with a sheen of sweat, but he made no sound.

Brogan nodded to herself, then restrained Chisnall's arm

using small metal straps attached to the armrest. She checked the position of the broken bones once more after she had finished, earning a wide eyed silent scream from Chisnall.

"Sorry skipper," Brogan said.

"I keep telling you guys, I'm not the skipper," Chisnall said. His voice was feeble.

"Okay, let's talk about that," Price said. Anything to distract him from the pain. "You're the senior officer here. This is your team. I'm just the caretaker. Besides," she smiled, "You're Lieutenant Lucky, and I think we could use some luck today."

Brogan moved a portable machine over to the treatment bed and positioned it carefully above Chisnall's arm, using a video x-ray screen on the back to align two sets of cross-hairs directly over the break in his bone.

"Lucky," Chisnall did not smile back. "You know why they call me lucky?"

"No, why?" Wall asked.

"Because people around me get very unlucky and that makes me look lucky by comparison."

Price could see the pain in his eyes and she knew exactly what was on his mind.

"Ryan, you've got us out of all kinds of scrapes," she said. "You're the luckiest guy I know."

"Tell that to Hunter, or the Demons. Or the soldiers on Task Force Magnum," Chisnall said.

"You think you're the only one carrying that weight?" Price asked. "Do you want me to tell you about Emile, or Nukilik, or Wilton?"

The name Wilton hung strangely in the air, as if it were

somehow denser than the rest and took a longer time to dissolve.

Chisnall winced as the machine above his arm began to whirr softly, knitting the bones back together.

"Price, I've been watching you. You're doing a great job as leader. I'd be happy to be on your team," he said.

"Maybe we should give the others that option," Price said.

"Why don't you do that," Chisnall smiled.

There was a silence, and the other Angels all looked at each other.

"I can't speak for the others," Barnard said eventually. "But I'd follow this girl to the end of the earth."

Price looked at her in astonishment. Barnard was the last one she'd expect to hear that from.

"The same goes for me," Wall said.

Monster grunted his agreement. Brogan managed a quick shrug.

"Guys…" Price began, embarrassed.

"It's been asked, and answered," Chisnall said. "Now what are your orders, LT?"

For a moment Price was almost unable to speak. Most of the time she felt she was hanging on by her fingernails, yet her team seemed to have a different view.

"You're the one with the plan," Price said. "I'd like to know what it is. We'd like to know what it is."

"Okay," Chisnall said. "But you're going to think it's seven kinds of crazy."

NZGALI

[Mission Day 1, July 1st, 2033. 0950 hours local time]
[Shopping Mall, Canberra]

The scene commander was a young Nzgali captain. She was examining the interior of the fire truck when Nokz'z arrived. She stepped down and visibly paled when she saw who was with him.

"Colonel Nokz'z," she said. "Commandant Goezlin."

"This is Captain Jazki," Nokz'z said. "One of my most competent officers."

Jazki waved away the compliment with a brief touch of one hand to her face.

The yellow truck, battered and blackened, peppered with shrapnel, had crashed into a pillar just by the large glass doors that led into the mall. The nose of the truck was crumpled like tissue paper and all the windows were shattered.

A trail of blood droplets led through large glass doors into the mall itself, but petered out just past the entrance.

A body lay on the ground beside the truck, surrounded by soldiers.

"Your report, captain," Nokz'z said.

"When we arrived we found the scene much as you see it," Jazki said. "The occupants had escaped, except for one who we found unconscious on the floor in the back of the truck."

"Alive?" Nokz'z asked.

Jazki nodded. "Badly injured though."

"From the crash or the shrapnel?" Nokz'z asked.

"Neither," Jazki said. The dressings aren't ours. Looks like he was wounded earlier and they patched him up as best as they could. He should be in hospital."

Nokz'z leant over the injured Angel, examining the face. "It is the one they call The Tsar," he said.

"They left him behind?" Goezlin asked.

"They had no choice," Nokz'z said. "They could never have escaped dragging him along with them."

"If you want my opinion," Jazki said. "They left him behind deliberately. They knew we'd get him to a hospital. He wouldn't last much longer without proper medical treatment."

"I want to talk to him," Goezlin said.

"He is not conscious," Jazki said.

Goezlin stared at her.

"I'll see what we can do," Jazki said.

* * *

"That is crazy," Barnard said.

"Have you got a better idea?" Chisnall asked.

"No," Barnard admitted. "But that doesn't make it any less crazy."

Brogan was examining the screen on the back of the machine that was mending Chisnall's arm.

"Can it go any faster, Brogan," Chisnall said. "We gotta get moving."

"We're not going anywhere till Humpty's together again," Brogan said.

"Tell us about these positronium bombs," Barnard said.

"Is that even a real thing?" Price asked.

"It might be," Barnard said.

"According to my source, Ferzerkers have hidden one of these bombs in Washington," Chisnall said.

"A decapitation strike," Barnard said.

"A what?" Wall asked.

"Decapitation," Barnard said. "Cut off the head. Then the orders to fire our nukes would never be given."

"Wouldn't the subs fire them anyway?" Price asked.

"They can't," Barnard said. "All our nukes are strictly controlled, to stop a rogue commander from starting a nuclear war. They can only be launched with codes supplied by the Pentagon. Without that, they're just expensive paperweights."

"So what is a positronium bomb?" Price asked.

"I don't really know," Chisnall said. "Any idea, Barnard?"

"Maybe," Barnard said. "I know what positronium is."

"Tell us. But try and use little words," Price said.

"When antimatter and matter collide, it releases tremendous amounts of energy," Barnard said. "But you can stop them colliding, temporarily, by getting the particles to orbit each other. That creates a mass called positronium. But there're two problems. Firstly, it's not stable. We've never been able to make it last for more than a few billionths of a second."

"Billionths?"

"Yeah. Blink and you'll miss it. A billion times. Here's the second problem. A gram of positronium would produce an incredibly powerful bomb, but in the entire history of the earth we've never managed to create more than a millionth of that. And it disappeared almost as soon as it existed."

"So where did the Pukes get all their positronium?" Price asked.

"I don't know," Barnard said.

"From the engines on their transporters," Brogan said.

"Their spaceships?" Chisnall asked. "That means they have thousands of them!"

Brogan shook her head, "Most of the transporters jettisoned their drives into space as a safety precaution before beginning their entry into earth's atmosphere. Remember that transporter that crashed? Imagine if that one had had its drive on board."

"Boom," Wall said.

"That's why when we inspected the transporters we found no sign of a power source," Barnard said.

"Yes. Mostly. Of the thousands of transporters, a very small number risked atmospheric entry with their drives on board. Any one of those drives has enough of this 'positronium' to create a dozen bombs, each bomb a thousand times more powerful than any nuclear weapon."

"Now you see the problem," Chisnall said. "The Pukes are backed into a corner. As soon as they feel there is a real possibility of defeat, they'll decide there's no other alternative but to blow us humans off the planet. First step: take out Washington."

"So how does Azoh help us stop this?" Price asked.

"They revere Azoh above everything," Chisnall said. "To them, she's like Mother Theresa, Ghandi and Jesus Christ all rolled into one."

"I still don't see how that helps," Price said.

"If someone kidnapped Jesus, wouldn't you do your best to get him back," Brogan asked.

"Exactly," Chisnall said. "If we could spirit Azoh away somewhere, we'd have the biggest bargaining chip of the war. Plus, if the Pukes don't know where she is, they not going to start blowing up cities in case they kill her."

"Nobody want to nuke Jesus," Monster said.

"We may be able to force the Pukes to negotiate some kind of truce with ACOG," Chisnall said.

There was a silence as they all thought through the implications of that. Price looked around at the team, noting the furrowed brows.

The very idea of kidnapping the spiritual leader of their enemy was outrageous.

"We'd have to get past all her guards, and somehow get her out of the country," she said.

"We'd be in the middle of the biggest manhunt in human history," Barnard said.

"You're right, it's crazy," Chisnall said.

"You'd have to be crazy to even think of attempting it," Barnard said.

"Monster crazy always," Monster said with a grin.

"I'm with the big guy," Wall said.

"Chisnall, you put me in charge," Price said. "So it's my decision. And I think it's suicide."

"You know what your problem is, Price?" Brogan asked.

"I'm sure you're going to tell me," Price said.

"You're still hoping to come out of this alive," Brogan said.

"And you're not?"

"I honestly don't care," Brogan said. "And that means I can function as a soldier. You'll never achieve anything unless you're prepared to put your life on the line."

"And the lives of those around me," Price said.

"Exactly," Brogan said.

"She's right," Chisnall said.

"It may be crazy, but at least we die in style," Brogan said.

"I'm starting to like this chick," Wall said.

"What about security?" Price asked.

"Very light," Chisnall said. "Bzadians don't have crime. Humans go around shooting their own leaders, the idea wouldn't even occur to a Bzadian." He stopped and corrected himself. "Usually."

Price wondered what he meant by that but didn't ask.

"Okay, we go back to the original plan, gain access to Azoh's private quarters," Price said. "Knock out her guards with some puke spray, tie her up, sling her over our collective shoulder, and whistle a jaunty little melody as we saunter on home."

"And live happily ever after," Wall said.

"It just might work," Chisnall said.

"If we can get her to the tunnels we might have a chance," Price said. "There'll be panic and confusion once the bombing raid starts. ACOG are sending in a rotorcraft to pick us up."

"In the midst of Bzadian territory?" Wall asked. "How's that going to work?"

"Same way it worked in Uluru," Price said. "It'll have hospital ship markings. Even if they suspect it, they wouldn't dare to shoot it down. How's that arm coming?"

"Almost there," Brogan said.

* * *

The Nzgali checked weapons and equipment as they finalised preparations for their search and assault of the mall.

Their equipment was impressive, and unique to their unit. Designed specifically for the kind of situation they were now in.

Spiderbots, modelled on a self-camouflaging Bzadian spider, were low, flat silent autonomous robots. Giding easily on eight legs with silent rubber feet they changed colour to match the surface they were rolling over, making them almost invisible. They were equipped with high resolution cameras and packed a powerful stun grenade.

BZB's were flying camera-bots, no larger than an insect, with a top speed faster than most birds, allowing a rapid and covert surveillance of a wide area. Their bodies were crystalline and their wings translucent. They were silent, and almost invisible.

There was a grunt from the prisoner, as he was moved onto a low gurney in preparation for transportation to hospital. Still unconscious, despite the best efforts of the medic.

The medic was clearly not used to treating humans, and was reading notes from a computer screen, comparing images to results he was getting on his equipment.

Goezlin was hovering over him like a predator about to pounce, but the medic ignored him, focussing on his job. Either he did not know who Goezlin was, Nokz'z thought, or he genuinely didn't care. Nokz'z though the former was more likely than the latter.

"We are ready, sir," Jazki said. "What are your orders?"

"Any sign of movement at any of the mall entrances?" Nokz'z asked.

"Nothing yet sir," Jazki said. "Every entrance has been sealed, and nobody has got in or out. Nor did any vehicles leave after the fire truck entered. They are in here somewhere."

Nokz'z nodded. "Search floor by floor. Every corridor, every cupboard. Start on this floor. Find them."

"Look for a medical centre," Goezlin said, eying the trail of blood on the floor.

"I know this mall. There is a medical centre on the second floor," Jazki said.

* * *

"So how do we infiltrate Azoh's quarters?" Price asked. "And why do we need Brogan for it?"

"I need a Vaza," Chisnall said.

"What are you talking about?" Barnard asked.

"My cover is that of a chef," Chisnall said.

"Is good," Monster said. "I could go a burger and fries right now."

"But a chef would never get through the layers of security," Chisnall said. "My plan was to impersonate a high ranking officer. To do that, I need a Vaza."

"I could have been your Vaza," Price said. "Or Barnard. Or Monster."

Chisnall laughed. "Not Monster. No offence big guy, I love you dearly, but not Monster."

"Are Vaza's always female?" Monster asked.

"Mostly," Chisnall said. "For male officers."

"And male for female officers?" Price asked.

Chisnall nodded.

"Why is that?" Price asked.

"Why do you think," Wall said.

"It can be a long, cold, hard winter when you're stuck on the front lines," Chisnall said. "A Vaza is…"

"More than just a bodyguard," Brogan said.

"But why Brogan?" Price asked.

"A Vaza must be able to speak the high language," Chisnall said.

"Do you speak it?" Price asked.

"I do now," Chisnall said.

"How do you know Brogan speaks the high language?" Price asked.

"All Ferzerkers do," Wall said.

"How does that feel?" Brogan asked, disengaging the machine from Chisnall's arm. "Try it."

Chisnall lifted his arm and stretched it out. It felt odd, as if not quite part of him. The pain was gone but there was a shadow, like a memory of it, a slightly numb, bruised feeling. He bent the arm back and forth a few times, testing it.

"How strong is it?" he asked.

"I wouldn't go lifting weights," Brogan said. "The bone is still knitting, but the rest of process is natural. It'll take a few days to completely heal, but it'll be strong enough for today."

"Okay, we are Oscar Mike," Price said.

"Wait," Brogan said, looking up.

"Why?"

"I thought I heard something outside," Brogan said.

* * *

Nokz'z and Goezlin watched from the temporary command centre set up next to the battered fire truck. The Nzgali had set up a perimeter around the medical centre.

A set of sliding glass doors led into a reception area and waiting room. Behind that was a recovery room and leading off from that area were the treatment rooms.

Each end of the corridor was blocked off by troops.

"Remember that we want them alive," Goezlin said.

"Get some thermals and visuals on that place," Jazki murmured into a microphone.

A soldier crept forward and placed a small device on the corner of the glass panel. He crawled backwards silently.

Another screen sprang to life. A fuzzy pattern gradually resolved into coloured contours, outlines of shapes, warmer than the cold walls around them.

"There are at least three people in there," Jazki said, pointing out different coloured patterns. Not in the front room, but somewhere in the rear."

"Anything on the acoustics?" Nokz'z asked.

"Indistinct," Jazki said. She had been listening on an earpiece, but switched the feed to loudspeakers. There were voices, but it was just a blur of overlaid sounds.

"You can't get any better quality?" Goezlin asked.

"The voices are coming through two walls and a pane of glass," Jazki said. "We are lucky to hear anything."

"At least we know where they are," Nokz'z said.

"Movement inside," Jazki said.

"They may be preparing to leave," Goezlin said.

"We could draw back, allow them to leave, and trap them in the corridor," Nokz'z said.

"No," Jazki said. "I think we can contain them better in the medical centre. Wait till they congregate in the recovery room, then take out the glass door. Hit them with a spiderbot, and assault the room while they're still trying to work out what happened. That way we should get them all alive."

Nokz'z glanced at Goezlin as Jazki spoke, confident that the PGZ officer would be impressed by her planning, and her care in avoiding a gunfight.

Goezlin was not watching. His attention was on the one Angel they had captured, and on the medic who was examining him. His eyes flicked back to the trail of blood. He was clearly considering something.

"Thermal imaging shows four people now in the recovery room," Jazki said. "Go, go, go!"

The tiny hovering cameras of the BZBs brought the images clearly to them.

A spiderbot walked straight up to the twin glass sliding doors of the medical centre. It stopped and waited as one of the soldiers extended a metal boom in front of the door sensor. The doors slid quietly open and the spiderbot slipped inside, changing colour as it did to that of the carpet.

It rolled around the front reception desk and towards an open door that led into the interior of the centre. A BZB followed, bringing back images.

A group of people were gathered in the room. One looked around, noticing the spiderbot.

"Hit it," Jazki said.

The flash of light and sound whited out their screen for a moment and the audio cut out under the overload. Then it was back. Nzgali soldiers were pouring into the room.

No one in that room would have had any chance of escape, Nokz'z thought. He glanced at Goezlin again, surprised to find that he was more interested in the patient than in the operation. On the video screen the scene inside the medical centre was chaotic, a number of people in doctors' uniforms lying on the floor, their hands neck-cuffed.

"They planned to disguise themselves as doctors," Nokz'z said. "I told you they were clever and resourceful."

Goezlin barely glanced at him.

One of the captives was made to roll over, bringing his face to the camera. Blood was trickling from his nose.

"That's Doctor Zutte," Jazki said. "I know him. He works there."

A hostage? Nokz'z wondered.

By the fire truck, Goezlin was talking to the medic.

"What do you mean conscious?"

For an answer the medic pointed to a medical scanner. "His eye reactions and heart rate indicate that he is wide awake. I think he is only pretending to be unconscious."

The Tsar coughed as Goezlin's boot caught him violently, just under his ribs. His eyes did not open.

"You are sure?" Goezlin asked.

"Certain," the medic answered.

"Could he have driven the fire truck?" Goezlin asked.

"I don't see why not," the medic replied.

"What's going on?" Nokz'z asked.

Goezlin turned and looked him straight in the eye. "You incompetent fool!" he said. "The Angels are still in the Congress building."

"Kick me again and I'll break your neck," The Tsar said.

INNER SANCTUM

[Mission Day 1, July 1st, 2033. 1000 hours local time]
[Bzadian Congress, Canberra]

The first security point was an elevator. It was the only way in or out of the bunkers. A classic defensive position, Chisnall thought, just a single point of entry. The bunker system could not be overwhelmed by a large force. The elevator was only large enough for maybe six or eight people.

To gain access to the elevator required the insertion of valid id tubes. Chisnall and Brogan had valid ID tubes. Daniel Bilal's people at the Pentagon had seen to that. Uniforms had come from a Bzadian general and his Vaza. They had been a little unwilling to give them up but had been persuaded by a can of puke spray.

The elevator doors opened smoothly and Chisnall and Brogan stepped inside.

The first hurdle had seemed easy. Perhaps too easy. The next would be more complicated.

The elevator began to descend. There were no indicators to say how deep they were, or how fast they were descending. It was a long trip down. Something about the rapid descent made his arm ache. The recently repaired one.

"You're wondering about me, aren't you," Brogan said, almost as soon as the doors closed.

"Did they teach you to read minds at Uluru too?" Chisnall asked.

"Nope," Brogan said. "But if I were you, that's what I'd be doing. Especially here. Especially now."

"Suppose I am," Chisnall said. "Suppose I am wondering if you are going to let us get within spitting distance of our objective, and then do your best to sabotage the mission."

"I'm not," Brogan said.

"It's happened before," Chisnall said.

"Not this time," Brogan said. "I've made a choice. I'm sticking with it."

"And I should believe a liar," Chisnall said. "I still don't understand why you agreed to come on this mission."

There was silence for a moment. The lift whirred. Lights on the ceiling panels flickered slightly.

"I wanted to see you," Brogan said.

"I don't know why," Chisnall said. "Some things can be undone. And some things can be forgiven. But some things can't."

"I didn't come to apologize," Brogan said. "I'm not looking for forgiveness. Perhaps to explain."

"Then explain," Chisnall said.

Brogan turned and stared directly at him. "I did what I did because that's who they made me," she said. "But that's not who I am now."

Chisnall returned her stare but said nothing.

"You know what really got to me," Brogan said. "As I was sitting alone all day long in a cinderblock cell. It wasn't patriotism or a feeling that I had betrayed my race. Nothing like that. Yes I'm human. But I was brought up a Bzadian. That thinking goes round in circles till it all just became a blur. What really got to me was the fact that I had hurt people who cared about me."

"Really," Chisnall said, more harshly than he intended.

"Really," she said. "In the end, that's all that really matters."

The elevator stopped moving before Chisnall could think of a response.

After a brief moment, long enough for him to wonder if something had gone wrong, and they would be sent back to the surface, the doors slid open.

They emerged into a circular room, bare of furniture or decorations. Behind twin glass doors on the opposite wall a pair of burly, and heavily armed security guards sat, both wearing the sand coloured robes of the Azaykin, Azoh's personal guard.

"Whatever happens," Brogan murmured on the comm. "Don't get in a fight with one of the Azaykin."

"I'll try not to," Chisnall said.

"I'm serious," Brogan said. "You won't win. They are bred and trained for one purpose: to protect Azoh. They are even more highly trained and dedicated than the Vaza corps. If it comes down to it, just shoot them in the face, and try to keep out of their way while they're dying."

"Cheerful," Chisnall said.

"Just telling it like it is," Brogan said.

"I hope it won't come to that," Chisnall said, his fingers grazing the grenade concealed within his jacket.

* * *

"You are The Tsar," Goezlin said.

He was standing directly behind The Tsar who was neck-cuffed and chained to a chair, facing a blank concrete wall.

Concern about The Tsar's well-being seemed to have vanished when they discovered that he was only feigning unconsciousness. Not that it had been hard to feign. The effort of the hair-raising drive to the mall had been draining and there had been little left to drain. The crash inside the mall had not been intentional.

He had blacked out as the truck had hit the ramp and only come to when he crashed into a pillar by the mall entry.

Voices outside the truck had given him just enough warning, just enough time to drag himself out of the driver's seat and into the back before the truck was invaded.

If he hadn't blacked out, then he might have been able to escape and hide. Not for long, just long enough for the Angels to do what they needed to do. Every minute might have made a difference. After that he didn't mind getting found. That had been part of the plan. Better to be a prisoner in a Bzadian hospital than a corpse in a human morgue.

But he had been caught, far too quickly, and his only defence had been to pretend he was unconscious. That had worked for a short while. Then he had been taken by an ambulance to this building, where-ever it was, and wheeled into this room.

He had been treated well enough, if you didn't count the neck-cuffs and the chain that attached him to the heavy metal chair. But he had a feeling that was about to change.

"I am not asking you, I am telling you," Goezlin said, right behind his ear. "You are The Tsar."

"Actually you got that wrong," The Tsar said. "I am the king."

"Tsar means King, yes?" Goezlin asked.

Goezlin's voice was high, and constricted, as if he had a problem with his throat. It added to the air of menace. His position behind The Tsar's chair was no accident. It was unnerving. The Tsar could hear Goezlin's voice but could not see him. The only person The Tsar could see was a guard who stood to attention at the left. He focussed on the guard instead of his soon-to-be torturer, behind him.

"I'm not that kind of king. I'm the king of Rock'n'Roll," The Tsar said. He winked at the guard who did not respond.

"You are wasting time, Mr Nicholaev," Goezlin said.

"Elvis," The Tsar said. "I won't answer to anything else."

"I think you are deliberately wasting my time," Goezlin said. "And you will regret it."

"I regret it already," The Tsar said.

"Your friends are somewhere in the Congress," Goezlin said. "We are searching it, and we will find them. But you could save us a lot of time if you told us where they are, and what they are planning to do."

"They're having a dance party," The Tsar said. "And I'm missing out. You should see me twerking."

"Perhaps you should listen, while I talk," Goezlin said.

"Why talk when you can sing?" The Tsar asked. "We could sing together. A duet. I am the king of rock'n'roll. Baby."

"We know all about you, Dimitri, and the other Angels," Goezlin said. "We have identified all of you from photos, and tracked down your identities, through... sources."

"Who's Dimitri?" The Tsar asked.

"Dimitri Nicholaev," Goezlin said. "A regular member of Angel Team Four, along with Ryan Chisnall, Trianne Price, Retha Barnard, and Janos Panyoczki."

"Never heard of any of them," The Tsar said.

"You might be surprised how much information we have compiled on you all," Goezlin said.

"Your spies were uncovered a long time ago," The Tsar said. "They've been feeding you false information for years."

He waited for a response to that but did not get one. There was no sound at all except for the slow tapping of Goezlin's shoes, a light tread on a concrete floor. Was he pacing the room? Was he tapping his feet? The Tsar could not tell without twisting his head around and he was not going to give Goezlin that satisfaction. The footsteps moved away, then returned. There was a light rustle of paper. When Goezlin spoke again it was in a softer voice.

"It may surprise you to learn that I have a son, about your age," Goezlin said. He sighed. "What I would feel if he ever found himself in your position, I cannot imagine. But of course that would never happen. We do not send our children out to fight. And do not think for a moment that will prevent me from doing my duty. My having a son, will not save you, if you do not tell me what I need to know."

"What's your son going to think when we kick your Bzadian asses of our planet?" The Tsar asked.

"I need to find out what your friends are up to, and to stop it," Goezlin said, as if he had not heard The Tsar's question. "Let us examine my options. There are drugs I could use, but they would take too long."

"Say no to drugs," The Tsar said.

"I could subject you to pain that you could not withstand," Goezlin said. "But your history and ours shows that people will say anything to stop the pain."

"Whip me, beat me, make me listen to rap music," The Tsar said.

"Fortunately, I have a better option," Goezlin said.

"Oh God, not the rap music," The Tsar said. "I was only joking. Anything but that! Peace out."

"I think we should discuss your family," Goezlin said.

Now the Tsar was silent.

"And at last we get a reaction," Goezlin said.

"There's not much point in talking about my family," The Tsar said.

"Is that what you believe?" Goezlin said.

"You know it as well as I do," The Tsar said.

Goezlin said nothing, but reached around and held a photograph in front of the Tsar who stared at it for a long moment.

"It's a fake," he said.

"You know it's not," Goezlin said, handing him more photographs. "And neither are these."

* * *

"Identification and purpose?" the voice came out of a speaker in the centre of the ceiling. The language was the high language.

Chisnall looked carefully at the doors as he considered his reply. The glass was thick, no doubt bullet and bomb proof, and the two sliding panels completely overlapped, providing a double layer of protection. In front of the doors a heavy metal shutter protruded from a ceiling panel, ready to slam shut in the event of an attack. This was what Kozi had called 'light protection'.

"I bring an urgent report on the new human jets," Chisnall said.

"We are in security lockdown," the second, more senior guard said. "Please give us the information and we will pass it on."

"The report is red-listed," Chisnall said. "High security."

"Then it can wait," the senior guard said.

"No, it cannot," Chisnall said. "As it concerns an imminent attack on this building."

There was silence as the two guards conferred with each other.

"There is no admission to this secure area until the situation above has been resolved," the guard said. "If it is urgent, you will have to submit the report electronically."

As he spoke, a Bzadian female in Azaykin uniform stepped into the security area behind him, talking urgently on a radio. She wore insignia denoting her rank. A captain of the guard. She looked up and caught Chisnall's eye.

Chisnall kept his face impassive, giving no indication that he recognised or knew her. But he did. And his world had just turned upside down.

It was Kozi.

* * *

"Here they come," Wall said.

"Had to happen," Price said. "The Tsar bought us a little time, but we always knew it wouldn't take them long to figure out where we were."

"We served him up on a platter," Barnard said. "We shouldn't have done that."

"He volunteered," Price said. "And besides, if this works then it won't matter."

"And if it doesn't?" Barnard asked.

"Then it won't matter for any of us," Price said.

The main entrance doors to the Congress slid open, silently, but the doorway remained empty.

A head appeared, just a quick stolen glance, checking the corridor was clear. Satisfied with what he or she had seen, a soldier appeared, crouching, weapon at the ready. Another appeared on the opposite side of the doorway. Their weapons traversed the grand entranceway.

"Hold your fire," Price murmured. "Let's see how many we are dealing with before we engage."

The two soldiers moved forward, scanning all angles, but did not detect the Angels, concealed behind pillars, deep within the great art gallery at the rear of the atrium.

The uniform of these soldiers was different, Price noted. There was something hard and clean about them. Something very efficient about the way they moved into position.

"Nzgali," Wall said. "Best of the best."

"So are we," Price said.

The two on point moved forward and four more joined in behind them. They moved forward and another complete squad entered after them.

"A little closer," Price breathed into the comm. "Now."

They had dialled their coil-guns up to maximum. Maximum noise, maximum damage. The noise, echoing off the great pillars was deafening.

The return fire was withering, the pillars exploding in shards of concrete and plaster around them.

"Fall back, fall back!" Price said. "They're coming in."

The nzgali advanced in combat formation, moving in pairs, leap frogging each other. One providing constant covering fire while their partner moved forward.

"You're sure this is a good plan," Barnard said, ducking back behind a pillar as the edge of it exploded, right where her face had been a half second earlier.

"We're about to find out," Price shouted over the constant gunfire. She emptied a clip around her pillar without looking or aiming, then slid silently sideways as the other Angels retreated deeper into the gallery. Price moved to a box-like sculpture she had scouted out earlier. A flat panel on the side was hinged and lifted quietly. She slipped inside and waited, listening to the gunfire as the other Angels continued to move away, making sure the nzgali heard them.

"Okay, we're out," Barnard said in Price's ear. "Have locked the rear door. It's just you and them now."

"Just the way I like it," Price breathed on the comm.

The nzgali did not see her. They did not hear her. They did not detect her. In groups of two and three they moved past her, smoothly, professionally, covering each other as they began their sweep of the gallery.

"You ready?" Barnard asked.

"Do it," Price breathed.

All the lights in the gallery went out.

* * *

"On the floor, now!" the voice gave him no choice, and neither did the vicious kick at the back of his knees. Chisnall went down, hard, Brogan beside him.

A quick glance up showed a squad of heavily armed Azaykin surrounding them. There was no chance to reach for a weapon, no chance to pull at his puke-spray grenade. The guards had slipped into the room behind them through some secret, silent door.

Only now did the double glass doors in front of them slide open and Kozi, flanked by more guards, stepped through.

What was Kozi doing here? The last time he saw her she was a clerk. But here she was, part of Azoh's inner circle. And it was more than that. If Azoh could read the minds of those close to her, then couldn't she read Kozi's mind. Whose side was Kozi really on? What was going on?

Kozi raised her radio. "Commandant Goezlin," she said. "We have them. Two of them. Trying to sneak into the bunker."

She listened carefully then replaced the radio on her hip.

"Search the female," she said. "But be careful. She has Ferzerker training."

One of the guards relieved Chisnall of his weapon, but when he began to search him, Kozi held up a hand. "I will do it," she said. "This one is Chizna."

With Azaykin weapons pointed just centimetres from his head and body, Chisnall felt Kozi's hands forcefully and expertly patting him down. No area was left unchecked. He was forced to roll over and the process began again. Kozi's hand passed over the slim shape of the grenade without comment although her eyes met his.

She straightened and pulled out her radio once again. "They have been secured. We will hold them here until you get here."

With that, Chisnall and Brogan were hauled to their feet, and marched in through the double glass doors, inside Azoh's inner sanctum.

"Put them in the secure room," Kozi said. "I want them under constant guard, at least three guards to each prisoner. Do not take your eyes off them for a second. Is that clear?"

That was clear. That was also when Chisnall's little finger found the pin of the grenade.

* * *

The Tsar stared at the photograph for a long time without speaking. It was, yet it could not be, a photo of his two sisters and his younger brother. They had aged, especially his brother, the chubby cheeks firming into a strong jawline, the smiley eyes now hollow and haunted. It all could have been faked, but The Tsar was sure that it wasn't.

"Katya, Oksana and Mikhail," Goezlin said. "As you can see they are very much alive, and in our custody."

"You hurt them and I will roast your boy bits over a slow fire," The Tsar said.

"Yes of course, this is what you would say," Goezlin said. "But it is you who is strapped in a chair, and I who have command over your life, and those of your family. I spoke before about pain. Perhaps that pain would be better inflicted on those you love, than on you."

"Don't you touch them," The Tsar said.

The sound of a door behind him was followed by footsteps and a low voice. The Tsar heard Goezlin reply, and although he could not make out the words, it was clear that it was a matter of some urgency.

Then Goezlin was back, right behind him.

"I will let you dwell on that image for a moment or two," Goezlin said. "You will have a few minutes to consider my request. It is a very generous offer. Your life, and those of your siblings, for a very small piece of information, that I would find out anyway in a short time."

Footsteps receded. The door opened and shut once more.

* * *

Chisnall couldn't take his eyes off the chair. It was not really a chair, more of a throne. A seat suited to a king, or a great leader. A chair for Azoh. Yet she was dwarfed in it, like a child in furniture made for adults, her legs did not reach far enough for her knees to bend, and her feet stuck out horizontally.

The chair itself was made of some kind of burnished Bzadian metal, a colour that seemed to change and flux when you changed the angle you were looking at it. The armrests were adorned with the faces of gargoyles, forever smiling in a knowing grin.

Azoh sat calmly, patiently, as if waiting for them.

The other Bzadians in the room lay where they fell, watching in mute fury as Chisnall and Brogan stepped carefully past them. Already the ventilation system was removing the haze of puke spray, but it had done its work, circulating through the underground bunker, room after room, doing its work.

Azoh's face was blurred, softened, by some kind of covering, a plastic film of some kind. No, not that, Chisnall realised.

"I think we just walked into a trap," Brogan said. "Something's not right here."

Something was strange, but not wrong, Chisnall thought. There was no coldness in this place. If anything it radiated a warmth that had nothing to do with the heating and ventilation systems.

"We're okay, I think," he said.

"Really?" Brogan asked. "Did you notice that she just happens to be wearing an oxygen mask?"

Thin tubes from the plastic covering on Azoh's face led away behind her, and the mask itself lifted and flattened slightly as she breathed.

"Maybe she has asthma," Chisnall said.

"Yeah, really," Brogan said. "Asthma. I think she knew what we were going to do before we did."

Chisnall stood in front of Azoh. The one previous occasion he had stood before her he had had his eyes lowered, and caught only glimpses of her face. She was extraordinarily beautiful, but in a soft, child-like way, a glimpse of innocence. The beauty was only part of it though. The tattoos that covered her face were both elegant and intricate, weaving complex patterns, perhaps telling a story, like the facial tattoos of the Maori.

Over the tattoos was the jewellery, attached to her ears, eyebrows, nose and lips, thin chains of the unusual silvery metal hung in loops, connected by bright, almost iridescent gemstones.

Her hair was long, brown and tightly braided beneath the cowl of her robes.

Chisnall hesitated, unsure what to say, feeling like a fraud. Feeling unworthy to be standing before this incredible creature, let alone to do what he was about to do to her.

Violence in the presence of this person was unthinkable. He hesitated, unsure how or what to say, unsure what he would do if she refused to come with them. He stared at her and she stared back. She was the first to break the silence.

She removed the oxygen mask and laid it on the armrest beside her. It was no longer necessary. The air was now clear. Her eyes met Chisnall's and her outer lips curled upwards in an expression that could be taken for a smile.

She spoke in the high language. The words were simple but so unexpected that his brain struggled to take meaning from them.

"We should go now," she said.

BOOK THREE: AZOH

Even monkeys fall from trees
Japanese Proverb

THE TUNNEL

[Mission Day 1, July 1st, 2033. 1010 hours local time]
[Bzadian Congress, Canberra]

Price activated her night vision lenses as she moved around the wide columns of the gallery. There was light. Just not much. The light from the outer doorways, channelled by the gallery entrance, filtered in, bouncing off pillar after pillar sifting throughout the wide expanse of the gallery.

It was like a forest. At night. And that, more than anything, made Price feel at home. On her own, operating in shards of darkness where no one would think to look. Dependent on no one. Responsible for no one. Ever since she could remember this had been her best defence. If you didn't get noticed, you didn't get hurt.

Except it was soldiers she was up against, not her drunken foster-father. And they were armed with guns, not a leather belt.

But she was armed too, and that made all the difference.

So did the night vision gear. The nzgali were not wearing it, possibly not seeing the need for it in the brightly lit congress building. That would be an oversight that Price intended to ensure they regretted.

Her gun was dialled down to silent. She was noiseless. The nzgali, for all their training, were not. She heard the sounds of movement, of low conversations as they adjusted to the sudden darkness in the gallery. Price moved in the darkest shadows, in slow, silent movements that would not catch the eye or alert the ear.

A peek around a pillar showed her four soldiers, standing in a small group, crouching, weapons scanning in all directions. A defensive posture. They were nervous, and rightly so. They were trapped in a dark concrete forest. And they were not alone.

Price eased her head back around the pillar, the muzzle of her weapon leading the way. She took careful aim at a pillar on the far side of the group, and gently squeezed her trigger.

The sound of the puffer pellet hitting the pillar was a sharp tap and the soldiers all instinctively looked in that direction.

Price put two puffer pellets onto the back of the furthest nzgali, knocking him forward, creating a cloud of puffer dust that the ones behind him could not help but breathe in.

As they dropped, the first one spun around, his gun seeking a target, just as another pellet exploded on his chest. He fell on top of the others, an untidy heap of bodies on the floor, moving only with the gentle motion of their breathing.

A gunshot came from Price's right and a pillar by her head exploded under the impact of a bullet.

She dived forward and rolled as more shots cracked out behind her, seeking shelter behind the four fallen nzgali.

There! She caught a glimpse of the shooter, concealed by the width of a column. She had no shot. She aimed for the very edge of the round pillar and fired. The pellet exploded into dust against the hard edge of the pillar, and the soldier reeled backwards, clutching at his face.

He fell and did not get up.

Price kept a mental count. She had seen twelve soldiers go in. Five were now lying on the floor. Seven to go.

She moved deeper into the artificial forest.

* * *

Chisnall studied the map Price had given him. A tunnel had been bored at the time of construction of the new Australian Parliament house, back in the 1980s. It joined onto an existing tunnel that already connected the original historic parliament house with the US Embassy building.

The tunnel entrance, according to the map, was in a storeroom, deep in the bowels of the building. They found the storeroom without problem. But there was no sign of a tunnel.

The walls were solid concrete, with no sign of cracks that might indicate a panel or a door. The only doorway was the double-width one that led in, and that was no help.

There was some furniture scattered around the room, and some plastic boxes. Chisnall and Brogan moved around a couple of desks in case they concealed anything on the floor, but to no avail.

The room was bare.

* * *

Price's coil-gun made a soft phut and the nzgali staggered, tried to raise his gun towards her with muscles that refused to respond to commands from his brain, sank to his knees and toppled forward onto the floor.

Two more, Price thought, but even as she thought it a mule kicked her in the back, and her coil-gun went flying from her grasp. She had unhooked it from the holster spring for silence and freedom of movement, but now that proved to be a mistake. It skittered across the floor out of reach.

She made to get back to her feet, but a second shot,

crashing, reverberating around the pillars, kicked up chips from the floor tile just by her head.

She stayed where she was, spreading her hands so they could see she was unarmed.

She was aware of two shapes standing over her, and a heavy boot was pressed between her shoulder-blades, pinning her to the ground.

"Cuff her and check for others," a Bzadian voice said. "Nokz'z wants them al…"

He never finished the sentence. Again Price heard the soft phut of a coil gun, once, twice, and the two figures above her, dropped, choking and retching to the ground on either side of her.

She rolled onto her back to see Wall now standing over her. He extended a hand, helping her to her feet.

"What are you doing here?" she asked.

"Someone had to watch your back," Wall said. "Is that all of them?"

Price nodded.

"Then let's go," he said. "Chisnall's made contact. They've got Azoh and are heading for the tunnel."

Monster and Barnard were still waiting at the gallery entrance when Price and Wall emerged. Price gave them both the thumbs up.

"We are Oscar Mike back to the tunnel," Price said.

Wall looked suddenly at the main entrance doors.

"What is it?" Price asked.

"Get down. Now!" Wall said.

Price hit the floor with the others just as the doors exploded, showering the room with broken glass and twisted fragments of metal. Smoke from the explosion was still billowing into the room when the black suited nzgali appeared, dark shapes in the haze, muzzle flashes lighting the smoke around them. Not two squads this time. This was an army. A river of black pouring in through the shattered doorway.

"Smoke grenades and covering fire!" Price yelled.

* * *

The Tsar was having bad thoughts. Bizarre thoughts. That was nothing new, all his life he'd had bizarre thoughts. Like what would happen if he chopped his own head off. Would he watch himself die? Or what if he could turn himself inside out, so that all his organs were on the outside of his body.

When he was young he had told his mother about the bad thoughts and she had said that all people had odd thoughts, sometimes bad thoughts, but only bad people acted on them. She said that every time you had a bad thought it was like there was a little devil sitting on one shoulder whispering in your ear. But if you just listened carefully you would realise that there was an angel sitting on your other shoulder whispering good things and the first thing she was telling you was to give the devil the flick. So that was what The Tsar did. He imagined himself reaching up to his shoulder and knocking the devil whisperer off with a well-aimed flick of his fingers. That almost always worked and then he could focus on what the angel was saying.

But not this time.

He turned his head as far as he could in the awkward restraints.

"Get Goezlin," he said. "Tell him I'll talk."

There was no response from the guard.

"You, dumbass, I said I'll talk."

Still no response.

"I'll tell him exactly what he needs to know, but if I don't tell him in the next ten minutes it's going to be too late."

The guard was staring at him now but remained silent.

"Ten minutes, you got that, after that it's all over, and it's going to be on your shoulders."

The Tsar raised his voice. "Unlike your head, which is going to be on a stake in the garden," he said.

The guard looked uncertain.

"Nine minutes," The Tsar said.

* * *

Chisnall was pacing out the floor of the room, trying to find what he had missed, when Price's voice came on the com.

"We are Oscar Mike to your position," she sounded short of breath on the com and the background was full of the sound of gunfire. "Being pursued by a large Bzadian force. We're becoming in hot."

"I guess we'd better get off our asses and find that tunnel," Brogan said.

Chisnall made no comment. They had explored every inch of the wall and the floor without finding any sign of a tunnel entrance.

No wonder the Bzadians had missed it, despite ten years of use of this building.

If it even existed.

"It's not here," he said.

"Then where is it?" Brogan said. "We have to find it, and fast."

"Let me think," Chisnall said, desperately scanning the room one more time. What if this was not the right room? In that case the tunnel could be anywhere. They did not have time to search the entire complex.

Azoh stood calmly in the middle of the room, beside a dusty table. She had made no attempt to escape.

She spoke now. The first time since they had left the bunker.

"Do not think, Chizna," she said. "Dream."

"What the hell does that mean?" Brogan asked, but Chisnall somehow knew. In the same way he felt the strangeness when bad things had happened, that he had known Brogan would not betray them, that he had felt the warmth in the throne room. That was what Azoh meant.

He looked at her and Azoh nodded.

How? He thought. How did you dream your way to a secret tunnel entrance. He closed his eyes for a moment, trying to clear his mind. Trying to blank out everything except his own emotions. It was not easy. He could hear the others breathing, the sound of his own heart, the brush of cool air on his skin.

The brush of air?

For there to be air movement there needed to be ventilation. He looked up, noticing a white plastic grill set into the ceiling. It was too small to be an entrance.

But the ceiling? They had examined the walls and floor, it had never occurred to him before to look upwards. Tunnels went down, everyone knew that.

Yet here, in the bowels of the building, they were already deep below the surface of the earth. Might not the tunnel be above them?

"We'll be at your location in about twenty seconds," Price sounded unsettled. That was understandable when you were running from an army of pukes.

"The ceiling," he said, looking upwards.

"Where?" Brogan asked.

That was the question. The ceiling was covered in white panels, any one of them could be an entrance. But what use was an entrance if you could not reach it.

You could climb up with a ladder, but somehow Chisnall doubted that was the answer. In an emergency situation, which the tunnel was for, you could not depend on having a ladder handy.

There was a way to get up, and it was in this room. The furniture and boxes did not count. They could easily be removed.

Apart from them there was nothing permanent in the room. Concrete walls, a doorway with a wooden frame, a light switch by the door.

A light switch!

Suddenly he knew, and he did not know how he knew, that the light switch was the answer.

He ran to it and flicked it off. The room plunged into darkness. He turned it back on. Off and on. Some kind of a pattern, was that it? If so he was stuck, because they did not know the code.

Brogan was with him now, pressing the two plastic covered screws that held the switch to the wall. Nothing.

Chisnall tried to lever the switch panel from the wall. It would not budge.

"Ten seconds," Price cried on the comm. "We're coming in real hot."

The sounds of the running battle were echoing around the corridor outside the room now.

Chisnall turned the light off one more time. He tried to clear his mind as before. He turned it on, this time noting the slight sponginess of the switch. It actually pressed on further than it needed to, before springing back slightly. He pressed it hard, as far as it would go, and held it there.

Nothing.

He was about to let go when there was a slight sound from above him.

"Azoh!" Brogan said. She glanced quickly at Azoh, a little embarrassed.

A small gap had appeared in one of the ceiling panels.

Chisnall kept pressure on the switch and the panel began to descend, at the base of a metal staircase extending, concertina like, to the floor.

"Brogan, get up there and look for a switch to raise it back up," Chisnall said.

She nodded and leaped for the bottom stair before it had even touched the floor, disappearing up through the gap in the ceiling.

"Got it," she said. "Get up here."

The moment the bottom of the staircase touched the floor, Chisnall let go of the switch, gesturing to Azoh, following her up the staircase, close behind, half-enveloped in her flowing robes.

Price burst into the room below him as he reached the top. She wasted no time, asked no questions, leaping for the staircase and hauling herself up, firing from the hip back out through the open doorway as she went. The other Angels followed.

Monster was last and even before his foot touched the bottom step, the staircase began to retract, bringing Monster with it.

Bullets sparked from the metal stairs as two Bzadian soldiers dived and rolled into the room below, firing from the hip as they came. More gunfire came from the doorway, the bullets punching holes through the light metal of the staircase.

"Move it move it move it!" Price yelled.

The crawlspace above the ceiling was low and dark, but rapidly growing brighter as automatic fire punched rows of holes in the ceiling below them. Monster staggered a couple of times as bullets glanced off his body armour, but he kept coming.

The crawlspace led them to a tunnel cut into the face of a rock wall, and ten or twenty metres inside the tunnel was a heavy metal door. Chisnall stayed at the door, helping and urging the others through. As soon as Monster dived through the gap, just ahead of a hail of gunfire, Chisnall slammed the door shut but could see no way to lock it.

"That won't stop them for long," he said.

"Already the door was clanging with the impact of bullets.

"This might slow them down," Monster grinned. He produced a C4 charge from his belt-pack and busied himself, rigging it to the door as the others hurried onwards.

Rough-hewn stone stairs led down deeper inside the hill, arriving at a long, straight tunnel with a rounded ceiling, leading in two directions.

"Left to the US Embassy, right to the museum," Price said. "We're going left."

They ran, and Azoh ran with them, without question or complaint.

"What's up with this chick?" Price asked. "She doesn't seem at all concerned about being kidnapped, shot at and dragged through tunnels."

"I don't know," Chisnall said.

Monster caught up with them as the tunnel took a sharp turn to the left and began to slope downwards.

"All set?" Chisnall asked.

"They open door, they will regret it," Monster laughed.

* * *

It was Jazki who found the switch to the ceiling staircase. While her soldiers were assembling ladders she was examining the room.

Nokz'z left her alone. She was smart and competent, and would be soon due for a promotion, if he had anything to do with it. And he would. After rescuing Azoh and capturing her abductors he would be a hero of Bzadia. There would be a ceremony, a sash presented by Azoh herself. Surely a promotion, perhaps a chance to lead troops into the Americas.

But even without that, his name would go down in history. He would be the rescuer of Azoh, and he would share the glory with those who helped him achieve it.

"Is it true?" a tight voice came from behind him. He did not have to look to know it was Goezlin.

"They have Azoh," Nokz'z said. "They somehow gained access to the bunker and gassed her guards. When backup arrived Azoh was gone. But they will not have her for long, nor will they have the opportunity to harm her. My troops will see to that."

"Two squads of your troops are currently staring at the ceiling of a hospital ward," Goezlin said. "Do not assume confidence that you have not earned."

"And what information have you learned from your prisoner?" Nokz'z asked. "What is their plan? Where does this tunnel lead?"

Goezlin was not the only one who could play that game. Goezlin smiled but did not deign to answer. What that meant was anybody's guess.

Troops were at the top of ladders, hammering at the ceiling with the stocks of their weapons when Jazki said, "I have found it."

A mechanical staircase began to lower from the ceiling.

"Nzgali, nzgali, nzgali!" Jazki shouted, the rallying cry of the fearsome warriors, urging her soldiers up the staircase before it had even reached the floor.

Two squads raced up, with Jazki right behind them. Nokz'z, on impulse, put a foot on the staircase after them. A thin metal handrail had unfolded on one side as the staircase had lowered, and he kept one hand on that for stability as he climbed. He was half way to the ceiling when there was a hand on his arm, stopping him. He looked back at the stern face of his Vaza.

"Two squads of nzgali against a few scumbugz children," Nokz'z laughed with a quick glance at Goezlin. "You think I could be in danger."

"Yes."

"All right, dear Vaza," Nokz'z said. "You win again. But in the meantime I want a plan of this tunnel."

"Nobody knew it existed, until now," the Vaza said.

"The scumbugz knew," Nokz'z said. "Plans must exist somewhere. In the old human records. Find them."

The Vaza did not reply. Or if she did, he did not hear it. His ears filled with a sound so loud it seemed solid. He was flying into the Vaza, embracing her, and now they were both falling in a whirlwind of rock and dust and smoke.

A TOOTHLESS DOG

[Mission Day 1, July 1st, 2033. 1020 hours local time]
[Beneath Bzadian Congress, Canberra]

"Get down!" Price shouted, grabbing at Azoh's arm and pulling her to the floor beside her. The roar of the explosion was followed by a wave of heat and dust, channelled by the narrow confines of the tunnel. It gushed over them.

When it had subsided, she said, "Monster get back and see what damage we did. Everyone else, keep moving."

Azoh stood, not bothering to brush the dust from her robes. Price resisted the temptation to do it for her.

They had reached a staircase, just a narrow series of cuts in a steep rock face, when Monster caught up with them again. "Tunnel blocked," he said.

"How blocked?" Price asked.

"Side tunnel she is complete gone," Monster said. "Roof collapse."

"Good work. What about the main tunnel?" Price asked.

Monster nodded. "Lots of rubble, but ok."

They came to another large metal door studded with bolts. In the centre was a heavy wheel like those on a submarine. Price turned the wheel until it clicked, then eased the door open a crack, peering through to ensure the room beyond was empty, before ushering the others through.

The room was small and sturdy looking. The walls were utilitarian, concrete and metal. There were no windows. There was only one other entrance into the room, a large sliding door set into a solid metal frame.

At one end of the room were a few rows of simple plastic chairs. They looked dusty and unused. At the opposite end of the room were rows of control desks with built in computer screens and keyboards. A row of large video screens covered one of the walls.

Monster, who was last to emerge from the tunnel, turned and pushed the door shut, spinning the wheel to lock it.

"Where are we?" Wall asked.

"It's a secure area," Barnard said. "Like a keep in a castle. In the event of an attack on the embassy, the staff were supposed to retreat to this room, and then use the tunnel to escape."

"Somebody figure out how this equipment works and get me Daniel Bilal on the phone," Chisnall said.

Wall sat at one of the consoles and began experimenting. Almost immediately the video screens on the wall sprang into life, showing scenes from throughout the building and outside. There was a constant flurry of activity through the corridors.

"Seems a good a place as any to stay," Chisnall said. "How long till the air raid?"

"I don't know," Price said. "But I agree. I don't think the Pukes know this room exists. And if they find us we can retreat back into the tunnel."

"Unless they manage to dig through the rubble," Wall said.

"Don't even think about that," Price said.

"We got some fancy weapons systems here," Barnard said, sitting at another of the consoles. "This place was supposed to be able to defend itself."

"What have you got?" Price asked, walking over.

Barnard indicated various screens. "Automatic machine guns with motion sensors. Built into pods in the grounds."

"Pods?"

"Near as I can figure, they pop up out of the ground when needed," Barnard said.

"Like lawn sprinklers," Price said.

"Yeah, like that."

"What else have you got?" Price asked.

"Forty-four mike-mike Bofors auto-cannons mounted in the dormer windows of the central building," Barnard said. "That's some serious firepower."

"Okay, I want all systems booted up and operational," Price said. "But don't pop up any of those lawn sprinklers until you have to."

Wall was the first one to see what was happening. "Azoh!" he yelled.

Price looked up from the console to see Azoh standing at the sliding door, her hand on a small panel next to it.

"Stop her!" Price shouted, but it was already too late.

A bleeping sound from the door was followed by a low whirr and a grinding sound, as if the door had not been opened for a long time. It shuddered briefly, then began to move.

Brogan was the first to reach the door, slamming her hand down on the panel. It juddered to a halt, about halfway open, then began to slide shut.

It was already too late. A pair of Bzadians, a male and a female, in clerical uniforms, stood there open-mouthed in shock at what, to them, would have seemed like a hole suddenly appearing in a solid wall, and Azoh standing in it.

They disappeared from sight as the door ground to a close.

Brogan escorted Azoh firmly away from the door, leading her to the seating area.

"Dammit!" Price said. "Why wasn't anyone watching the prisoner?"

"Why weren't you?" Brogan said.

"Now they know where we are," Chisnall said.

Azoh says kidnapping will not work (C)

"I should have known this Little Miss Nice routine was too good to be true," Barnard said. "Don't let her fool you into thinking she's on our side."

"She's not on anybody's side. Azoh does not take sides," Brogan said.

"Then why did she try to escape?" Price asked.

"Ask her, not me," Brogan said.

Price looked at Chisnall. "You do it, LT. You speak her language."

"Shouldn't we be getting out of here?" Wall asked. "They'll be coming for us."

"The building is well defended," Price said. "And as long as they think we have Azoh, they'll treat us with kid gloves."

"When the air-raid comes there'll be confusion and panic," Barnard said. "We'll slip out the back door into the woods, just like the plan."

"Why don't we go back down through the tunnel?" Wall asked. "Hide out at the museum?"

"Inside the secure area?" Barnard asked. "We might as well give ourselves up. Besides, when the air-raid comes, that's a target. This building is not."

Chisnall picked up one of the plastic chairs and turned it

around to face Azoh. He sat and stared at her for a moment, taking in the intricate facial tattoos and the ornate jewellery.

"Why did you open the door?" he asked, in common Bzadian, then repeated it in the high language.

"It was necessary," Azoh replied in perfect English.

If he was surprised to hear the English, Chisnall gave no sign of it. "What does that mean?" he asked.

"I cannot explain that to you," Azoh said.

"Can't or won't?" Chisnall asked.

"I cannot, Chizna," Azoh said. "Not yet."

"So you know who I am," Chisnall said.

Azoh nodded. "That is known to me, yes."

"What do you know?" Chisnall asked.

"You are Lieutenant Ryan Chisnall of Recon Team Angel, Team Four," Azoh replied. "Who called himself Chizna in the Bzadian tongue. Son of Val and Cliff Chisnall, an only child, now an orphan."

"Go on," Chisnall said.

"My people have been hunting you for a long time," Azoh said. "They fear and respect you. You have taken on a certain mystique among our soldiers."

"Undeserved," Chisnall said.

"Your modesty does not alter the truth," Azoh said. "Your humanity and compassion have also earned our respect."

"What are you talking about?" Chisnall asked.

"You refused to take the lives of Yozi and his team in the desert at Uluru," Azoh said.

"They were unarmed and tied up," Chisnall said.

"You cried and sang when one of Yozi's team, your enemy, died," Azoh said.

"He was just a child," Chisnall said.

"As you are just a child," Azoh said. "At Wivenhoe, the loss of so many lives, Bzadian and Human, weighed so greatly on your heart that you lost your own will to live."

Chisnall started to argue, but Azoh held up a hand. "A few hours ago you believed that killing me would end the war, and yet you would not do it."

"You know about the salt," Chisnall said.

"The poison," Azoh said.

"How do you know this?" Chisnall asked.

"I am Azoh," she said, as if that were answer enough.

"I'm not much of a soldier, am I," Chisnall said, thinking of the words of an SAS officer, so long ago, in the sands near Uluru.

"There is more to being a soldier than killing," Azoh said.

Chisnall smiled grimly and glanced around at Brogan. "She'll answer anything I ask?"

Brogan nodded.

Chisnall turned back to the Bzadian leader.

"Azoh, we are going to take you away from here. We will not harm you, but we will use you as a bargaining chip to try and avoid the use of..." he hesitated, "terrible weapons."

Azoh was silent.

"Will this plan work?" he asked.

"No," Azoh said.

* * *

Flight Captain Molly Shaw gave no show of emotion as the last of the wreckage was pushed over the side of the USS Apple.

Seventeen people had died and twenty-four had been rescued from the water, with injuries ranging from moderate to serious. Sixteen jets had been shot down but all except three of the crews had ejected and been recovered.

Mostly importantly, the USS Apple had lost only five scream-jets out of the full complement of twenty-four. Without those scream-jets her only option would be to put her tail between her legs and run for cover, back in the Americas.

Forty-seven casualties. On a ship with a crew of over five thousand that was almost a miracle, considering what had nearly just happened. However each one of the twenty-three deaths was a human being, and the six flight crew were friends of hers.

Even while the clean-up teams had been clearing the flight deck, technicians had been at work, checking and testing the catapult system, without which the planes could not take off.

Now the massive elevators were bringing up the scream-jets and their attendant carrier jets, four at a time.

It had taken less than an hour from fending off the attack, to being ready to launch an attack of their own.

The Bzadians would pay for what they had done to the ship, Shaw thought grimly. Just as they would pay for what they had done to the planet.

The Bzadians had sent just a single dragon. That aircraft had almost destroyed an aircraft carrier.

The next time it would be five dragons. Or ten.

They were not going to wait for that to happen. The raid, planned for noon, had been brought forward an hour.

The Pukes were going to get hurt today.

* * *

"Why will the plan not work?" Chisnall asked.

"Everything is connected, in every possible way," Azoh said.

"What is this?" Wall asked. "A Buddhist retreat?"

"I tell you guys many time," Monster said. "There is plan to universe."

"Your friend is wrong. There is no plan," Azoh said. "But everything that happens, from the quiver of a single leaf to the fall of a nation, are the product of an infinite number of other, seemingly random events. Everything you do has an effect on all that is around you. A single bird cannot see the beauty of the flock as it soars and swoops yet without each single bird there would be no flock."

"I don't understand," Chisnall turned to Brogan. "I asked a direct question. Why am I getting all this?"

"Azoh will answer, but in her own way," Brogan said.

"To understand the answer, it is often necessary to fully understand the question," Azoh said.

"Then help me understand the question," Chisnall said, frowing.

"Evolution," Azoh said.

"What are you trying to tell us," Barnard asked.

"Just as an ape cannot understand a future as a human being, so a human cannot foresee what lies in its future," Azoh said.

"But you do?" Price asked.

"Of course," Azoh said. "We are your future."

"Forked tongues and vomit coloured skin, no thank you," Price said.

"The form is immaterial," Azoh said. "The nature of the being is not dictated by the colour of its skin, nor the shape of its tongue."

"So you're more evolved than we are?" Barnard asked.

"It is not an insult," Azoh said. "Our species is much older than yours. If anything it is a compliment."

"How's that?" Price asked.

"Humans have achieved in a few thousand years what took Bzadians tens of thousands," Azoh said. "Had our ships arrived a hundred years ago there would have been no war. Bzadian technology was vastly superior."

"Do we have time for all this?" Wall asked.

"You got some place better to be?" Barnard asked.

"Our history is a savage one," Azoh said. "Two Bzadians would fight over a sack of food. If we favoured different sports teams, we would brawl in the streets. If we came from a different side of a border, we would fight to the death over the position of that border. If we disagreed about our gods, we would burn each other alive."

"Sounds familiar," Barnard said.

"Humans are not that bad," Price said.

"Are you kidding," Barnard said. "A few hundred years ago it was a legal form of execution to boil a person in oil."

"That's ancient history," Price said.

"No, we gave that up in favour of suicide bombers, necklacing, and crashing airliners into buildings," Barnard said. "Rape, robbery, kidnapping, kneecapping. We murder our prophets and abuse our children." She glanced at Price who held her gaze for a moment, then dropped her eyes to the floor.

"Man's inhumanity to man is inventive and limitless," Barnard said.

"This was our past also," Azoh said. "It is your present, but it is not your future."

"You seem sure of this," Chisnall said.

"The evolutionary journey is a long one," Azoh said. "In the early days this savagery was necessary for survival. Then came civilisation, but the traits of your distant ancestors remain. In time these will be gone, as you complete the journey from savage beast, to human being, from savage man to true being. Crime, as you know it, will disappear. So will war. So will poverty and starvation. And then will the Fathers return, when the process is complete."

"What fathers?" Chisnall asked.

"The longheads," Azoh said.

"With long skulls like this?" Barnard demonstrated, using her hands.

Azoh nodded.

"Holy crap," Barnard said.

"What are you on about?" Price asked.

"Throughout human history there have been cases, all over the world, of people binding their skulls to elongate them," Barnard said. "The Nazca did it, and early Europeans, so did Australian aborigines and pacific islanders. Societies on the opposite sides of the world which had no contact with each other. No one knows why."

"This was true on Bzadia also," Azoh said. "Our forefathers believed that looking like gods would make them into gods."

"These are the Fathers?" Chisnall asked. "Ancient gods?"

"Not gods," Barnard said. "Aliens."

"The bringers of life," Azoh said.

"Whoa, wait a minute," Barnard said. "You're saying the Fathers created you?"

"That is our belief," Azoh said. "That they guided the evolution of our species."

"And they're our creators also?" Chisnall asked.

Azoh nodded again.

"So the gods that Christians and Muslims and all the other religions in the world have been worshipping for thousands of years are just some cranially challenged space invaders?" Barnard asked.

"That is not what I said," Azoh said.

"Then what are you saying?" Price asked.

"To a goldfish swimming in a bowl, its owner must seem like a god. But that does not make them a god. To early humans, the Fathers would have seemed like gods. But that does not make them gods either."

"So there are no gods," Barnard said.

Azoh smiled lightly and adjusted her cowl. "Who do you think the Fathers pray to?" she asked.

"LT, you need to see this," Monster said.

Chisnall stood up, then realised that Monster had been talking to Price.

He remained standing as Price moved over and studied the video screens.

"They are evacuate building," Monster said.

Bzadians were streaming from the doorways. They seemed subdued. It reminded Chisnall of fire drills at school.

"Either that or the ice cream truck is at the front gate," Wall said.

Wall flicked through the different camera angles until he found a view of the main gates. Queues had formed, moving forward slowly. The holdup was clear. A group of soldiers stood at the gates, scanning every face with a hand-held scope.

"They're planning an assault," Price said. "They want to make sure we don't try and slip out amongst the regular folk."

"We'll be ready for them," Barnard said, at the weapons console.

Chisnall sat back down in front of Azoh. "Tell me more about the Fathers," he said.

"The Fathers were the ones who showed us the way here," Azoh said. "They gave us the technology for interstellar travel. Our planet was dying, and we would have died with it. But the Fathers warned us of the primitive, savage nature of Earth. Even as we were preparing our transporters nearly a hundred million humans died in two world wars. We had to defend ourselves. Old blueprints were brought out and studied. We rebuilt our old armies."

"What is she saying?" Wall asked.

"She's saying that Earth is the Wild West, they are the plucky settlers, and we are the savage injuns," Barnard said.

"Why Earth?" Chisnall asked. "Why choose our planet?"

"The choice was made by the Fathers," Azoh said. "Perhaps it was the only planet within range. Perhaps the only planet with the atmosphere to support our kind. Perhaps the only planet with inhabitants similar to our own."

"Perhaps the Fathers intended Bzadians and humans to live together," Barnard said. "Maybe that was part of their grand plan."

"Yeah, or perhaps this war is just their way of amusing themselves," Wall said. "Maybe to them we're just two scorpions in a cardboard box; two fighting dogs in a pit. Maybe they're up there right now taking bets on which side is going to win."

"This is all bull, any way you look at it," Price said. "You think you're more evolved than us. You're the ones who started this war."

"That's not entirely true," Barnard said.

"Why do you keep saying that?" Chisnall asked. "How was it our fault? They attacked us."

"We forced them to," Barnard said.

Chisnall turned back to Azoh, who nodded.

"Your governments restricted us to arid deserts, in which we could not subsist. For months we pleaded and reasoned, but to no avail."

"But you came from a desert planet," Chisnall said.

"One with great underground oceans," Azoh said. "We cannot live without water. We had to defend ourselves, to take more land, in order to survive."

Azoh sat quietly for a moment as the Angels digested that.

"The war has not been good for my race," Azoh said. "Aspects of our nature that we thought were gone forever have resurfaced. To fight Savage Man, we have begun to descend back into savagery ourselves."

"Like in Indonesia," Price said. "Bzadians have committed some of the worst atrocities of the war."

An image came to Chisnall's mind from Operation Magnum. A simple farming family, men, women and children, callously murdered at their dining table.

He did not mention it. All he said was, "War changes people."

"What you say is true," Azoh shook her head sadly. "I do not like what some of my people have done. I do not like what we have become. Indonesia was a particularly unfortunate case."

"We met him. Colonel Nokz'z, the Butcher of Jakarta." Price said. "We had the misfortune of running into him in the Bering Strait."

"Azoh, you said that kidnapping you would not alter the course of the war, would not stop your people using their super weapons," Chisnall said. "Why is that?"

She was silent for a moment and when she spoke, it was reluctantly.

"I am a toothless dog," Azoh said. "A leader in name only. To my people I am a spiritual guide, but to the councillors and generals who rule our society, I am a joke. An inconvenience. I am not even welcomed at High Council meetings."

"The chair is always empty," Chisnall said. "I assumed you did not lower yourself to such trivialities."

"I have been kept a virtual prisoner in the bunkers beneath the building," Azoh said.

"Even so," Barnard said. "Would it not change their thinking?"

"My disappearance would allow the High Council free reign," Azoh said. "Without my presence, the howling of the wolves of war would go unrestrained."

"There is a group of Bzadians who believe the only way to end the war is if you were killed," Chisnall said.

"The Peacemakers," Azoh said.

"You know of them?" Chisnall asked.

"Of course," Azoh said.

"Did you know it was them who sent me to poison you?"

"Of course," Azoh said again, without a trace of emotion. "They work for me."

SACRIFICE

[Mission Day 1, July 1st, 2033. 1025 hours local time]
[Bzadian Congress, Canberra]

Field Marshall Leozii was a small, pudgy creature with the hands of a farm worker. When he talked those hands moved, illustrating every sentence with short, brutal gestures. It was a very human trait. Nokz'z could not take his eyes off those hands, even though he knew he should be staring Leozii in the eye, or at least gazing respectfully at the floor.

Leozii's office was on one of the lower levels of the government building, indicating his importance, his seniority.

How someone with such coarse hands had achieved his status was a mystery to Nokz'z, yet Leozii was the supreme commander of Bzadian Coast Defence forces. In meetings he sat at the central table.

"You know Colonel Kriz?" Leozii was asking.

Kriz was seated in a chair by the window, her hands clasped in her lap, tightly, as if to stop her from doing something else with them, or was that taking his imagination too far, Nokz'z wondered.

Colonel Kriz had been a major the last time Nokz'z had met her. Severly injured at Uluru and transferred to the Coastal Defence Command centre at Brisbane. She had a good reputation although her prospects for advancement were probably limited by her fear of flying.

He acknowledged her with a touch of his hand to his shoulder, wondering what she was doing in this briefing. Goezlin sat at the back.

"Your report, Colonel Nokz'z," Leozii said.

Nokz'z hesitated, wondering how much to reveal. Only what he had to, he thought, especially in front of Goezlin. He shifted slightly in his chair, his back ached from the impact of debris from the explosion, but his armour had saved his life. That and his Vaza. He had landed on top of her. It wasn't the first time she had saved his life, and it probably wouldn't be the last.

He raised a hand to his forehead and cautiously touched the bandages there, suddenly sure they were leaking, but they were dry.

"We know the location of the Angels. We are confident that Azoh is still in their custody," he said.

"But what are you doing about it," Leozii asked.

"We have surrounded the communications centre," Nokz'z said. "We are evacuating all Bzadian personnel. The Angels cannot escape. We will contain them there and negotiate for the safe return of Azoh."

"Our beloved leader is in the hands of scumbugz," Leozii said, and you want to wait? To negotiate? With these primitives?"

"If we attack, it might place Azoh's life at risk," Nokz'z said. "But in the meantime we are digging through the rubble in the tunnel. Once we are through, we can come up behind them, and surprise them."

"How long?" Leozii asked.

"I am unsure," Nokz'z said. "It is slow work. We don't want to bring the rest of the tunnel down on our heads."

Leozii was silent for a few minutes. His pudgy, workman fingers tapped lightly on the desk.

"I should go and continue to co-ordinate the search," Nokz'z said, after a moment.

Leozii looked up. "You allowed enemy soldiers to penetrate the Congress," he said.

Nokz'z dragged his eyes away from those jabbering hands. "Sir…"

"Colonel Nokz'z, are you interrupting a senior officer?" Goezlin asked from behind him. Nokz'z was silent.

"You are responsible for the defence of the capital," Leozii said. "Yet you have failed to stop infiltrators entering our city. You have failed to protect the Congress and now you have failed to protect Azoh."

"Sir—" Nokz'z began but Leozii was not finished.

"Just as you failed in the Bering strait!"

The Field Marshall's next words seemed to be coming through a thick fog. Nokz'z could barely hear them. But he didn't need to. He knew what was being said.

"Colonel Nokz'z, you are relieved of command," Leozii said. "Colonel Kriz will be taking over, effective immediately. You will return to your quarters and await re-posting."

"That would be a mistake," Nokz'z said calmly. "I have first-hand knowledge of these Angels."

"So does Colonel Kriz," Leozii said. "Including the leader, Chizna. You are relieved, Colonel."

Nokz'z glanced at Kriz and got an apologetic wave of a hand over her face in return.

"Of course, Field Marshall," Nokz'z said. "I understand completely. An unfortunate set of circumstances. I have no doubt that an opportunity will arise which will allow me to redeem myself."

"I doubt it, Colonel," Leozii said. "One way or another, this war will be over before that opportunity arises."

Nokz'z said nothing further and waited where he was until he was dismissed with a curt nod of the head from Leozii.

His Vaza was waiting outside the door and joined him as he marched furiously down the corridor.

A black rage was welling up within Nokz'z, a seething fire and he fought to contain it. At least until he was alone. At least until he had one of the Angels within range. He had been a rising star in the military once. On track for General. Until Jakarta. He had done what had needed to be done in Indonesia, and his reward had been a demotion.

It had taken years of grovelling and playing the political games to restore his reputation. Then after the debacle in the Bering Strait he had been pulled from Chukchi and given a lesser post.

Now he had been removed, even from that. It was a long and ignominious fall.

His Vaza put a hand on his arm, he furiously brushed it off. She put it back, stopping him from walking further.

"I have information," she said.

"It had better be important, Vaza," Nokz'z said.

"My sister works in the computer records section," she said. "She has been scouring the old human databases as you asked."

"And?"

"And she has discovered the plans of the tunnels."

* * *

"You knew I was going to try to poison you," Chisnall said.

"And I knew you would fail," Azoh said. "And I knew why. But it would have been easier had you succeeded."

"And you knew we would try to kidnap you," Chisnall said.

Azoh nodded. "It was the most likely of the possibilities that I had considered."

"How many possibilities did you consider?" Barnard asked from over on the weapons console.

"All of them," Azoh said.

Chisnall was silent, trying to get his head around that. What she was saying was almost incomprehensible. Azoh had thought through every permutation, every possible action of every person, and had accurately predicted the future.

"You knew what we were going to do before we even decided to do it," Chisnall said.

"To some extent, yes," Azoh said. "You took actions that had to be taken, given the circumstances. I simply had to evaluate all the variables and decide on the most likely outcome."

"That is incredible," Barnard said.

"You seek to flatter me," Azoh said. "But compared to my predecessor my thinking skills are very basic. My vision is very limited. And my predecessor was like a blind infant compared to the Fathers."

"The Fathers taught you these skills?" Chisnall asked.

In the process of becoming I was trained in some of the ways of the Fathers," Azoh said. "But other things cannot be taught."

"What kind of things?" Chisnall asked.

"I think you know," Azoh said.

Chisnall thought she might be right, but there was no time to dwell on that.

"Azoh," he said. "If kidnapping you would not help stop the war between our races, then what would?"

"The world is a complex puzzle," Azoh said. "Everything is interconnected. A change here causes a change there. A tap of a finger, carefully placed, can cause a million year boulder to topple."

"I do not understand what you are trying to tell me," Chisnall said.

"I will answer your question," Azoh said. "But you will not like the answer."

* * *

Goezlin made a point never to hurry, never to seem in a rush, or under pressure. It unnerved other people. But he was hurrying now.

The fool of a guard had had express instructions not to leave the prisoner alone under any circumstances. Yet somehow the prisoner had convinced her to do exactly that.

He had a dangerous kind of charm, this prisoner. 'The Tsar' they called him, although that was not his name. And for a number of minutes he had been alone. That worried Goezlin. The Angels had a reputation for resourcefulness.

Perhaps he should not have left, but the business with Nokz'z could not be avoided, nor delayed.

He waited calmly as the guard unlocked the door of the interrogation room.

His prisoner sat securely, still facing the far wall, shoulders slumped in defeat.

It was a far cry from his attitude previously, his head held high in false confidence, a cocky grin hiding the fear that he must surely have been feeling.

Goezlin allowed himself a small murmur of relief at the sight of the boy. The room was secure, the building was secure, the compound was secure. But even so it was good to see The Tsar still where he had been put.

The Tsar's wrists were secure in the neck cuffs, the cable that secured the neck cuffs to the chair was intact, and the chair was still bolted to the floor. Not even an Angel could escape from these bonds.

The Tsar sat quietly, unmoving. Defeated.

Sometimes that was all it took, a little time. Time for the prisoner to anticipate the horror that was to come. To dwell on whether the price was worth it. The carefully masked lighting, and the grim concrete block walls were carefully designed to increase the mental pressure.

"You have been lucky," Goezlin said. "We have located your friends, and your information is no longer required or relevant."

The Tsar remained silent, although Goezlin thought he detected a small sigh of relief.

"You will be taken to the cells now," Goezlin said. "You will not be mistreated."

When that got no response he walked around to the front, to face The Tsar.

He was wrong.

The Tsar had not been lucky.

Somehow he had twisted his hand around enough in the cuffs to reach the dressing on his neck. The bandages hung loose, and the wadding that had been stuffed into the hole in his neck lay in his lap, sodden and red.

The front of his uniform was soaked in blood and it was pooled on the floor below him.

Goezlin stood and stared at the body of the young man for a long time. Too long. There were things he needed to do, places he needed to be, but the body had become a magnet, and he could not pull himself away.

Was there a likeness to his own son? Not really, but still his mind transposed the face of his son onto the body of this enemy soldier.

He considered calling for medics, but he knew there was no point. It was too late for that.

The Angels' reputation for resourcefulness was not unwarranted.

The Tsar had found his own escape.

MOUSE BAIT

[Mission Day 1, July 1st, 2033. 1045 hours local time]
[Old US Embassy, Canberra]

The strangeness came over Chisnall as he was talking to Daniel Bilal. He pushed it aside, desperately afraid of what it meant.

The phones in the room had not worked, but Wall had figured out a way to patch them through a satellite communications system. Chisnall wasn't sure it was secure, but it was all they had.

"It is an honour to hear your voice, son," Bilal was saying.

Chisnall forced his mind to focus on the telephone. On the voice on the other end. Everything depended on the outcome of this call. Everything.

Communications equipment in the safe room connected via a secure line straight to Washington. Chisnall was a little surprised to find out that it still worked after so many years, but not at all surprised to find Bilal waiting on the other end of the line. Bilal had been expecting his call.

Bilal was some kind of bigwig in Military Intelligence. Nobody seemed to quite know what, but that was kind of the point for these spy types, Chisnall thought. All his previous communications with Bilal had been through Barnard, or – and the memory brought a heaviness to his heart – Wilton.

"Thank you sir," Chisnall said. "We don't have much time so let me lay it out for you real quick. You need to call off the air-strike. If ACOG attacks Canberra with their new jets, it will start, well let's just call it a nuclear war, and ACOG will lose."

"That's a moot point," Bilal said. "In a nuclear war, everyone would lose."

"Not according to the information I have uncovered," Chisnall said, and explained briefly about the positronium warhead.

Bilal reflected on that for a while. "That does change things, if it's true," he said. "Do we have any verification of this information?"

"No sir," Chisnall said. "Except the source. It came from a Bzadian on Azoh's inner circle."

"That's not a good reason to trust the intel, in fact it may be the opposite," Bilal said. "Look I believe you, but I have to convince ACOG, and they're going to want something more substantial that what you've given me. It could be a ruse to prevent us using the scream jets. A carrier strike group got hit in Auckland Harbour this morning and ACOG are not going to just let the Pukes get away with that."

"All I know is what I've told you," Chisnall said. "But I honestly believe that if you target Canberra, most human cities are going to end up as giant smoking craters."

"I'll take it to them," Bilal said. "Any idea where we would find this bomb?"

"Only that it was placed by the same man who put the Ferzerkers on Little Diomede," Chisnall said.

"Colonel Reid?"

"Yes sir, maybe you can persuade him to talk."

"If you can find out anything else get back to me straight away," Bilal said.

"Of course, sir," Chisnall said shut his eyes as Bilal broke the connection.

Now the strangeness could not be denied. The coldness in his soul. The Tsar was dead. He knew it without understanding how he knew it. But it was not a vague feeling. It was a fact.

Chisnall looked grimly around at the others. Barnard was at a weapons station, studying the controls, reading the help screens, she was nodding and murmuring to herself. Wall was doing something similar at the video station. Monster was standing at the video wall, watching as they cycled through different views of the building and its surrounds.

Brogan and Price had gone. Back into the tunnel with Azoh. She had been right, Chisnall didn't like her plan, not even with the modifications he had insisted on, but he could see no other option.

He pulled up a chair and sat down at the desk next to Barnard. This was not going to be easy. Price had told him how close Barnard and The Tsar had become.

"We've got a lot of firepower," Barnard said. "All of it controlled from this room. We should be able to hold off the Pukes for quite a while."

"Barnard…" Chisnall began.

She looked at him and raised an eyebrow.

"It's The Tsar."

"What about The Tsar?" she asked.

"It's bad news," Chisnall said.

"Dead?" Barnard asked.

Chisnall nodded.

Monster came and stood behind him. There was silence for a while. Wall broke it. "You can't know that."

"I do," Chisnall said.

Barnard was silent.

"He should never have been allowed to drive the fire truck out of the parking garage," Wall said.

"He volunteered," Monster said softly. "And if no for him, then we are no here now."

"How did he die?" Barnard asked.

"Bravely," Chisnall said. "That's all I know."

"You're sure?" she asked.

"I'm sure," Chisnall said.

Barnard pointed at the controls. "Bofors auto-cannons," she said. "You've got two of them, hidden in dormer windows on the main building, and on the old chancery."

"He really was a hero," Chisnall said.

"Yes he was," Barnard said. "You can only control one gun at a time. If they take out your first, switch to the second. Do you know how to work the controls?"

Chisnall glanced up at Monster, who gave a tiny shake of his head.

"Show me," Chisnall said, turning back to Barnard.

"It's a touch screen," she said. "Touch the target and the gun locks on. You can zoom if you need more accuracy and pan around with gestures."

"Just like a smart-pad," Chisnall said.

"A little," Barnard said.

The arming and firing buttons were large red and green buttons at the bottom of the screen. Chisnall selected his first Bofors gun and armed it. A series of indicators flashed up on the side of the screen, diagnostic functions. They all turned green. The gun was ready to fire. He disarmed it and tried the alternative gun. That also checked out without a problem.

"What about the machine guns?" he asked.

"They're automatic," Barnard said. "You have five of them, scattered around the gardens." He pointed them out on the console. "When you activate them, they rise up out of the ground and start shooting at anything that moves."

"Anything?"

"If it moves, it's a target," Barnard said.

"Nice," Monster said.

"I wouldn't leave them up too long," Barnard said. "They're protected by an armoured metal casing but they'd still be vulnerable. "I'd pop them up and down at random. That way the Pukes will never know where you're going to strike next."

"Got it," Chisnall said. Monster grunted his agreement.

"Barnard," Chisnall asked. "Are you okay?"

She shrugged. "I'm good, lieutenant. Why wouldn't I be?"

"Just checking," Chisnall said. He turned back to the controls and studied them for a few moments. "This is just like playing a video game."

"Except if die, you no get to respawn and start over," Monster said.

"No, you don't," Chisnall agreed.

* * *

They dared not use explosives for fear of causing another collapse.

Colonel Zara Kriz clasped her hands behind her back. An old trick to stop herself pulling at the skin on her forearms, regrown after the rotorcraft crash that had killed so many of her colleagues. That was a long time ago, and the skin was no longer soft and new, but the habit remained, and the clasping of the hands remained also.

The urge to pull at the skin came on much more strongly when she was nervous, and the events of today went way beyond nervousness. They were terrifying.

She had been called to the capital to take over its defence, when Nokz'z, a person who made her skin creep just to look at him, had been removed from his position. That had meant a trip from Brisbane to Canberra, and Kriz did not fly. She hadn't since the crash. But the call from Canberra had left no room for argument, and with the help of a powerful sedative she had made the flight. The anti-sedative that had woken her up at the other end had left her with a mild headache, which added to the tension she was feeling.

She had been thrust into the command of the operation, unsure whether it was because she was a valued and trusted commander, or if the High Council needed a scapegoat.

Azoh had been kidnapped! The enormity of it was almost overwhelming.

If Azoh could not be rescued, if the infiltrators could not be caught, then it would be on her head.

She stood at the base of the rocky staircase, watching them work in the confined and dimly lit space and clasped her hands even more tightly together.

She held a damp cloth to her face to filter the fine rock dust that drifted in strangely flat layers through the air of the tunnel.

The soldiers attacked the concrete and stone rubble with pick-axes and shovels, manhandling large stones backwards where they were passed along a line of workers and spread out along the length of the remaining tunnel.

They worked furiously, but no one knew how far they would have to dig. The collapsed section might be just a metre or so, and they could be nearly through it. Or the entire tunnel could have collapsed.

The Angels, with their captive, were holed up in the Communications Centre. A rescue mission was being planned. That was surely a big mistake. Assaulting the building would put the life of Azoh in very grave danger.

Kriz had said as much to Field Marshall Leozii, and he had agreed with her. But the High Council had voted otherwise. A bunch of old politicians with no grasp of the realities of warfare. The kidnapping of Azoh was seen as slap in the face of all Bzadians, and the Bzadian leaders had to be seen to be taking direct action.

Nokz'z's plan had been a good one, in Kriz's view. To enter the building the same way the Angels had, through the tunnel, coming up behind them in a surprise attack. But time was running out. So Kriz waited, and watched. She smiled thinly at one of the workers who quickly looked away and threw himself into the work redoubled.

Jazki, a worthy, but intense young captain came scrambling back along the tunnel towards her She was grimy and sweaty, helmetless. Her head was heavily bandaged from the earlier explosion, but the bandages were black with rock dust. "Air movement at the top of the pile," she reported. "We're almost through."

* * *

The blue fabric of Azoh's ceremonial robes billowed in front of Price as she, Azoh, and Brogan hurried back down the corridor. The robes, so delicate and elegant, were now stained with dust and dirt of the tunnels. This was no place for a princess, and as much as she understood Azoh's role in Bzadian society, it was hard for Price not to think of her like that, a princess. A flawless, unblemished beauty, accustomed to a life of perfection and luxury, not a tunnel rat.

They reached the cross tunnel where an avalanche of rock and rubble had flowed across the passageway, leaving little room for them to climb through. Price could hear the sounds of hammering and scraping from the other side. It sounded close. Even as she watched, a large stone fell from the top of the pile, bouncing and skidding down the uneven slope.

"Come on," she said. "Hurry."

She took Azoh's hand and helped her climb, trying to avoid the jagged razor-sharp edges of the broken rock. They had to crawl over the last bit, squeezing below the low ceiling of the tunnel, then slipped and skidded down the other side.

She tried to reach Chisnall on the com, but the rock of the tunnel blocked any chance of a signal.

She did not look back once they reached the far side of the rubble, and so she did not notice the small insect like creature that emerged from the rock pile. It crawled on spindly, wire-like legs through a small gap between the rocks. It turned one way, then the other. Sensing movement, filmy, translucent wings unfolded from its crystalline thorax and it hummed quietly into the air.

* * *

The Vaza led the way, following an old map that she had printed.

She hurried across the vast wooden floors of the old building, to a stairway that led down to a basement.

The basement was vast and divided into a maze of rooms and corridors. Several times the Vaza stopped, studied her map again, and backtracked where necessary.

"Here," she said at last, arriving at a small, non-descript office.

"Where?" Nokz'z asked.

"That is not clear," the Vaza replied. But the tunnel emerges in this room.

Nokz'z looked around. There were no obvious doors leading from the room. The floor was wooden, with no sign of trapdoors, nor even a break where a tunnel could emerge.

"You are sure?" he asked.

The Vaza nodded.

"Then we wait," Nokz'z said.

"You are sure that they will use this tunnel?" the Vaza asked.

"They cannot return to the Congress," Nokz'z said. "The tunnel is blocked and crawling with our troops. The Communications Centre is surrounded. They must come here. They have nowhere else to go."

He watched her closely for a moment.

"Vaza."

"Yes Colonel," she said.

"Your fortunes are closely tied to mine," he said.

"Of course," she said.

"When I succeed, you succeed with me," he said. "But

when I fail, you must suffer because of me."

She moved to him and placed her hands on his shoulders before leaning forward and kissing him directly on the lips. It was a tremendous breach of protocol. It should always be the superior who initiated physical contact. But they had served together for far too many years, and protocol was merely a guidebook for beginners. He restrained himself from wiping his lips with his fingers after she released him. Protocol or not, that would be crass.

"I do not want you to suffer," Nokz'z said.

"I would have it no other way," she said.

ASSAULT

[Mission Day 1, July 1st, 2033. 1000 hours local time]
[Old US Embassy, Canberra]

"ACOG are taking your request under advisement," Bilal sounded worried and frustrated.

"Request!" Barnard exploded. "It's not a request. Don't they understand that they are picking a fight they can't possibly win?"

"Barnard's right," Chisnall said. "It's mass suicide."

"I explained it in words of one syllable," Bilal said. "They're asking for proof, but frankly, the impression I got was that ACOG are so determined to show off their new military might, to teach the Bzadians a lesson and tear them a new asshole, that they won't change their minds."

"Proof!" Chisnall said.

"They are looking for this bomb of yours," Bilal said. "They're interrogating Reid and analysing his every movement over the last four or five years. They are taking this seriously."

"Not seriously enough," Chisnall said.

"One other thing," Barnard said. "The scream-jets just took off. They're climbing to launch altitude as we speak."

Chisnall was silent. There was nothing to say.

"I'll keep trying," Bilal said. "What's your plan? What are you doing with Azoh?"

"Azoh seems to believe that if she addresses the High Council, she can convince them not to retaliate." Chisnall said. "Brogan and Price are trying to get her there. But ..."

"What is it, Ryan?"

"I'm not going to say," Chisnall said. "In case there is any chance that the Pukes are listening in."

"It's supposed to be a secure line," Bilal said. "But okay. Whatever she's up to, I just hope she's on our side."

"She's on nobody's side," Chisnall said. "She's Azoh."

"Pukes moving up to the main gates," Wall yelled.

"Gotta go," Chisnall said. He hung up the receiver. "Okay kids, time we showed them our teeth and claws. Lock the gates and arm the weapons."

"Praise the lord and pass the ammunition," Barnard said. "Here they come."

The big screens showed all angles of the compound and its grounds. The gardens, once manicured, now overgrown under the reign of the Bzadians, the tennis court, the swimming pool, emptied and disused. Swimming was not considered a recreational pastime by the aliens.

The black-suited nzgali and the grey uniforms of the regular soldiers were advancing steadily across the open ground, in combat profile, moving in pairs, covering each other, using what shelter they could find: trees; shrubs; fences. Some glided across the ground on T-boards, a three-wheeled, motorized Bzadian skateboard.

"Keep coming," Chisnall said. "Let them think this is going to be easy. Start with the machine guns. We'll keep the Bofors as an ace up our sleeve."

Still the creeping tide of Bzadian soldiers flowed towards the old ambassador's residence.

"Hold your fire," Chisnall murmured. Then, "A little further."

The first of the soldiers was almost at the doors when Chisnall said, in a mock Cuban accent, "Say hello to my little friend.'"

The chatter of machine guns came about three seconds later. On the video screens they could see circular plugs of grass rise up out of the lawn, at first unnoticed by the Bzadian troops. Then the dragon-breath stream of fire as the high velocity bullets squirted from the muzzles.

Soldiers fell. Some merely stunned, protected by their armour. Others injured.

Even as the Bzadians identified the threat it was gone, the pods melded seamlessly back into the grass, leaving just a drifting pall of smoke, a ghostly presence over the battlefield.

The alien soldiers scanned around desperately, seeking targets, trying to return fire. But there was nothing to fire at.

"Count to three," Chisnall said. "Now."

Just as the soldiers were beginning to restore some sort of order, a different set of guns emerged up, and the thunder began again.

There were clear signs of panic among the regular soldiers, but the nzgali were too good for that. Calm, under control under fire. Chisnall nearly lost a pod when a nzgali grenade exploded on the ground above it just after he retracted it.

A third set of pods opened up and now the troops were retreating, unsure where the next attack would come, they dragged their wounded and their unconscious, perhaps dead, comrades with them.

"Boo-yah!" Monster cried.

"They'll be back," Chisnall said. "And it won't be so easy next time."

* * *

"Scream Leader to Scream Team, we got a lot of wild life ahead of us," Shaw said. Her radar scope was bright with targets. The air was uneven and the cockpit of her jet was jolting around the sky like a car on an old dirt track. She glanced out at the wings, above and below the plane, and wondered exactly how much of this they could take. The scream-jets had been developed in furious haste, without the usual time for testing and refining. If the wings were going to fail, now was when they would find out. And at Mach five, ejection was not an option.

"Scream Four to Scream Leader I'm counting at least seven Dragons."

"Then make like St George," Shaw said. "It's nothing we can't handle. On the first pass focus on the air cover. We've got Type Ones, Type Twos as well as those Dragons in the air and that means a lot of ordnance coming our way. Stay high, that will give the SAMs a longer ride and we should be well out of range by the time they reach our height. The Dragons are going to be our biggest problem. Fire as soon as we're in range, then go for the moon, gain as much height as you can as quickly as you can without dropping below hypersonic velocity. The Dragons are big and heavy and they won't be able to match us on the climb. Drop your countermeasures as you go and we should be past them before they can do anything about it. Once we've cleared the sky, we'll come back for the SAM sites. We need to cut the spikes off this cactus before we go for the juicy bits. Are we clear?"

She got a chorus of assents from the team.

Ahead of them their long-range cameras showed a fiercely burning fire line less than a kilometre from the city and closing in fast. A grey pall of smoke covering almost all of the target area. That wouldn't affect the scream-jets, their major targets had been locked in before they had left the USS Apple, but if it got any thicker it would seriously impede visibility over the target area.

"Scream Two to Scream Leader, do you see those tanks. Whole bunch of them on the scope at our ten. They appear to be surrounding the old US Embassy. Didn't you say that was where the Angels were going to be?"

"Solid copy and confirming, Scream Two, that is the safety point for the Angels," Shaw said.

"Do you want me to light 'em up," Scream Two asked. "Give those Angel kids a helping hand?"

"Negative, Scream Two," Shaw said. "It's too dangerous while the Pukes still have air assets in our vicinity. Concentrate on the fighters."

* * *

The next attack was by a smaller force, nzgali only, the regular soldiers confined to the perimeter. They came in armoured cars, charging through the gates on three sides of the compound.

"Can we play with the big guns now?" Wall asked.

"Yes, keep the pods down," Chisnall said. "They're waiting for them."

Teams with rocket launchers were creeping in behind the armoured cars, trying to identify the sites of the pop-up machine guns.

"Light up the vehicles as soon as they're within range," Chisnall said.

"No, wait," Wall said. "Those cars are heavily armoured. But when they reach the building the sides will drop, become ramps for the assault troops."

"Okay, wait for the ramps," Chisnall said.

He armed his first Bofors gun, and somewhere in a dusty garret, a heavy metal screen drew back and the long snout of the automatic cannon protruded.

Six of the armoured cars skidded to a halt at the building's main entrance. The sides dropped and suddenly nzgali were everywhere.

"Now!" Chisnall shouted and the crack, crack, crack of the huge guns filled the air around them, shaking the walls of the saferoom.

The forty-millimetre Bofors auto-cannon is one of the longest serving artillery pieces in the world, first seeing service in the second world war as an anti-aircraft weapon. Variants of the weapon have been used for nearly a hundred years. The machine-gun of the artillery, it fires forty-millimetre high explosive shells at a rate of nearly 200 rounds per minute.

The results were devastating.

Even if the armoured walls had been up, Chisnall doubted they could have withstood the volume of fire that encased each of the armoured cars. With the walls down the cars disappeared in a teeth-shaking series of explosions and balls of flame as their fuel tanks ignited.

"Pop up some pods!" Chisnall shouted. "And turn the Bofors on the rocket teams."

The nzgali were just starting to pick themselves up off the ground where they had been thrown by the force of the explosions, when the machine guns started. Even the finest troops of the Bzadian army could not cope with the smoke, the firing of the guns, the shock and disorganisation. They broke and ran for their lives. Those on the ground stayed there.

Chisnall saw a rocket team lining up on one of the pods, and switched to his second Bofors which had a clearer angle at them. He touched the ground just in front of them and hit the firing button. Dirt and lawn erupted, scattering them like tenpins.

Another team, another burst from the Bofors, and now the rocket teams were in full retreat also.

"Run like the wind, mother-shippers!" Wall yelled, standing and punching the air.

"Next time it will be tanks," Barnard said.

"Not as long as they think Azoh is in here," Chisnall said.

*　*　*

Kriz sat at the back of the council chamber, horrified by the drama that was playing out below.

"Human warplanes fly with impunity over our heads, while our mighty dragons fall from the sky," Field Marshall Leozii said. "I can no longer defend the capital. In fact I can no longer guarantee to defend any Bzadian city or base. We have nothing to match these new jets. This war is now lost, unless we take action."

"We came to this planet to make a home for our people," a councillor said. "Not to destroy its inhabitants."

"Yet the natives will wipe us out, if we don't take direct action," Leozii said. "We came offering friendship and new technologies. They spurned us, tried to quarantine us, and now try to kill us."

Another councillor spoke up, a female, completely bald, the oldest of all the councillors. "Leozii is right. For all our best intentions, it has come down to us or them. There is no room for both species on this planet."

"They will retaliate," a third councillor, heavily bearded, said. "Their nuclear weapons are crude and clumsy, but they have thousands of them."

"Which cannot be launched without direct orders from the Pentagon," Leozii said. "And that will cease to exist before any orders can be given."

"You are sure of this?" the female councillor asked.

"Absolutely," Leozii said, although Kriz did not understand how he could be so sure. "But we must act now, while we still can."

Kriz's phone was buzzing with an urgent message. A quick glance at the screen showed her it was Jazki. She stood and moved quickly to the back of the chamber before answering.

"Azoh is no longer at the communications centre," Jazki said.

"You are sure?" Kriz asked.

"I have a cam-bot following her, with two of the infiltrators, along a tunnel that leads away from the building," Jazki said.

"I will be right there," Kriz said.

On the council floor below her, a vote was being held. She did not wait to see the result. It was a foregone conclusion.

* * *

Lajes Field on the island of Terceira, in the Azores, lies midway between North America and Europe. Formerly a combined US Air force/Portuguese Air force base, it sits less than four thousand kilometres from Washington DC.

ACOG was aware of its use as an airbase for the Bzadian military, but was unaware of its real purpose. Had they known, they might well have bombed the island into the sea.

The 74th Squadron of the Eastern Atlantic Bzadian Air Command had never seen combat. There were twenty four planes in the squadron, all of them Thunderclouds, what ACOG referred to as Type Twos, air to ground attack planes.

These planes were special. They each carried just four missiles, in addition to their defensive armament. Each missile carried just a single warhead.

But each warhead was a weapon that had not yet been used in the Great War of Earth. An anti-matter weapon that would later be called positronium by historians, although scientists would argue that this term was incorrect and misleading. Whatever the name, it was a stable form of anti-matter and matter, it required little to detonate, and the resulting explosion would make Hiroshima and Nagasaki look like mere firecrackers. Yet the weapons left no residual radiation.

At exactly TIME, the thirty-two aircraft of 74th squadron took off from Lajes Field. Altogether they carried one hundred and twenty eight positronium weapons. Enough to not merely destroy the North American landmass, but to wipe it clean.

* * *

"Tanks moving up on the south side," Wall yelled. "Time we were Oscar Mike."

"Okay team, we're out of here," Chisnall said. "Monster, get the door."

"One of those tanks is right up our ass," Wall shouted.

"They won't fire," Chisnall said. "They won't risk killing Azoh."

Almost immediately the sound of the tank's main gun, resounding distantly through the walls of the room, proved him wrong. On the video screen there was a flash from the muzzle of the tank then the image disappeared into grainy static.

The whole building shook and all the lights flickered. The video screens went blank for a few seconds before recovering. Monster ran for the door to the tunnel.

"What the hell?" Wall shouted. He touched his firing button and on the remaining screens they saw the tank light up like a Christmas tree as the 40mm shells exploded uselessly on its spinning hull.

"Are they trying to kill Azoh?" Chisnall asked.

"They know she's not here," Barnard said.

"Hurry!" Chisnall said, "We've..." his sentence was cut off by the next explosion. All of the video screens died.

"Door stuck!" Monster shouted.

He was wrenching at the wheel that opened the door. His entire body was straining, blood vessels standing out on his forehead, shoulders bunched, feet planted, but Chisnall could see that the frame was buckled and the door was thoroughly jammed.

Wall joined him, the two strongest members of the team, but even together they could not budge it.

Chisnall raced over to help.

"Barnard have you still got coms?" he asked.

"Yes," Barnard shouted over yet another explosion. The Bzadian tanks were taking the building to pieces, shot by shot.

"Get hold of Bilal," Chisnall started, but could say no more as another explosion, much closer, threw him to the ground.

The wall of the safe room bulged then collapsed inward with a groaning roar and a hurricane of dust and bricks. It enveloped Chisnall, wrapping him in a blanket of swirling debris.

When the storm finished he was lying in rubble. The wall was gone, he could see daylight outside. Above him broken fluorescent light strips that fizzed and sparked above him.

He tried to talk, to tell the others to get out, although he himself could not move, but he had no voice, sucked out of his chest by the vacuum of the explosion and the weight of rubble on his chest.

Then the weight lifted. A shadow was over him, blocking the garish flicker of the fluorescent lights.

Concrete blocks were being lifted off him and he could breathe again. Immense chunks of grey concrete and steel were being tossed aside like lego blocks.

That made Chisnall smile, because there was only one person in the world he knew who could do that.

"LT! LT, you are okay?" Monster's voice came thickly through the soup in his ears.

Chisnall sucked in enough air to say, "Okay." And then Monster's face was above him.

It was a red mass of blood, but Monster did not seem to notice.

The concrete around them began to vibrate, rock pebbles dancing on the shimmering dust.

Chisnall looked up, and past his friend, and he saw death.

The tank was moving into position to fire directly into the hole it had already punched in the side of the building. Its muzzle lowered until it pointed directly at them.

Then came the flash.

REDEMPTION

[Mission Day 1, July 1st, 2033. 1030 hours local time]
[Old Parliament House, Canberra]

Nokz'z looked again to the ceiling as another series of explosions rocked the world above them. The ceiling shook and dust filtered down between the cracks, but the explosions were too far distant to do any damage. So far. He did not feel in direct danger. They were in the basement of the building, a safe enough place unless the humans directly targeted the building. And what interest would they have in blowing up a load of dusty old relics.

A sound drew his eyes back to the wall, and a section, that looked solid, suddenly shifted and what had been an almost invisible seam grew darker and larger as though a pencil line had been overdrawn with a thick black pen. Without speaking, Nokz'z and the Vaza moved to that wall, flattening themselves against it. The hidden doorway opened further and a head came through, a quick glance around, checking out the room, but not seeing the two shapes, hidden by the half-open door.

The door opened further and a combat suited figure stepped through, followed by another, then then flowing blue robes of Azoh. She did not appear to be resisting her abductors.

Moving as one, Nokz'z and the Vaza stepped silently up behind the two Angels and on a quick nod from Nokz'z kicked simultaneously at the back of the Angels' knees. Both went down, face-down on the ground, arms flailing, and before they could hit the release buttons for their coil-guns, or grab at their sidearms, Nokz'z and the Vaza were standing over them, weapons pressed against a weak point in the armour on the back of their suits.

"Unclip your weapons," Nokz'z said.

The two Angels complied, reaching up over their backs to disconnect their coilguns then pushing them away from them. Their sidearms followed. The Vaza kicked the weapons out of reach.

"Stay face down," Nokz'z said, as one of the Angels made to roll over.

Azoh stood quietly to one side, apparently neither concerned nor pleased by what had just happened.

"Colonel Nokz'z," Azoh said.

"Azoh," Nokz'z said, lowering his eyes and bowing his head.

It was less a show of deference that to hide an expression of exuberance.

Against all odds, on the very verge of defeat, he, Nokz'z had done it. He had rescued Azoh from the clutches of the enemy. He had saved her. He would be a living hero for all Bzadians. Senior command would have no choice but to reinstate him. He was redeemed.

And then, he was not.

"Release these soldiers," Azoh said. "And help us get to the High Council. It is extremely urgent."

"Azoh, they are dangerous enemy agents," Nokz'z said. "You are safe now. I will escort you to the Congress, while my Vaza deals with your captors."

"These are not my captors," Azoh said.

"Surely…" Nokz'z started.

"They are working with me to stop a terrible mistake," Azoh said.

"A mistake, Azoh?" Nokz'z asked.

"The High Council is about to authorise a strike against the human territories," Azoh said. "It must be stopped. I believe we can now negotiate a peaceful end to this war."

One of the Angels spoke, lifting her face off the floor. "Colonel Nokz'z, we can stop this war right now, and end the killing and the suffering."

It was the one called Price, who had mocked and bested him in the ice desert of the Bering strait. Nokz'z smiled briefly to conceal a sudden flame of anger. Azoh was working with Price!?

"Colonel Nokz'z, these humans will not harm me, nor you," Azoh said. "Please lower your weapons, and escort us quickly to the Congress."

"You believe we can end this war?" Nokz'z asked. "And negotiate for peace?"

"I know this to be true," Azoh said.

"Azoh, your wisdom is beyond question, but these are humans," Nokz'z said. "A violent, savage sub-species. One step from wild animals. They cannot be trusted."

"And yet we must trust them, if we are to live together peacefully on this planet."

"Live together peacefully," Nokz'z repeated the words.

"Yes."

"The High Council will never agree to this," Nokz'z said.

"They will when they hear what I have to say," Azoh said.

"What is that?" Nokz'z asked.

"That you tried to kill me," Azoh said.

"I did no such…" Nokz'z voice trailed off. He had not tried, but he had thought about it. From the moment she had spoken of ending the war. The idea had been in his mind. And this Azoh. She knew what was in his mind. She had seen his intent, even though that was all it was, an idea, a thought. Not an action. He would be an outcast, a criminal. A renegade who thought of killing the Bzadian leader.

The war was over. His career was over. He was over.

The sudden flutter of the blue robes was something that Nokz'z watched dimly, faded into insignificance by the red curtain of blood that seemed to have been drawn across behind his eyes, and the only sound he could hear was a roaring in his ears as though a great wind had blown into the room. Even the gunshot was barely audible through the sound. He observed with interest, not emotion as Azoh's body jerked backwards, her hands twitching towards her heart, before going limp, as did her face, and her legs.

He saw one of the Angels trying to rise and being viciously kicked back down.

Then Azoh fell, no longer a living being, now a lifeless collection of body parts, her ceremonial robes now a funeral shroud. Her own prediction now come to pass.

* * *

There was a clear hole at the top of the rock pile when Kriz arrived. A shout came from one of the soldiers and a large boulder came crunching down the slope in the midst of an avalanche of smaller stones. Kriz stepped quickly to the side as the boulder smashed into the wall right where she had been standing. She looked back at the top of the pile.

What had been a hole large enough to put an arm through, was now large enough to climb through.

"Move aside!" she ordered. She scrambled up the pile of rocks, which shifted and skittered under his hands and feet. She had to lie on his stomach and squeeze through the gap. Lieutenant Jazki was at her heels, scrambling and falling down the loose rocks on the other side. Then they were in the tunnel and running.

* * *

The scream-jet was so fast that time on target was very limited. The window for identifying, targeting and firing was no more than a few seconds.

Multiple SAMs were chasing her as she fled the target area. But they would not catch her, and her wingmen would already be targeting those launchers with anti-SAM missiles.

The order had come from the USS Apple, relayed directly from the Pentagon. The Angels needed help. The tanks had become a target.

She had fired four missiles, which had split almost immediately after launch into twelve independently guided smart warheads.

The rising plumes of smoke and flame on her rear cameras were a testament to the accuracy of those bombs.

The proximity warheads were design to explode just prior to contact with a Bzadian tank. Not even the spinning armoured hull could withstand such tremendous force so close. The outer shells crumpled like paper then tore themselves to pieces, exploding in sheets of flame and debris that tore gaping holes in the nearby buildings. The old Ambassador's residence, already shattered by tank shells, collapsed in on itself.

Shaw never saw this however. She was already nine kilometres away and accelerating by the time the warheads struck.

"Scream Leader this is Scream Four," a voice came in her earphones, "All air cover and SAM sites in the vicinity have now been destroyed. We are clear for a run against ground targets."

"Clear copy, Scream Four," Shaw said. "Scream Team commence turn. Let's light this place up like Christmas. Final target reminder, we are not, repeat not going to strike the Bzadian Congress. We are trying to shake up the Puke leaders, not to wipe them out. Anything else is a legitimate target."

* * *

Nokz'z mind was clear. The red haze had lifted and he knew exactly what he was doing as he emptied the cartridge of his sidearm before pressing it into the reluctant hand of one of the Angels.

He registered every detail of the shocked face of his Vaza as he turned, so calmly towards her.

"We could not stop them," Nokz'z said. "The scumbugz, the murderers of Azoh. "But we will avenge her death."

The Vaza stared at him for a moment before an iciness came over her and she nodded, just once, short and sharp, and placed the muzzle of her weapon on the back of the neck of the one called Price, just below the helmet, where there was little protection.

"We will be heroes," Nokz'z said, but as he said it there was a small twitch, and a sound like a weak cough from Azoh's body.

He turned quickly and knelt beside her, reaching around her neck and feeling for a pulse.

The realisation that there was one came at the same time as he noticed the short, buzz cut hair beneath the cowl; the body armour under the robes. Her ceremonial tattoos were smudged. Smudged!

Then he saw the sidearm in her hand.

* * *

Chisnall was conscious of someone near him, a light amidst the darkness that enveloped him. His eyes were open, yet he could see nothing, nothing but black. He could feel nothing. He could smell and taste nothing. He was in complete emptiness, weightless. Alone.

Except for a pinpoint of light. It was Azoh, he knew that, although he could not see her.

Azoh?

Yes, came the response.

Am I dead?

You are alive.

But...

The tank was destroyed. But the explosion knocked you unconscious.

So this is a dream?

A kind of dream. But you are real, and I am real.

And you are here?

No. I am far from you.

Then how…

Your consciousness and mine are touching.

But I am not Bzadian.

I cannot reach out in this way to other Bzadians. Except for a very few.

Then I do not understand. Why me?

I think you already know why. You call it the 'strangeness'.

* * *

"Tell your gorilla to put down her weapon," Brogan said, the sidearm in her hand pressed against his temple.

Price could only watch, her head pressed into the cold concrete of the floor, by the weight of the Vaza.

Nokz'z stared at Brogan for a moment nodding slightly as he comprehended the subterfuge, the hastily attached jewellery, the tattoos drawn on with surgical pen.

The entire building shook from the impact of another huge explosion, jolting the solid concrete floor and sending drifts of fine dust from the wooden floorboards and beams above them.

"Kill them," Nokz'z said.

Price was already moving. She rolled over, grabbing the barrel of the gun and wrenching it away from her, away from where Azoh still lay quietly in Barnard's combat uniform.

It pulled the Vaza off balance and Price hurled herself off the ground, shouldering the Vaza so that she stumbled forwards, the coil-gun clattering over the floor towards a wall.

The Vaza was on her feet like a cat, though, spinning around towards Price, feinting with a swinging arm while her leg swept at Price's feet.

Price, still recovering her own balance, went down hard, but recovered instantly, rolling across the floor and back up onto her feet, just as the Vaza caught her around the midriff, slamming her back into the wall. She wrapped her legs around the Vaza'z chest, and grabbed at her helmet, twisting until she was sure the neck would break.

Another explosion shattered the fabric of their world, rattling and shaking their underground cave, and part of the ceiling gave way in a shower of splinters and broken wood.

Still Price twisted. Somehow the neck held together, but it forced the Vaza to let go and grab up at Price's arms. Price unwrapped her legs from the Vaza's chest, and thrust them behind her, pushing off from the wall and toppling both of them over.

They would have landed on top of Azoh, but she had moved, as if she knew exactly where they would land. She was now standing quietly in one corner.

The Vaza hit the ground hard and Price tried to get an elbow into her neck, but the Vaza, with incredible strength, twisted Price off the top of her, forcing her down, pinning her arms with her knees. Price grabbed at her utility knife on her belt, but the Vaza beat her to it, crushing Price's hand in one of her own and picking up the knife when it fell from unresponsive fingers.

Now Price's own knife was at her neck and she felt a sharp sting on her skin.

"In the Bering Strait you told me you were a match for a Vaza," the Vaza said. "You said a human child could beat a Bzadian soldier." She switched abruptly to English, heavily accented. "You lose."

She wrenched Price's chin upwards, exposing more of Price's neck and the knife grazed her skin then suddenly the weight was gone. The Vaza was gone, wrenched sideways, rolling across the floor.

"You're the loser, you loathsome toad," Brogan said. "Get your hands off my friend."

* * *

I do not understand.

Yet you feel it, this strangeness.

Yes.

Then you have a glimmering of what it is like to be Azoh.

I do not, I cannot...

You must listen to me carefully.

I am listening.

Then I will tell you your future. Your people are on a journey, and it has been a long one. From savage animal to savage man, from savage man to true being. Compassion and peace are the future of your species. Greed and violence will fade into your history. I see the future of your people.

How can you see this?

I see it in you.

Chisnall was silent, digesting that.

Azoh, you are right that I feel a strangeness when something terrible happens. And I felt it a few moments ago. What was it that I felt?

Your friend, The Tsar.

The Tsar?

He is gone. He died bravely. Protecting you. That is all I can tell you, for now. That is what I feel.

You knew Nokz would be waiting.

I did.

You knew what he would do.

I knew what he might do.

And you were prepared to die to end this war.

I was. But you would not let me. That is the real lesson.

* * *

The Gelman Library is situated on the main campus of the George Washington University, in the amusingly, but appropriately, named Foggy Bottom suburb of Washington DC. It is a seven-story building, built in the 1970s.

The ground floor of the library is home to a café, long since closed, although the counters and rusting espresso machines are still in place.

The storeroom of the café had been disused for over ten years and any of the patrons of the café in its heyday, mainly latte-sipping fine arts students, and psychology majors, would be amazed to see the kind of attention it was receiving now.

A full complement of SWAT officers in full combat gear surrounded the storeroom, ensuring that no one could get anywhere near it.

Inside, a small team of technicians and scientists surrounded a plain, unlabelled wooden crate. It looked, and was about the size of a fruit crate. But it did not contain fruit. It contained a bomb. Someone knowing that might wonder why the technicians did not wear bomb-proof suits. The answer to that was simple. No suit in the universe could protect the wearer against this bomb.

The components of the device had been identified. A warhead, of Bzadian origin. A radio receiver, of very human origin. In between the two, a detonation device. Just a small explosive.

Unlike a nuclear bomb, which had to be detonated in exactly the right way in order to achieve critical mass, and nuclear fission, all it would take to detonate an anti-matter weapon was to disrupt the delicate dance in which the positrons and electrons found themselves. Even a heavy jolt could be enough to set it off, the scientists had decided, which was why they did not consider moving the bomb, but rather worked on dismantling it.

The detonator had already been removed from the radio receiver, and they were slowly working on removing it from the warhead also.

They worked in short shifts, as their focus had to be extreme.

Although the radio receiver had been disconnected, and the bomb was safe, it was still with a sense of great relief and a silent handclapping from those present when the chief technician disconnected the last turn of the thread of the final screw and moved the detonator away from the warhead, placing it in a Total Containment Vessel, that would prevent any damage even if the detonator did somehow explode.

The warhead itself, for which no kind of containment vessel was possible, was left in place. With the radio disconnected and the detonator rendered safe, all that now remained was to keep watch.

It happened almost immediately. Less than ten minutes after the bomb had been rendered inactive.

The arming system made a light humming sound and a red light began to flash. It flashed exactly six times then turned green. The technician's face turned white and he turned to his colleague for confirmation.

His colleague said, "Detonation activation confirmed."

The technician reached immediately for his radio with sweaty hands. He spoke only one word.

"Boom."

The word was received and understood in the Operations Command Centre, in the now repaired and restored bunker, deep beneath the Pentagon.

General Harry Whitehead, head of ACOG forces, closed his eyes and let out a deep sigh.

"Oh. My. God," he said, making the sentence into three distinct words.

"Any chance the information is wrong?" The speaker was the liaison officer for the ACOG oversight committee, Emily Gonzales.

"None," Daniel Bilal answered. "Our experts have studied the device extensively. As far as the Pukes are concerned, it just blew Washington, Maryland and most of Virginia into the sewers of hell. That includes all of us."

"Thank God we found it and disarmed it in time," Admiral Lynette Hooper, CiC ACOG Naval Forces, spoke up for the first time.

"Thank God?" Whitehead asked. "Thank God?! If the Pukes tried to detonate that bomb it can only mean one thing. A decapitation strike. They want to prevent us from retaliating with our nuclear weapons. And the only reason we would even think of retaliating with nukes?"

"Is if they attacked us first," the admiral said softly.

"We must now assume that an enemy strike is inbound and we must launch our retaliatory strike immediately," Whitehead said.

"There is no evidence of a first strike," Gonzales said.

Whitehead turned to her. "Emily, you know me. I am no hawk. I am not a war-monger. I wish dearly for all this not to be true. But the Pukes just tried to destroy us. They failed. But maybe there is a second bomb. Maybe when they realise the first one failed, they will switch to a backup."

"Reid said nothing about a backup device," Gonzales said.

"He may not have known about it," Bilal said.

"We have to strike back while we still can," Whitehead said.

"I have to obtain authorisation from the oversight committee," Gonzales said.

"No you do not," Whitehead thundered. "In the event of a first strike by enemy forces, we have automatic authorisation to launch a retaliatory strike."

"There is still no proof of a first strike by the Bzadians," Gonzales tried, but her words sounded weak and unconvincing.

"General Whitehead," a new voice intruded. Colonel Cheryl Watson was the command coordinator for the operations centre, responsible for relaying information and intelligence.

"Yes Colonel?" Whitehead asked.

"AWACs patrolling the eastern coast report a squadron of Type Twos inbound. Looks like their point of origin was Lajes Field in the Azores. Heading right for us."

"Enough proof for you?" Whitehead demanded.

Gonzales nodded mutely.

"Release the nuclear codes," Whitehead said. "And I'll see you all in hell."

* * *

The tunnel was not even, nor were the walls smooth. They had been hewn by hand out of bedrock, and the ceiling was not level either, but dipped and raised, sometimes so low that Kriz had to duck to get underneath. In places, heavy wooden beams held up metal girders and considering the age of the tunnel it was amazing that these places had not also fallen when the infiltrators explosion had ripped through here.

A glow in the distance, just around a slight curve in the tunnel, indicated an opening, or a doorway.

Kriz withdrew her sidearm and nodded to Jazki whose coil-gun was already in her hands. She gave some silent hand signals to the troop of soldiers behind them.

A doorway in front of them was partly open, and the light was spilling around three edges of it. Jazki moved forward, but Kriz restrained her with a hand. She moved in front and pressed lightly on the door, peering through the gap, evaluating the scene. Only then did she take a step back and nod at Jazki.

* * *

Price jumped as the tunnel door burst open with an explosive snap, smashing back against the wall with a sound like a gunshot. Bzadian soldiers spewed from the opening, combat ready, guns high, fingers tight on triggers. She froze, sensing the slightest move would earn her a bullet. Brogan also was unmoving. She was standing over Nokz'z, Price's knife at his throat. His Vaza lay against a wall, her head on an unnatural angle. She was neither moving nor breathing.

Kriz emerged from the tunnel. A sidearm in her hand. She replaced it in its holster, seeing that the situation was under control.

"Put the knife down," Kriz said. "And make no move towards your other weapons. Or you will die, unnecessarily."

Price slowly raised her hands to her neck and saw Brogan do the same after tossing the knife well away from Nokz'z.

"Thank Azoh," Nokz'z said. "Just in time."

"Who is this, who wears Azoh's robes?" Kriz asked.

"A traitor," Nokz'z said. "One of our elite. A Ferzerker, gone native. Now fighting with our enemies."

"And where is Azoh?" Kriz asked.

"She is here," Nokz'z said, gesturing towards a far corner of the room. "In the guise of our enemy."

Kriz's eyes swept over Azoh, taking in the combat uniform, acknowledging her identity with a short nod, but nothing to reveal surprise.

"Azoh works with the humans," Nokz'z said. "She is a traitor to Bzadia."

There was a long silence during which Kriz's eyes flicked rapidly between Azoh and Nokz'z.

"I do not understand," Kriz said.

"Azoh has betrayed us," Nokz'z said. "She has betrayed all of Bzadia. She works with the scumbugz against her own people."

"This cannot be true," Kriz said.

"Ask her," Nokz'z said. "She cannot lie."

Kriz turned towards Azoh and bowed her head, on an angle, Bzadian style. "Azoh," he said. "I seek only to understand what the Colonel is saying."

"He speaks in part-truths," Azoh said. "I work with these children of our enemies, not against our people, but to prevent future bloodshed."

Kriz seemed visibly shocked.

"Just as we are about to erase our enemy from this planet, she wants to capitulate," Nokz'z said. "She would surrender in our moment of triumph, and leave future generations of Bzadians to a life of slavery, or worse, at the hands of these savages. She is no longer Azoh. She renounced this role when she betrayed her own people."

"I work for our people," Azoh said. "I work to avoid more Bzadian deaths as well as more human ones."

"She will destroy us all," Nokz'z said as another explosion shook the walls of the room and part of the ceiling sagged.

"Is that why you shot her?" Jazki asked.

"Shot Azoh? I don't know what you are…"

Jazki held out a hand and made a specific hand movement. With a quiet hum, and a flutter of translucent wings, a small insect-like bot landed on her palm. Nokz'z stared uncomfortably at it for a moment, clearly considering his next words carefully.

"That was not Azoh," he said. "It was one of the Angels."

"You did not know that," Kriz said. "Not then."

"It makes no difference," Nokz'z said. "This traitor cannot be allowed to continue as Azoh. It is time for a new Azoh, one that will not stand in the way of the Bzadian people."

He smiled grimly and gestured at the broken ceiling. "Perhaps Azoh was tragically killed in the bombing of the museum."

Even as he said it, part of the wall gave way and a wooden beam crashed down in a corner of the room raising mushroom clouds of dust.

"Our glorious leader, killed by the humans who were attacking our capital," Nokz'z said. "There will be an outcry such as never been heard on Bzadia. The High Council will chant with a single voice and the human race will be eradicated from this planet. From our planet."

Kriz stared at him, evaluating him, her eyes intense and unblinking.

"This building remembers and commemorate tens of thousands of years of our history," she said.

"A great and glorious history," Nokz'z said.

"A short while ago one of these humans, merely a child, gave up his own life to protect those of his friends," Kriz shook her head. It was a gesture of sadness. "Whereas you would take the life of our leader in order to protect yours."

"Colonel –" Nokz'z began, but Kriz cut him off.

"Take her," she said to a young female captain. "Our leader. Our Azoh. Take her now. Take her to safety. Take the humans with her. Get her into the tunnel, and back to the Congress."

"Colonel Kriz, is it possible that you also are taking the side of the humans?" Nokz'z asked.

"It is not up to me," Kriz said. "Azoh can speak for herself to the High Council."

VENGEANCE

The USS Oracle received the signal at 1109 hours, the exact same time as it was received by other submarines around the world.

Lieutenant Setefano brought the digital order, and the associated authorisation code, to Captain 'A-Sam' Weiss. There was no discussion of the rights and wrongs. No questioning of the orders. They were unequivocal.

Five minutes after receiving the signal, it had been electronically confirmed by a secure burst transmission. Ten minutes after receiving the signal, the USS Oracle's full complement of twenty-four Trident III ballistic missiles began to emerge from the ocean, one after another, soaring into the sky on fiery tails.

The targets were varied, but all were major cities, or military installations, all on the Australian mainland.

The USS Oracle was maintaining position a few hundred kilometres from the coast, so close that the missiles would fly a depressed trajectory, without the need to leave Earth's atmosphere. Those aimed at Canberra would have a flight time of just over twenty minutes.

***

Ryan.

Yes.

It is time for you to return.

Return how?

Chisnall looked around, but all he could see was the black,

black sky and the infinite galaxies of stars.

We need you now, Ryan. You must return.

Another star, much brighter than the rest, a sun, burning intensely in the blackness. It seemed to be rushing towards him, swallowing all around it, filling his vision and...

Chisnall sat up with a jerk, and lay back down just as quickly, unable to rise more than a few centimetres off... what was he lying on... a hospital gurney. His wrists were manacled to the sides of it and a plastic strap ran around his neck. It was that that had stopped him rising.

In front of him, on a table barely a metre away, was a bowl of salted sierfruit. One of his specialties. The careful cuts to remove the heavy skin without leaving the fleshy underside, the even sprinkling of salt and the drizzle of lemon, staining the fruit blue, but adding a hefty zing to the flavour. He had prepared this very dish. Many hours ago. It still looked fresh and edible, the salting helped with that.

His focus began to widen. There were other dishes on the table, some half-eaten, along with empty plates and bowls. There was a roaring in his ears, and as his focus widened even further, and the sounds became more distinct he realised he was in the council chamber. Right in the centre, inside the rows of seats, on the raised speakers' platform.

The other Angels sat on the floor around him, neck-cuffed. He looked around for Azoh and found her gazing intently at him from her seat in the ornate chair at the other end of the oval. She nodded briefly.

It was not a dream. Nor was it an hallucination.

He looked around as best as he could, trying to make sense

of the circus he was seeing. The council chamber was an orderly place where high officials sat with dignity and decorum, discussing in a civilised way, the issues up for debate.

Not today. The entire chamber was in a state of pandemonium, people were standing, shouting, running. In the centre of the storm, the eye of the hurricane sat Azoh, unmoving, unblinking, staring at him.

Chisnall closed his eyes for a moment, trying to gather all the consciousness he could. And consciousness was there, but not in the way he expected. All of the people in the room, the Angels, the generals and high commanders, Nokz'z, Kriz, Goezlin he still saw them all, or rather he felt their presence. It was as if, while unconscious, his eyes had been more fully opened than ever before, and having been opened, they did not entirely shut again.

He opened his eyes again. Faces and voices swam into clarity.

The reason for the bedlam became clear.

In the air above the central oval, the 3D projectors were displaying a radar image of Australia. Overlaid on it were the tracks of what could only be missiles, too many to count. Thin lines showed the trajectories and regular dots on those lines gave an indication of speed. Many of the missile tracks were clearly aiming at Canberra. Others at Sydney, Brisbane, Uluru.

"There is no time to evacuate!" a councillor was shouting. "We have less than ten minutes. We would not escape the blast radius."

"Even if we had time, we are trapped. The wildfires have cut all the roads on three sides of the city," another yelled.

"And if we take to the air, they will shoot us down."

"What happened?" another was gesticulating wildly, "You assured us that the humans would never have a chance to launch their weapons!"

Leozii stood to speak.

"All we know is that the warhead did not detonate," Leozii said. "Washington still stands."

"Then we are lost," a councillor said.

"And so are they," Leozii said.

"We must call back our planes," this was a new voice, but one he recognized. Chisnall turned to try and find the speaker, but could not.

"And let them win?" Nokz'z thundered. "We must have vengeance!"

Chisnall looked around at the faces of the Angels. They were grim, frightened. He had never seen them look as scared before. It was the helplessness, he decided. Restrained and guarded, there was nothing they could do.

Price caught his eye. "Why doesn't Azoh speak?" she asked. "Why is she letting them do this?"

"She cannot," Chisnall said. "If they do not ask for her advice, then she cannot give it."

Chisnall twisted his head back to look at Azoh. She turned also, and again looked Chisnall directly in the eye, and in that moment, that singular, instantaneous, point in the timescale of the universe, Chisnall understood fully for the first time what Azoh meant about the interconnectedness of all things.

That a tree falling in a forest in Africa creates ripples in the universe that are felt on the other side of the world; that the death of a peasant can change a government; the position of the moon changes weather on the earth, a schoolboy crosses a wet road in a hurry and the consequences of that seep into the future. The world will be different, because of the orbit of the moon around the earth.

With that deep understanding came knowledge. He knew the minute change he needed to make in the universe, the place where the prod of a finger could dislodge a million-year boulder. He knew the question he had to ask.

He waited for a brief lull in the uproar then raised his voice so that it filled the room, conscious that it was a young voice, the light smooth tones of someone who had not yet fully formed into the adult that he would one day become.

"I wish to speak to the High Council," he said in the high language.

There was silence, the most powerful Bzadian leaders shocked at hearing him speak.

"He is human, he cannot address the High Council," Nokz'z said.

"Anyone may address the High Council," Leozii said. "If their opinion is sought by a member of the council."

"No one here wishes to hear the voice of a human," Nokz'z said.

"If you do not, then your own may be the last voices you hear," Chisnall said.

"The question must be asked," Leozii said. "Will anyone here call for the voice of this human."

"I wish to hear the voice of this human," The voice was high, strained and instantly recognizable. "I call for the voice of Chizna," Goezlin said, and for the first time there was complete silence in the room.

Chisnall turned to face Azoh. He felt weak, propping himself up on his elbows. She sat calmly in her chair, knowing what he would ask before he spoke a word.

"How did we meet?" Chisnall asked.

He collapsed back on the stretcher as Azoh raised a hand and pointed a finger at Chisnall.

"This human was sent to kill me," she said.

* * *

The screen in the operations centre showed the position of the Bzadian planes, they had split up as they had approached the US coastline.

"Any chance we can get to them in time?" Whitehead asked.

"None," Hundal said. "They will fire their long-range missiles well before we are in range. Our scream-jets may be able to shoot down the planes as they return to their base, but they won't be able to stop the missiles.

"And what is the status of our nukes?" Whitehead asked, turning to Admiral Hooper.

"Locked on targets," Hooper said. "First impact will be in less than ten minutes."

"How did it come to this?" Whitehead asked, but nobody answered. "Ladies, gentlemen," he said. "It has been an honour serving with you."

"General Whitehead," Colonel Watson said, "You're going to want to see this."

* * *

"He was sent to assassinate me, not by humans, by Bzadians, by my own people." Azoh said. "But he refused, even though it put his own life in great danger."

The silence in the chamber was complete.

"A few minutes ago this officer tried to kill me," Azoh said, gesturing at Nokz'z. "My life was saved by two young humans."

"Is this what we have become?" Her voice, previously calm, now rose in anger. Coming from her soft young face, and unblemished skin, it was like hearing thunder from a clear blue sky. "Thousands of years of evolution, yet civilisation, it turns out, is just a thin veneer. Our wild and brutal past still lurks, just below the surface. We came here expecting to fight savages and found that the savages were us."

"What would you have us do?" Leozii asked softly.

"We should learn from the children of our enemy," Azoh said. "We must call back our planes."

"Then we will die without vengeance," Nokz'z was back on his feet and shouting.

"Vengeance?" Azoh's voice was quiet again, yet somehow cut through the echoes of Nokz'z's outburst. "Vengeance is a bitter and toxic fruit. Vengeance would not change our fate. We will die. But this is their planet, not ours. We should not seek vengeance. We should turn back our planes, accept our fate, and leave this planet to the humans, what is left of it."

"You are crazy!" Nokz'z shouted.

"Is it crazy to do the right thing, instead of the easy thing?" Azoh asked. "We must act now, while we still can and then pray for forgiveness."

"Pray? You rely on the fathers?" Nokz'z asked. "The fathers will not come. The fathers will not turn back the missiles."

"The fathers are already here," Azoh said. "They have always been here."

"You have killed us all," Nokz'z cried.

"No colonel, we did that to ourselves, when we gave the order to destroy Washington," Leozii said.

"May I speak," Chisnall asked.

The rushing and shouting of earlier had subsided. There was a quiet acceptance of what was coming.

"You may," Leozii said.

"No one needs to die today," Chisnall said.

"That is now unavoidable," Leozii said. "We have only minutes."

"Let me state this very clearly," Chisnall said. "You have turned back your planes, and you would now seek peace with ACOG?"

"It is too late to seek peace," Nokz'z said.

"I can stop the missiles," Chisnall said. "But if I do, will you seek peace? Will you put an end to the barbarity, this insanity?"

"We will," Leozii said. "In our fear and folly we have descended far from the ideals of our ancestors."

"Is that the decision of the High Council?" Chisnall asked.

"Yes," Leozii said, after a quick scan around the oval.

"No! We must have vengeance!" Nokz'z shouted.

"And the hawks in your war council will be replaced," Chisnall asked.

"Yes," the leader said.

Chisnall did not see what gesture or signal was given, but Nokz'z's arms were suddenly in the grip of two strong nzgali, Kriz directing them as they pulled him away from the table and towards an exit.

"Even Azoh cannot turn back ballistic missiles," Nokz'z cried as he was dragged away. "No one has that power."

"I do," Chisnall said.

Now the eyes were no longer on him, but on the 3D radar projection hovering above the oval. The tracks of the missiles were changing. The straight, determined trajectories were beginning to bend, to curve in new directions, out over the ocean or to open desert where they could self-destruct without scattering radioactive material on populated areas.

One by one, the icons representing the missiles began to disappear from the screen.

Kriz began to applaud, human style, clapping her hands together in front of her. Others in the room looked at her in confusion at first, then slowly joined in, until the entire chamber filled with thunder.

"How did he do that?" Price asked.

Chisnall ignored her. He waited until the sound diminished enough for him to speak.

"The missiles are gone," he said. "As I said they would be. And ACOG will negotiate for peace with Bzadia."

Chisnall turned and crossed the raised central platform to where Barnard stood quietly by herself.

He stopped in front of her and allowed himself a small smile.

She looked around, making sure nobody could see, then winked at him.

"Best magic trick ever," Chisnall said quietly.

"Best ever," she agreed, and held out her hand for a low fist bump. She did it with her left hand. Her right hand was occupied. It held a small device, no larger than a thumbnail. It was the colour of her skin, but that was the point of the device. It changed colour to that of its surroundings. It was the kind of device that could be placed discreetly under a table or stuck to a wall and would never be noticed or detected.

* * *

"That sly devil," Gonzales said as the image on the screen steadied. For a moment all they had had a view of was Chisnall's mid-section.

"It wasn't some kind of a ruse?" Whitehead asked. "The Bzadian planes are definitely heading back to Lajes Field?"

"Yes sir," Watson said. "It's all clear."

"And our missiles?"

"We stopped them all," Watson said. "Just."

"That was close," Hooper said.

"Too close," Whitehead agreed.

* * *

The other Angels, somehow now freed of their restraints, gathered around him. Chisnall gazed around at their faces, nodding and acknowledging each of them. Monster, his best friend since the first day at training camp, he reserved a small smile for.

"You guys will be heading home soon," Chisnall said. "And there won't be any more missions."

"You'll be right there with us," Price said. "There'll be a hero's welcome for you after this."

"A tickle-tape parade," Monster agreed with a huge grin.

Chisnall shook his head. "I need to stay," he said. "Right now is our best chance to secure peace. We've opened the door to it, but there is a heck of a lot of work still to do. If I stay here for a bit, and work with Azoh, liaise with ACOG, maybe we can build something that will last."

"The Pukes seem to think you're some kind of a god right now," Price said.

"And I'll keep fooling them as long as I can," Chisnall grinned. "Whatever happens, I'll see you guys soon."

"Yeah bro," Wall said. "See you soon."

* * *

Monster was the first to emerge from the building, into the swirling smoke and uncertain air outside. Price was immediately behind him, conscious of the lack of a weapon: no coil-gun adding its weight to her back; no side-arm on her hip. It had been so long that she felt almost naked without them.

Bzadian soldiers watched them curiously, aware of whom they were, but did not raise their weapons towards them. Orders had clearly been given and received.

Barnard, Wall and Brogan emerged next, blinking against the harsh sunlight, filtered only slightly by the gauzy haze of the smoke. They were herded into lines, awaiting their transportation. The entire city was being evacuated, the wildfires, now completely out of control, were encroaching on three fronts.

"I know you think I'm an idiot, but I don't get what just happened," Wall said. "So Azoh knew in advance that Nokz'z would try to kill her?"

"She knew," Barnard said. "And she knew how that information would affect the High Council."

"But why did Brogan dress up as Azoh?" Wall asked.

"Chisnall wouldn't let Azoh go through with it, even wearing Barnard's body armour. There was too much risk. Nokz'z could have shot her in the head," Barnard said.

"But Chisnall was happy for Brogan to get shot in the head?" Wall asked.

"Brogan volunteered," Barnard said. "But basically yeah. Chisnall was okay with that."

"She was willing to risk her life to save Azoh," Monster said.

"To save the world," Barnard said. "Are you starting to see the picture?"

"I think so," Wall said.

Price stared at the entrance to the building for a long time, as if expecting to see someone else emerge. But she knew no one would. Not The Tsar. Not Wilton. Not Emile. Not Hunter. And not Ryan Chisnall.

"You remember our first ever mission together?" she asked, of no one in particular.

"I do," Monster answered.

"It seems so long ago now," Price said.

"Like lifetime," Monster said.

"We won't see him again, will we," Price said, blinking away tears from the smoke.

"I thinking he be quite busy for a while," Monster said.

His arms slipped around her waist from behind and he pulled her close, clasping his hands across her stomach. They remained like that for a moment, watching the empty doorway, until their attention was distracted by harsh cawing as a trio of birds flew overhead, fleeing the fires to the east.

Barnard was watching the birds also, Price saw, and there was something in her eyes. A kind of wistfulness that was so unlike her that Price might have laughed, if she had been capable of it at that moment. The expression softened the German girl. It made her seem more human. What was going on inside, Price could only guess. She reached out and took Barnard by the arm, pulling her closer.

Barnard tried to shake her off. "I'm not much of a hugger."

"Get over it," Price said, putting her arm around Barnard's neck and pulling her close.

There was silence for a moment then Barnard said, "Wilton gave up his life to save those of people he loved. I'm not sure how I feel about that. Emile gave up his life trying to aspire to some ideal of being a hero. I'm not sure how I feel about that, either."

"You not alone," Monster said.

"But I think I finally figured out what love is," Barnard said.

"I thought you didn't believe in love," Price said.

"It's when someone knows what's wrong with you and doesn't try to fix it," Barnard said.

"You nearly got it," Price smiled. "It's when someone knows what's wrong with you and doesn't want to fix it."

Monster's lips were by her ear now, murmuring things that were just for the two of them.

She twisted her head and kissed him softly on the cheek.

Was it fair? After all they had been through, that somehow both of them had survived? When she looked around, all she saw was heartbreak and loss. Wall had lost a brother. Barnard had lost The Tsar, possibly the only person in the world she had ever truly cared about.

At the end of the line, Brogan stood alone. Isolated by who she was. By what she had done.

When Price turned back she saw that Wall had latched onto the group, Barnard's arm around his waist.

"Though you weren't much of a hugger," Price said.

"Get over it," Barnard smiled.

Wall was gazing skywards and Price followed his eyes.

The trio of birds were disappearing noisily to the west and clouds had begun to form in an otherwise clear blue sky, swirling slowly around into a vortex, a whirlpool of white, gradually turning to grey, and spreading out through the dome of the sky like soap diffusing in water.

"What's going on?" Price asked.

"Is just clouds," Monster said.

"Strangest looking clouds I've ever seen," Barnard said, and for the first time since Price had known the German girl, her eyes were full of tears.

Price watched her for a moment then found her gaze drawn back to the sky as the unnatural clouds continued to darken and spread.

"Brogan," she said, and when Brogan looked at her, she said, "Get over here."

Brogan hesitated, then began to walk towards them.

"Everything is way it meant to be," Monster said.

And then it began to rain.

JULY 2, 2035

An unsteady and uneasy peace swathed the planet Earth for two full years following the events at Canberra in July of 2033. It had taken a glimpse over the edge of the precipice for both sides to see how deep and dark that chasm really was.

Disarmament began in 2034 and was finished by early 2035.

It was on the second anniversary of that day in 2033, the day the world nearly ended, that Bzadians and Humans signed the final treaty.

But to get to that point took a lot of trust, and spontaneous outbursts of hostility flared up like spot-fires in various parts of the globe as tensions rose and waned.

Two species, like twins separated at birth, gradually got re-acquainted with each other. Land was shared, the Bzadians building new cities in Earth's vast deserts, where they felt most at home.

An interesting change had happened on the human side also. They say that two brothers will fight against a cousin, but two brothers and a cousin will fight against a stranger. Faced with an enemy from outside, Earth's many nations and tribes had drawn together, bonds had been forged that were not to be easily undone. There existed a peace among humans for perhaps the first time on the planet.

The Treaty signing ceremony was held in the shadow of the great rock at Uluru. A place that had once been the heart of the Bzadian military machine.

It was attended by most of the top dignitaries from either side.

But there were some unexpected, and uninvited guests also.

The immense spaceship that descended slowly through the clear blue skies was easily visible to the naked eye yet had not been picked up by any radar stations. This was later confirmed to be due to the design of the spaceship, pyramidal in shape, without any surface to reflect radar back to the transmitter. It was the original and the ultimate in stealth technology.

All the participants at the signing ceremony, waiting patiently in the cool July sun, found their eyes drawn to the sky as the craft descended.

The participants in the ceremony did not see the pyramid at first as it fell softly to Earth. The shape of the object was not obvious until after it had landed. What the participants saw, humans with shocked, awed expressions, Bzadians with smiles of understanding and recognition, was a geometric shape. A circle of blue fire inside a square.

GLOSSARY

Everything about the Allied Combined Operations Group (ACOG) was a mishmash of different human cultures: tactics, weapons, languages, vehicles, and, especially terminology. The success of many missions depended on troops from diverse nations being able to understand all communications instantly and thoroughly. The establishment of a Standardized Military Terminology and Phonetic Alphabet (SMTPA) was a key factor in assisting this communication, combining existing terminology from many of the countries involved in ACOG. For ease of understanding, here is a short glossary of some of the SMTPA terms, phonetic shortcuts, and equipment used in this book.

Clear copy: "Your transmission is clear."
Coil-gun: weapon using magnetic coils to propel a projectile
Comm: personal radio communicator
Fast mover: fixed-wing aircraft such as a jet fighter
GPS: global positioning system
How copy: "Is my transmission clear?"
Klick: kilometer
Mike: minute
Oscar Kilo: okay
Oscar Mike: on the move
Puke: military slang for a Bzadian
Rotorcraft: helicopter with internal rotor blades at the base of the craft
Rotorbot: A small, unmanned rotorcraft
Slow mover: helicopter or rotorcraft

NOTE ON PRONUNCIATION

There is no equivalent in English for the buzzing sound which is a common feature of most Bzadian languages. As per convention, this is written, where required, using the letter z to represent this sound.

NOTE ON BZADIAN ARMY RANKS

The ranking system and unit structure of the Bzadian Army is markedly different from that of most Earth forces. There are many ranks which have no equivalent in human terms, and the organisation of units is different. For simplicity and ease of understanding, the closest human rank has been used when referring to Bzadian army ranks, and Bzadian unit names have been expressed in human terms.

CONGRATULATIONS

The following prize-winners in my school competitions have all had a character named after them in this book:

Retha Barnard – Albany Junior High School, NZ

Daniel Bilal – Woodcrest State College, Australia

Holly Brogan - St. Cuthberts College, NZ

Ryan Chisnall - Belmont Intermediate, NZ

Emily Gonzales – Santa Gertrudis School, Texas

Lynette Hooper – Ipswich West State School, Australia

Josh Allan – Hurunui College, NZ

Janos Panyoczki - Kaiwaka School, NZ

Trianne Price - Woodcrest State College, Australia

Leon Setefano – Murrumba State Secondary College, Australia

Molly Shaw – Faith Lutheran High School, Las Vegas

Hayden Wall – Padua College, Australia

Aidan 'A-Sam' Weiss – Alexander Dawson School, Las Vegas

Harry Whitehead – Waimea College, NZ

Blake Wilton - Orewa College, NZ

ABOUT THE AUTHOR

As a child Brian was a great reader and a fan of the adventure stories of Enid Blyton and Willard Price. Some influences from that early reading still show in his own adventure stories for young people.

A native of New Zealand, Brian still lives Down Under, but now on the sunny Gold Coast of Australia.

Find him online at brianfalkner.com.

THE RECON TEAM ANGEL SERIES

The Assault
Task Force
Ice War
Vengeance

ALSO BY BRIAN FALKNER

The Flea Thing
The Real Thing
The Super Freak
The Tomorrow Code
Brainjack
The Most Boring Book in the World
Northwood
Maddy West and the Tongue Taker
Rampage at Waterloo
Clash of Empires
Shooting Stars
1917: Machines of War
That Stubborn Seed of Hope
Cassie Clark: Outlaw

Tane and Rebecca aren't sure what to make of it. A sequence of 1s and 0s, the message looks like nothing more than a random collection of alternating digits. As they work to decode it, and the ones that follow, it slowly it becomes clear—the messages are being sent back in time.

Tane and Rebecca follow the message's cryptic instructions, but it's not long before they begin to suspect that worst—that the very survival of the human race may be at stake.

Fifteen-year-old Willem has been living in hiding in a small Belgian village since his father, a famous magician, fell out of favour with the French Emperor Napoléon Bonaparte. When a girl from the village is killed, it becomes obvious that there are hidden terrors in the forest and that they are connected with Napoleon's plans to conquer Europe. But Willem has a secret that could interfere with the emperor's plans and Napoléon will stop at nothing to find him.